Christine Coleman, a University of Auckland graduate, practiced optometry in both Australia and New Zealand. Her other accomplishments include being a violinist with the New Zealand National Youth Orchestra, a singer with the Hamilton Operatic Society, an actress with the Mairangi Players, as well as a creditable pianist and bagpiper. Christine is a prolific short story writer and lives in Auckland with her husband, Brian.

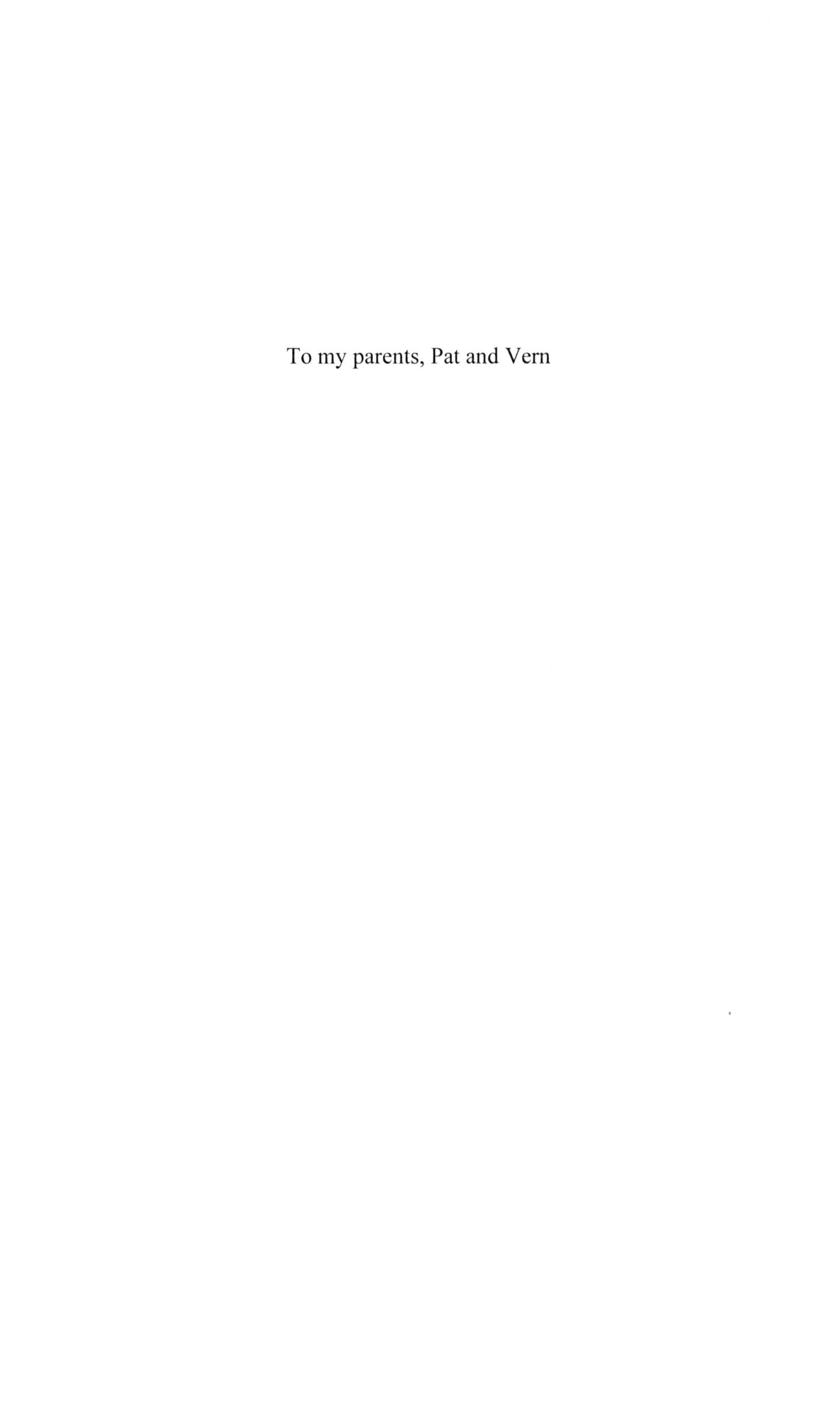

To my parents, Pat and Vern

Christine Coleman

THE SKY PILOT'S WIFE

AUSTIN MACAULEY PUBLISHERS™
LONDON ∗ CAMBRIDGE ∗ NEW YORK ∗ SHARJAH

Ordering Information
Quantity sales: Special discounts are available on quantity purchases by corporations, associations, and others. For details, contact the publisher at the address below.

Publisher's Cataloging-in-Publication data
Coleman, Christine
The Sky Pilot's Wife

ISBN 9798886933680 (Paperback)
ISBN 9798886933703 (ePub e-book)
ISBN 9798886933697 (Audiobook)

Library of Congress Control Number: 2023906380

www.austinmacauley.com/us

First Published 2023
Austin Macauley Publishers LLC
40 Wall Street 33rd Floor, Suite 3302
New York, NY 10005
USA

mail-usa@austinmacauley.com
+1 (646) 5125767

Acknowledgments

Pat Coleman, Brian Bahlmann, Lloyd Bahlmann, and Brian
Whitecliffe-Davies

One

But for the presence of a certain personable and fascinating young stranger at the Bingham church gala on that fateful day, things might have turned out quite differently. The ensuing chain of events happened as a direct consequence of his arrival. He made his appearance not long after the ritual toast and blessing of the bells by the vicar, who was known in common parlance as the local 'sky pilot'.

A small clannish group of men had gathered like bees around a pot of honey outside the belfry door. The center of their attention was an up-turned church bell implanted in the ground, full of vintner's brew and ripe for the tasting.

"Here's to you, Squire," said the vicar, as he sipped from a ladleful of the potent mix of ale, rum and port from the smallest of the newly re-cast bronze bells.

The vicar drank thirstily, wiped the tailored sleeve of his vestral garment tantalizingly across his lips, grinned and gestured for the squire to do the same.

"Oh, thank ye, Vicar. Cheers!"

The squire raised the ladle to his lips with both hands and held the vicar's gaze steadily over the top of the rim with his rheumy blue eyes as he partook avidly of the sweet nectar.

"Ahhh…a perfect brew. Perfect! And just when are we likely to see the likes of this again, Vicar?"

"Oh, not for another two hundred and fifty years, I shouldn't think. It was around 1650 that the bells were last re-cast, you know. They should last another two hundred and fifty years at that rate, but I doubt whether I'll be here for that…or you, for that matter! That would be in the year 2150!"

They both looked at each other incredulously and laughed. The squire's belly quivered like jelly and his salacious cheeks swelled up so as to almost obliterate his twinkly eyes as he threw his head back in raucous laughter. The vicar, being a much smaller man in comparison, felt a little disconcerted at being almost blown away, and losing his top-hat under the mighty blast of his friend's belly laugh. Meanwhile, the ladle was periodically plunged into the open mouth of the bell and its rich contents poured into the goblets of the eager church-goers, each awaiting with hands outstretched, their turn at this 'profane christening'. It was the treble bell of the cluster of five from which they were so freely imbibing. These revered bells had been a part of the parish church of Bingham out on the North Yorkshire Moors for over five hundred years. In fact, the vicar himself was the third generation as both his father and grandfather had been the incumbents of this very same parish before him.

"Here's to the village church!" the organist, Hugo, exclaimed, proffering a grandiose toast. He raised his goblet melodramatically and then quaffed fastidiously from its rim. The ladle was dipped and poured until the bell was empty and everyone present had partaken of the merry-making mixture. Then the vicar, clearing his throat, drew himself up to his full height and proclaimed in a loud voice:

"Thank you everyone for taking part in this little ritual. It is now time for me to bless the bells. Then we shall all join the other members of the congregation inside the church for a short service before adjourning to the village green for a fete. The ladies of the Guild will be organizing the refreshments and the Bingham Brass Band will be playing a few items for us as well. As you all know there will be the usual boating on the river and an archery target which the curate very kindly set up for us, as well as coconut shies, merry-go-rounds, sack-racing, market stalls…in fact, something for everyone. I must give special thanks to the squire for his assistance in arranging all of this for our church. I do hope you all enjoy the day."

With that, the treble bell and the other four bells were wiped with holy water, anointed with oil and duly blessed by the vicar. The service was held in the adjoining Anglican Church and the celebrations continued on the village green by the river. It was early October, autumn 1899, in Bingham near the River Rye. It was a crisp clear day and the vicar, a youthful fifty-two-year-old, was anticipating a good turnout to raise money for the parish church. His church was running about forty years behind the *Victorian Gothic Revival* which had swept through the churches of the rest of England. But as both he and his father before him had said, "Better late than never."

Structural alterations had been made to the chancel, nave and pulpit ten years ago and now the bells had been melted down, re-cast and re-tuned and the framework strengthened. They would be re-hung next week by an expert team of workmen, winched up on the outside of the tower and swung in through the belfry windows before the window louvres were replaced. He knew just how much blood, sweat and tears went into this dangerous work because he had heard that 250 years ago, a Thomas Bilbie had reached the promised land after failing to tune a bell correctly. And in 1810 in Liverpool a bell tower disintegrated during Sunday morning ringing after the bells had been hung erroneously side by side in the tower. Swinging in the same plane, the total stress and strain was much more than the masonry could withstand. He was just glad that in *his* bell tower, the bells had all been carefully and scientifically arranged in a circle. The last thing he wanted was for his church to fall down!

After the service, the vicar wandered over the church grounds to the village green, conspicuous in his short black coat, black trousers and top-hat. He spied his wife, Louisa, serving tea and scones with the Ladies' Guild under a canopy near a grove of oak trees by the river. He thought to himself how especially lovely and fresh she looked today with the sun catching her auburn hair, dressed in her cream lace mutton-sleeved blouse, khaki skirt and frilly apron. He had never regretted marrying her, the daughter of an ex-Admiral of the British Navy and now the wife of a third-generation vicar who had borne him six children.

"Hello, Louisa dear. I'll have Devonshire tea, thank you."

She smiled sweetly and said with a twinkle in her eye, "I *did* like your short sermon this morning, Alfred," and handed him a tray with tea things, jam and cream scones.

He grinned knowingly at her, tapped the side of his nose with one finger and thanked her for the compliment. Then he excused himself and took the tray to sit with the curate and his wife at one of the outdoor tables. The curate was a bright-eyed, wiry-looking fellow of about thirty-five, of animated demeanor, who always dressed impeccably whatever the occasion. He always looked so dapper. His wife Betty, in contrast, was short and plump and so no matter how hard she tried, never quite seemed to match the same degree of sartorial elegance as her husband. To make matters worse, she typically wore her hair in a low chignon, which had the unfortunate effect of drawing attention to her prematurely developing double chin. Apart from that slight impairment to her looks, she had a pleasant face and delighted in making a fuss of her husband, especially in public…a sentiment to which he seemed not quite so well enamored. Under public scrutiny, he would suffer her attentions meekly while she flew to the rescue with her handkerchief at the slightest threat of a rogue crumb falling from his cherubic lips and landing upon his freshly pressed trousers.

They were soon joined by the squire who immediately dominated the conversation and who was accompanied by his rather waif-like pre-Raphaelite-looking wife. The ladies all held parasols up because although it was autumn, they were very aware of retaining their peaches and cream complexions.

"My, look at that wife of yours at the tea stand, Vicar," said the squire. "Always working. She never stops. I don't know what you would do without her!"

"Neither do I," admitted the vicar. "Louisa is indispensable."

"Did she *really* make these scones?" asked the squire.

"If she did, you can bet that you will lose her to the bakery in the village if you are not careful! They're delicious!" He patted his round girth and smiled indulgently at his wife. "How is it you never make me scones like this, Milly?"

Millicent, who was as tiny as her husband was large, scowled slightly and replied tartly in her characteristically wispy voice, "Why do you think, my honeybun?"

She obviously considered that her husband's appetite was far too great and was concerned about him becoming even more rotund.

He chuckled and pinched her arm. Then changing the subject, he began to discuss village politics with the men.

Louisa in the meantime was busy amongst the ladies at the Devonshire Tea stand attending to customers. She was interrupted mid-morning by a very handsome stranger who had just joined the queue. He tipped his bowler hat and smiled charmingly across the table at her. She in turn, blushed. Who was this beguiling stranger who had the looks of a star actor? William Terris? She thought not. What would *he* be doing in this little corner of the world? Her heart gave a jump and she stammered somewhat girlishly for a woman of her tender, albeit forty-two years.

"What would you like, sir, tea? There's coffee if you prefer."

"Neither really. Just to look at you…that is to say, madam…I'll have tea if you don't mind. And scones with jam and cream. Thank you kindly."

Nervously, she clattered the teacups and cutlery together and set them on the tray before passing it to him. There was no doubt about it. They were both utterly taken with each other. He tipped his hat again, turned and left. She could feel her heart pounding in her chest as he ambled down the river bank to sit on the grass.

"What a perfectly gorgeous young man!" she marveled to herself. "He can't be any more than fifty-five…just a spring chicken! But those big brown soulful eyes! And those long eyelashes…! Oh, it's not fair!"

Consciously, she tried to detach herself from where her thoughts were taking her as she stacked plates and teacups until noon. Then her shift was over and she was free to enjoy the day.

Louisa's husband, Alfred, was nowhere to be seen amidst the throng of the crowd so she wandered off in the direction of the river bank, her long skirt carelessly skimming the grass as she shaded her eyes with one hand and carried her hat and a pack of scones in the other. To anyone who was watching, she was obviously a woman of great breeding and a lady of elegance. She was still a beautiful woman and still had an extremely tiny waist even though she had been married to Alfred for twenty-two years and borne him six children. She was endowed with beautiful pale porcelain skin, high cheekbones, soft doe-eyes and long silken hair which she wore up as was the fashion of the day. This accentuated her elegant neck which was adorned with a small silver locket.

Finding a shady spot, Louisa spread out her skirt, sat down on the riverbank and laid her hat on the ground. Several black swans kept her amused on the opposite side of the river as they dived underneath each other searching for food. She watched them closely and between mouthfuls of lunch, began throwing little pieces into the water to beckon them her way.

Before long, she heard a voice beside her say, in a barely discernible Irish brogue:

"Excuse me, madam. Allow me to introduce myself…Mr. Bycroft, Mr. Theodore Bycroft, businessman and florist, new to the village of Bingham. May I sit down?"

He tipped his hat with an engaging smile. Flattered by the attention, she said, "Certainly. Do sit down, Mr. Bycroft."

She waved her hand invitingly, indicating for him to sit down beside her. It was the handsome young man she had met earlier at the tea stand. Her heart began to pound.

"Did you enjoy your Devonshire tea?" she inquired shyly.

"As sure as I'm sitting here, ma'am."

"Are you Irish, by any chance?" she asked. "My mother was Irish."

"Right again," he said. "I'm from County Cork originally. So your mother was Irish?"

"Yes. But she died when I was twelve. I was only a child I'm afraid to say."

There was a pause in the conversation.

"Did you say you were new to the village?" she asked.

"Yes, I've just this week bought the florist shop in the main street…and a house near the squire on the south side of the village. It suits me really well because it has a greenhouse and a semi-detached conservatory. It's an ideal set-up for me as a florist."

"Oh, how lovely! We have a conservatory and a greenhouse at the vicarage too. They're both very useful on lots of occasions. We do quite a lot of entertaining in the conservatory you see. The extra room comes in quite handy."

He threw a pebble into the river and watched the ripples disappear slowly as a couple of rowboats went past. Then as a sudden idea struck, he said, "I say, would you like to come for a row?"

He stood up clutching his hat in both hands, then frowned slightly and said apologetically, "I'm sorry. I don't even know your name."

"Mrs. Picard," she replied. "Mrs. Louisa Picard."

She looked at him quizzically and then thinking there would be no harm to it, graciously accepted the invitation.

Soon they were out on the river amongst the other Sunday afternoon couples, enjoying the country air. Theodore had removed his hat and jacket and was rowing manfully in his rolled-up shirtsleeves while Louisa had carefully pinned her hat on and was sitting back and enjoying the scenery. She couldn't help making furtive glances at his handsome features whenever he wasn't looking. What a handsome brute he was! Expressive bushy eyebrows overhanging doleful eyes and a beautifully waxed handlebar mustache. Olive complexion and ruggedly handsome to boot. How honored she was to have met such a beautiful specimen of the male species! She smiled secretly to herself and remarked:

"You row so easily, Mr. Bycroft. I take it that you've done this sort of thing before?"

"Of course, m'lady." He laughed. "I rowed for Cambridge a couple of times so I'm not exactly out of my depth here!"

"Oh really! My second eldest son is at Oxford…that's Jeremy. He's studying entomology there. Being the second eldest son, he's destined for the church of course, like his father, grandfather and great-grandfather before him. But my husband fears he has Unitarian leanings and may become an Oxford don instead. I think we shall just have to wait and see!"

"And your eldest son?"

"Oh, he's in the navy. That's Thomas. Somewhere off the coast of Portugal, I think he is now. He's been all over the place, through the Suez Canal, to India and even Australia. Jeremy just wishes he would visit that place where Charles Darwin found all those strange animals so he can hear about them firsthand. The Gala…gala…"

"Galapagos Islands."

"Of course! I always mispronounce that. Yes, Thomas should be back home in port in around eighteen months' time, hopefully. We're all looking forward to that. He keeps sending us letters from ports all over the world telling us of his exploits."

There was a pause and Theodore looked at Louisa reflectively.

"You know, Mrs. Picard, from what you've been saying, you don't look quite old enough to me to have two grown-up sons, one in the navy and the other at university. How do you do it?"

"Well actually, Thomas is twenty-two and Jeremy is twenty. Then there's Emma, she's eighteen and a trainee nurse in London. And then there are my three girls at home with me…Geraldine, she's sixteen, Charlotte, she's fourteen and then my little one, Lucy and she's just turned six. And so, I keep myself pretty fit running around after them, looking after my husband Alfred, doing the Ladies' Guild's duties, keeping the reading room going at the vicarage, relieving the organist when he's on holiday, and last year I became lady captain of the bell ringers."

"Really! You amaze me!" He looked at her admiringly. "I mean, you look so young to have such grown-up children. And a bell ringer too! Very impressive. That would certainly keep you fit. It's kept me fit the past couple of years down in London. It's quite unusual to meet a lady bell ringer. In fact, I've never met one before. Tell me how you managed that?"

"Well, do you remember hearing about Alice White of Basingstoke? She became the first lady bell ringer in England three years ago. When I heard about that, I thought 'Why not? If she can do it, I can do it.' My husband had no objection. It's all for a good cause and it's good for the brain as well as the body!"

"Yes. How does that little ditty go now…?

'Like a breath of summer laden,
like a cheery ray of hope;
Is the sight of a gentle maiden
deftly handling of a rope.'"

They both laughed.

"So which bell do you ring, Mr. Bycroft? Tenor, treble or in between?" Louisa asked, dying to know more.

"Well, I started off on treble last year, but I'm pretty adaptable really. I ring whichever bell is available at the time."

"That's good. We may be able to make use of you then, that is, if you're interested," she hinted broadly giving him an encouraging smile.

"I'd be delighted, ma'am," he said grinning.

"That's settled then," she said, satisfied. "So, what made you decide to stay in Bingham?"

"Well, I had had enough of the big city life and working for someone else, so I decided to start my own business away from it all. I've always had an interest in floristry. My father and uncle were flower growers in Kent so I've been brought up in the industry. I have a natural affinity for flowers. I just love their color, their smell…their beauty…"

He looked at her strangely, let go of an oar and fished in his pocket. As he did so the boat veered slightly to the port side and the oar groaned in the rowlock. Louisa gripped the side of the boat and hung on to her hat.

"Here," he said. "Take this."

He was about to hand her what she thought looked like a slightly bedraggled cornflower when he suddenly changed his mind.

"Oh, sorry," he said. "This one's had it. I'll find you another."

He repeated the exercise this time checking the other pocket and by this time the boat had done a complete about turn.

"Oh bother," he said upon examining the piece of flora in his hand. "This one's just the same…I'm sorry I can't give you any cornflowers unless they're still fresh. It would mean bad luck for me you see, as a bachelor, I mean. This is what they call a 'bachelor's button' by the way," he said, holding up the flower. "Never mind, I'll make it up to you, I promise."

Louisa laughed. "Do you always carry cornflowers in your pocket?"

Theodore blushed and said, "Yes, it's a habit I try to keep. The trouble is they never last very long."

He dropped the second oar and the boat turned back in the direction from which it had come. He dug into his deepest pocket and found what he was looking for.

"Here it is!" he said triumphantly. "My little dictionary. I carry it with me everywhere." He held up a small volume bound with velvet cloth and waved it in the air. "This is my little 'Bible'."

Both oars dragged in the water and the boat began to slowly turn in a circle while at the same time drifting downstream. A trifle alarmed, Louisa grabbed both sides of the boat but listened nevertheless as Theodore quoted from the treasured book, which he held open in his lap, about *The Secret Language of Flowers.*

With a certain veneration, he spoke about the lily and the lotus from Asia as being the symbols of spirituality and of Buddha himself. Then he spoke of the classical Greek and Roman legends with allusions to particular flowers. He mentioned the *Dream book of Artemidorus* which described the meaning of every single bloom in floral decorations and ceremonial crowns. He described how Olympic winners in ancient Greece received garlands of wild olives and how the Romans scattered millions of rose petals in gay abandon during their licentious feasts. He spoke of the significance of the lily, ivy, the carnation and the rose to Christianity and how Shakespeare described the meaning of the flowers that Ophelia wore in her crown in *Hamlet.*

At this point, Louisa felt the need to interrupt. "Excuse me, Mr. Bycroft," she said, slightly distressed, "but do you not think it is a good idea to take the oars now for we are fast approaching the bank!" She pointed sharply behind him, holding her hat with the other hand.

"Oh, my goodness! I *am* sorry my dear lady. Here, would you like to read the book while I man the oars? I must have got carried away!"

So saying, he stuck one oar deep into the water and strained on the rowlock until the boat turned around in the opposite direction. He strained against the current on both oars until they were finally under way again up stream. When he finally got his breath back, he said, "If you read the book, you will find that in the early sixteenth century a certain Lady Montagu from England accompanied her ambassador husband to Istanbul to attend the Turkish court. She was supposed to have sent a love letter from there back to her lover in England. Inside the letter were the first interpretations of eastern flower gifts. She said that no flower was without meaning and that it was possible to send messages 'without even inking the fingers'."

"Well, that's fascinating," said Louisa. "I must admit I do already know the meaning of some of the more common flowers because of course, a lot of it has been passed down from mother to daughter over the generations. My husband's an amateur naturalist and botanist as well. But I certainly don't know the history behind it all. In fact, when I come to think of it, I suspect my mother had an old flower dictionary amongst her belongings that were passed on to me when she died. I vaguely remember seeing pictures of young maidens (or were they fairies?), wearing bonnets and holding up posies somewhere about. I think I must have given it to Emma. I wouldn't be surprised if she were into all this in a big way. You know what young women are like these days!"

"You may have my copy of this little lexicon if you wish," Theodore volunteered. "I have plenty of spare copies in my study at home."

"Oh really? I couldn't. But if you insist. I'm delighted really," enthused Louisa.

She smiled coquettishly at him, appreciating his generosity and blushed. Then deliberately avoiding his gaze, she strained her eyes northwards over his shoulder to where the banks of the village green loomed in the distance.

"Goodness, it's getting late, Mr. Bycroft. Half the crowd has left. I didn't realize we had been out on the river so long!"

"My apologies, ma'am. I will get you ashore as soon as I can," he said gallantly.

He rowed a while longer and before long they were alongside the jetty and she gave him her hand as she alighted.

"Well, thank you, Mr. Bycroft," she said with a certain sense of decorum. "Glad to be ashore. If you would care to join us at bell ringing practice, it's at seven o'clock every Wednesday night. But not next week because the bells still need to be re-hung."

"Why thank you, ma'am. I'll be there," he said and tipped his hat.

Louisa tucked the little lexicon into her pocket and hurried up the bank to the main marquee. There, she spied the squire standing by the entrance and holding a jug of ale.

"Oh, Squire, have you seen my husband?" she inquired of him.

"Not lately, me lady," he said gruffly. "He left here half an hour ago to go looking for you."

"Oh," she said and gulped.

Just then the village brass band struck up with *When the Saints Come Marching in*. Not knowing where to start looking for her husband, she smartly side-stepped the band which was marching towards the band rotunda and peeked into some side-shows and stalls. She watched as a local villager won a couple of coconuts and then caught sight of one of her daughters on the merry-go-round nearby. The hurdy-gurdy of the merry-go-round and the *oompah-pah* of the passing band ensnarled each other in an arresting cacophony until the band had well and truly passed and the merry-go-round stopped. Louisa breathed a sigh of relief and Charlotte dismounted from her pink wooden horse.

"Hello dear. Have you seen Father?" Louisa asked her daughter.

"No, Mama," she said, dusting off her frilly dress. "Have you seen Geraldine and Lucy? They were supposed to be waiting for me here before going to get ice-creams. Oh no…they've gone without me and Geraldine's got all the money in her purse!"

"Never mind, dear. We'll just wait here a few minutes and see if they turn up. If they don't turn up, we'll go and buy ice-cream anyway."

They waited together as patiently as was possible for a mother and fourteen-year-old daughter to wait and then Alfred arrived unexpectedly around the corner.

"Hello! Where have you been all this time?" he asked addressing his wife. And then turning to Charlotte he said, "I thought I told you to stick together with your sisters?"

"I…I…they went off to buy ice-cream."

"Oh, I see. Now come along you two."

Alfred marched them both gently with one hand on each of their shoulders back towards the vicarage.

"But I wanted an ice-cream," Charlotte complained.

"Later," he said and continued to march them both home.

"Darling, let me explain," Louisa began.

"Later," he said and tightened his grip on her shoulder.

Oh dear, thought Louisa. *Now I've got some explaining to do. I'm sure he will understand. He always does in the end.*

She smiled wanly as they passed one of the ladies from the Guild and Charlotte began to whine and snivel. Just then, Geraldine and her little sister, Lucy, appeared licking ice-creams.

"Oh no!" wailed Charlotte. "Those two said they would wait and they didn't! I want ice-cream too!"

"Geraldine…let Charlotte have a bite of your ice-cream. That's the way. Now, Lucy…give Charlotte a bite of yours," said their father.

"No!"

Lucy swung her arm defensively across her chest so as to keep her ice-cream as far away as possible from her sister.

"You can't have any! It's mine!" said Lucy indignantly.

"Lucy…" said her father.

"No!"

Catching a glimpse from on high of the little drama unfolding, a passing clown on stilts wearing long blue striped trousers cheerfully leant down and took a big bite out of Lucy's ice-cream. Then he patted her blond head, grinned and went on his merry way.

Lucy couldn't believe her eyes and stood transfixed in horror as the other two girls laughed heartily at her misfortune.

Then Lucy cried, "Wahhh…h!" with all her might and her face went red.

"Oh dear! I think we've all had enough for today. Let's go home, shall we?" Louisa suggested pleasantly.

She grabbed Lucy's other hand and the family traipsed up the slope back to the vicarage, being narrowly missed by a man on a penny-farthing as he flitted past them crossing the road.

Once they were all safely inside the vicarage, the girls all ran off to their rooms to rest and Alfred was free to speak to Louisa at last. Carefully in control of his tone, he asked:

"Now who was that strange man I saw you with out on the row-boat, Louisa?"

"Oh, just another bell ringer who's arrived in the village. He's just bought the florist shop in the main street. He used to row in the Cambridge Boat Races, he was saying."

"Oh, really. I trust he will be willing to attend church regularly then? Or is he one of those dissenters?"

"I'm sure he will attend, dear. He seemed quite keen to get back into his bell ringing. I told him about our practices on Wednesday nights." Then changing the subject, she said, "Do you think the fundraising for the church was a success?"

"It was a great turnout…all things considered. We will check the takings tomorrow morning and see how it all went. The squire seemed pleased by it all too, I might add."

"Yes. He seemed quite happy when I spoke to him last," she said evasively. She wandered into the scullery for a glass of water and then called out, "I'm just going to have a lie down on the couch in the conservatory, dear."

"Right-o," Alfred called back from the other room.

Louisa lay down and made herself comfortable on the wicker couch with her feet up and re-arranged the cushions. She reached for the little lexicon in her pocket on *The Secret Language of Flowers*.

The frontispiece contained an excerpt by Leigh Hunt from his poem *Love Letters Made of Flowers*.

It began:

'An exquisite invention this,
Worthy of Love's most honeyed kiss,
This art of writing billet-doux
In buds and odours and bright hues!
In saying all one feels and thinks
In clever daffodils and pinks;
In puns of tulips and in phrases,
Charming for their truth of daisies!'

"How utterly delightful!" she said aloud. "I will definitely make a study of this!" She read on and then stopped, thinking, *Of course, I remember my mother saying never to bring lilies into the house. And then yellow roses. She always used to say to never give or accept yellow roses. Mmm…I must try and find that book…I'm sure Emma knows more about this than I do now…*

Two hours later she had fallen asleep with the little book splayed open across her chest.

Two

"Lucy dear, keep Rusty away from the croquet ball, would you? That's a good girl. If he doesn't behave himself, we will have to tie him up around the back of the house."

"Oh no, Mama! Here Rusty, here boy! Good dog! Now don't you touch the croquet ball!" she said, admonishing the dog. "Mama's trying to play."

Louisa was playing a friendly match with Eleanor Duval from the Ladies' Guild together with Millicent, the squire's wife and Betty, the curate's wife in the front garden of the vicarage. Eleanor Duval was a patrician-looking woman, straight-backed, stiff upper-lipped with a slightly hooked nose, strong forehead and dark intelligent eyes. Her auburn hair was streaked with grey and worn coiled up on the top of her head as was the fashion of the day. She was married to Terence Duval, the treasurer of the parish church, who was in the drawing room at a meeting with the other menfolk.

It was a clear day in late autumn, unusually warm for late October and the leaves from the magnificent mulberry tree were still being blown everywhere about the garden. The other deciduous trees including the weeping flowering cherry had all molted some time ago although several clumps of pansies still peeked out from the undergrowth here and there.

"Clunk!" went Eleanor's mallet.

"Good shot, Eleanor!" Louisa called out. "How did you manage to do that?"

"Oh, just sheer good luck, my dear," she called back. "Either that or the dog was behaving himself for once."

"That was a good game. Thank you, ladies. We must do this again some time." Then turning to Lucy, she said, "Lucy, please take Rusty around the back and tie him up while we all go in for some afternoon tea. We don't want him drooling all over our laps asking for pieces of cake, do we?" Then addressing the ladies again, she said, "Come along ladies. Into the conservatory and we will all have a nice hot cup of tea."

She waved the ladies indoors into the conservatory which opened southwards out over the front garden. The conservatory was of the domed variety with a crested peak and was embellished with white painted scrolled ironwork. It was built on to the rectory which itself was made of fine stonework. Under the pelmets of the conservatory ran a double row of small red and green stained-glass panels which cast a rosy apple-colored glow upon the white floor-length table cloth that was draped over the small round table inside. The interior boasted of a nonchalant profusion of plants which appeared to swallow up the white wicker furniture arranged around the perimeter. There was the obligatory aspidistra in a *jardinière* in one corner, a parlor palm and a huge dwarf Cavendish which towered overhead at the gabled end. A plethora of red and white pelargoniums hung suspended from the ceiling and around the walls, almost obliterating the begonias and fuchsias from sight. And from the center of the ceiling hung a single gas lamp.

"Oh what beautiful climbing geraniums…or rather, pelargoniums, I should say!" exclaimed Betty, the curate's wife. "Don't they look lovely today!"

"Why, thank you Betty. We've got Mabel Grey and Cinnamon Rose in here. Try breaking off a leaf and smelling the scent."

"I will indeed," replied Betty and so, being a little on the short and dumpy side, she reached up on tip-toe and picked a succulent-looking specimen from one of the Mabel Greys.

She sniffed the scent deeply with much ceremony while Millicent who was a much tinier person and more bird-like in comparison, chirped up with, "Yes, this room has a distinct Christmassy look about it with all the red and white and green, doesn't it?"

"And it's still only October." Eleanor chuckled.

The three women sat down and made themselves comfortable. Meanwhile, Louisa called out to the men who had been discussing financial matters in the drawing room to join them and began busily making tea in the kitchen. Sensing that refreshments were soon to be served, Charlotte and Geraldine soon made their appearance and assisted by ferrying tiered trays of fancy cakes and cucumber sandwiches to the guests. By the time Louisa breezed back into the room with a hot teapot, the conversation had turned to bell ringing.

"You know, Vicar," the squire was saying in a rather loud and pompous voice, "now that the bells have been re-hung, I wouldn't mind giving them a tingle or two myself."

"Well, I'm sure that could be arranged, Squire," the vicar replied, leaning thoughtfully back in his chair. With both hands, he placed the tips of his fingers together carefully under his nose. "What do you think, Louisa?" he asked, peering over the tops of his fingers. "A good candidate for the tenor bell?"

Looking somewhat taken aback, she looked first from one and then to the other and becoming a little flustered she said at length, "Oh, I can't see why not. I'm sure Algie wouldn't mind showing you the ropes, so to speak. He might want some time out for himself now and then, quite possibly and welcome a break."

"He's a big man too, is Algie," put in the vicar. "You need a big man on the tenor bell."

"Yes, that's why I'm on the treble," explained Louisa to the squire. "I'm the smallest of everyone in the group so it's easier for me to pull on the lightest bell."

"Oh yes…that makes sense," said the squire. "So, you will have a word to Algie then?"

"Certainly, next Wednesday, at our next practice," said Louisa. She smiled and laid the tea things on the table. Then modestly adjusting her hair and smoothing her skirt, she said, "Did you know that the new florist in the village is a bell-ringer? He will be sitting in on the next practice. He's quite keen to pick up the ropes again after ringing down in London."

"Oh really?" said the squire. "What did you think of the man? I saw you talking to him at the fete. Do you think he will fit in here after all the high life down in London?"

"Oh, I'm sure he will, Squire. Such a nice gentleman! In fact, being a florist, he gave me a book of his to read which I have found absolutely fascinating. It's all about the history of 'the language of flowers'."

"Really?" said the squire. "Now how about that. And have you become an expert yourself on the subject yet?" he inquired, somewhat boorishly.

"Not yet," replied Louisa. "But I can tell you about our ancient old mulberry tree out there which has been in the family for three generations."

"Oh? Do go on…"

"Well, the mulberry tree as you know is an extremely slow grower. In fact, Alfred's grandfather planted it there when he was a young man…didn't he dear?" she said, looking to Alfred for support.

"Ah, yes…that's right." He nodded.

"Well, it is said that whoever plants a mulberry tree will never live long enough to taste its fruit. And that is exactly what has happened with us because our tree only started to bear fruit after Alfred's grandfather died and Alfred was ten. Isn't that right, Alf?"

"Yes, dear."

"So," Louisa went on, "if anyone ever gives you a sprig if mulberry it translates as 'I will not survive you.'"

"Well, I never…" said the squire in disbelief.

"And then," Louisa went on, "there's the classical myth about the doomed lovers, Pyramus and Thisbe, that Shakespeare wrote about in his *A Midsummer Night's Dream.* Thisbe arrived first at the rendezvous under a mulberry tree to find that a lion had just ripped an ox apart. Naturally, she fled but she left her cloak behind which the lion took much delight in pawing with his bloody paws. Then when Pyramus arrived he saw the blood-stained cloak and assumed the worst. So, he killed himself with sword right under the tree. Then later Thisbe returned and finding her lover dead, she killed herself as well because she was overcome with grief.

Their mingled blood was said to have been soaked up by the tree so that its fruit then changed from what had been previously white, to black."

"Well, then…" the squire spluttered in amazement. "So *that's* why the garden path always looks so bloodied every summer…there's been a marauding lion out there and a couple of suicides!" Alfred quipped.

"No…silly…" Louisa retorted. "You know it's those greedy blackbirds that gorge themselves all day on the ripe mulberries…which *we* didn't pick in time! The juice just spills down their beaks and onto the path so it looks like the floor of a gladiator's pit."

"Oh, I *had* noticed last summer…" ventured Millicent tentatively.

"No, no murders Milly," Louisa said solicitously, "but we *were* looking forward to the rain to come and wash it all away!"

Everyone laughed and had another sip of their tea while Millicent squirmed uncomfortably in a chair that was really much too large for her. Ideally, she and the squire should have swapped places because he was spilling over to a certain extent in *his* chair. The two girls handed around more cakes and sandwiches and then the squire drew a deep breath and took the floor, announcing magnanimously:

"Well, ladies and gentlemen, I can safely say that on behalf of the vicar and myself, the curate and the treasurer here, that the church fete was a runaway success. And thanks to the ladies here present (and to those not present from the Ladies' Guild) for their unstinting support, the parish church is now flourishing very nicely. Financially speaking I mean, of course."

"Of course, Squire," agreed the vicar.

The squire went on.

"We all know that in the past ten years or so, congregations everywhere have been shrinking…at an alarming rate really if I may say so…so to have done as well as we have is a credit to us all."

"And to the Squire, especially," added the vicar. "We could not have done it without your help."

"Why thank you, Vicar. If I may say so, Vicar, the reason for these dwindling congregations is founded in all the nonsense about Darwinism and the increased literacy rates amongst the masses. The common people are starting to think for themselves now. With respect, sir, they don't seem to need as much divine guidance from the church as they did say, even thirty years ago."

"You might be right, Squire," said the vicar. "There certainly has been disruption in the church. I personally have no problem reconciling Darwinism and Anglicanism and yet still consider myself a strongly religious person in the face of all these new scientific theories (which I must admit, I also have a strong intellectual affinity to). My amateur studies in botany and the natural world stand by me there. But what worries me is that Jeremy, my second eldest son, the one who traditionally follows his father as a vicar into the church, has become a dissenter. I fear he is turning towards Unitarianism. I mean to say, when *I* go, who the dickens will take my place?"

Suddenly, realizing his *faux pas*, he said, "Oh, I *do* beg your pardon, Curate. I quite forgot you were here. You are so quiet."

The curate coughed deferentially and said, "Apologies accepted, Vicar. I do understand how you must feel about your son. But if I am still around when you go, I will gladly step into the breach."

"Thank you, Curate. That would be much appreciated. But you do all understand what I'm saying don't you? Only the other day the vicar in a village not fifty miles from here was quoted in the newspaper on the decline of this parish… 'My congregation is waiting for me in the churchyard,'" he said.

"No, really? Is that so?" asked the squire.

"Yes. Quite so."

"Well, I must say," said the curate, now that he had a chance to get a word in, "there has certainly been an exodus lately of the flute and violin players from the church galleries to go and join up with the Salvation Army Bands. But all this has been happening very slowly of course since incorporating organs into the churches years ago. It's the new mechanization everywhere. Not that the Salvation Army isn't a good thing (I go along with teetotalism and 'no smoking' myself). And not that having a new electric organ installed in our church (thanks to the squire) isn't a good thing. But progress is progress. Or perhaps I should call it…*evolution*," he said with a hint of irony.

A slight titter went around the room. During the lull in the conversation that followed, Louisa piped up with, "Speaking of organs and organists…where's Hugo today? I thought he was going to call in for afternoon tea, Alfred?"

"Oh yes, he was, but then he decided to go cycling in the country with a couple of girls from the church choir. He's just bought a new bicycle and wanted to try it out. In fact, I think they *all* have bought new bicycles."

"Where Hugo…I go…" quipped the squire and laughed at his own joke.

When the squire had finished laughing, there was another pause in the conversation. Then Eleanor's husband, Terence Duval, the treasurer, who was a thoroughly well-read man, cleared his throat and announced in a clear voice whilst peering penetratingly through his round-rimmed spectacles, "Yes, with the turn of the century only two months away there are bound to be changes. It will be the year 1900 after all. But we just have to accept the changes and go with the flow. We cannot just 'extirpate curiosity' to use Dr. Pusey's words in his just published *Spiritual Letters*. Curiosity is not a sin in *my* view…pardon me if I speak out of turn, Vicar, and I appear to be giving a sermon…but I'm sure you will bear with me because I know you are a very tolerant man."

"Not at all," said the vicar.

"I mean to say," the treasurer went on, "let us remember Copernicus and Galileo were both unnecessarily condemned. That was sheer non-scientific theological prejudice. Remember what Professor Huxley himself said to

Bishop Wilberforce forty years ago…'I would rather be descended from an ape than a bishop.'"

The vicar, who had visibly stiffened at this embarrassing outspokenness, coughed and said almost apologetically:

"But you must remember, sir, 'doubt' is not the same as 'unbelief'."

"Of course," Mr. Duval agreed.

"And even as Beatrice Potter herself said after a long religious quest, 'Religion is love; in no case is it logic.'"

"Correct, Vicar. What I am merely trying to point out in my clumsy and blundering fashion is that in the past sixty years since Queen Victoria came to the throne there have been an incredible number of changes. Not so much in medicine as we would like perhaps, except for Louis Pasteur, the Curies and the discovery anesthetics…but in other fields. For instance, we now have telephones, railways, steamships, airships and moving pictures…ice-cream…I mean…what's next?"

He splayed his hands expressively and looked disarmingly at his audience.

"I understand what you are saying, Mr. Duval," said the vicar. "All this progress is undermining religion and the church."

"Exactly. Look at Annie Besant."

"Oh, you mean the suffragist?" asked his wife, Eleanor.

"Yes. She is the perfect example of intellectual and religious unsettlement. What did you say her religion was, Eleanor?"

"Oh, at first, she was an Anglican, then a Tractarian, then something else…I forget what…oh yes…I remember, a follower of Stopford Brookes. Then she was a Unitarian and now she's an atheist, I think. Goodness knows what she will become next!"

"There you are you see," said Mr. Duval significantly.

"Yes, it's a worry," admitted the vicar. "All those lost souls…Life has definitely become more secular in the past sixty years, especially in the big towns. I just wonder what life will be like in another sixty years!"

"I don't think you need to worry dear," interjected Louisa, "because it's quite likely that you won't be here!" There was general laughter as everyone relaxed a little more.

Then the squire spoke up with, "I say…I heard the vicar at Melplash in Dorset, Samuel Johnson, is doing alright. He's built himself a new vicarage with an observatory attached and he's quite an authority on astronomy I believe. Not that such a study would help with the work of his parish, of course."

"That's interesting," piped up Betty always keen to know the latest piece of gossip. "*I* heard that he draws up horoscopes at the top of his house."

"Really!" said the squire, not knowing quite what to believe. "I tell you what though, he must have some sort of a private income to sustain building that…his wife's I shouldn't think!" he said with a trace of innuendo as he folded his arms across his chest. Louisa and Alfred glanced at each other fleetingly then Louisa announced:

"Anyone for more tea? Tea? Go and put the kettle on Charlotte, thank you dear," and began offering the last of the sandwiches.

Suddenly, they heard barking coming from the back of the rectory.

"Oh, that sounds like there must be a hedgehog out there," said Louisa exasperatedly. "Lucy, see if you can find it and Geraldine will shift it."

Lucy ran out to attend to the dog and the hedgehog with Geraldine following obediently behind.

"Rusty's a Jack Russell terrier," Louisa explained to the guests. "We got him as a supposed-to-be descendant of one of the Reverend John Russell's dogs three years ago. But he can be a yappy little thing when he wants to be. He's definitely not a foxhound. Alfred doesn't go grouse hunting or hunting foxes on the moors anyway. He's too much of a softie when it comes to that sort of thing, aren't you, Alfred?"

Alfred grunted in reply. She went on, "So Rusty just gets the run of the vicarage grounds here and digs up the garden for us in all the wrong places. But we wouldn't be without him, would we, dear?"

"Definitely not," said Alfred. "He's one of the family even though he can drive us mad at times."

Suddenly, the barking stopped. It seemed the girls had solved the problem. They returned triumphant but with dirt everywhere on their hands and faces.

"Right, you two," Louisa said. "Off to wash your faces and hands and then you can sing and play some items for the guests."

"Oh, *must* we?" they groaned.

"Yes. You know we always entertain our guests. Now off you go."

The guests by now had all finished their tea and withdrawn into the rectory drawing room. The girls soon returned all spic and span and stood to attention.

One by one they gave their recitals, Geraldine and Charlotte both singing a duet accompanied by their mother on the piano and Lucy reciting a poem that she had memorized at school. The vicar gave a recital on his violin (as he was a keen amateur violinist amongst other things) and performed a creditably good rendition of *The Arrival of the Queen of Sheba* (his favorite) to a perfectly timed accompaniment from his wife on the piano. When they had finished, they invited the curate to play on his flute, but unfortunately, he had left the said instrument at home.

"You *what*?" asked the squire. "You left your flute at *home???*" he asked, addressing the curate in mock horror as if he were some miscreant schoolboy.

The curate blushed and apologized for his misdemeanor but was able to make amends by singing a sea-shanty unaccompanied instead.

The girls loved it and asked him to sing it again and again…In the end he was 'all sung out' and after the guests had gone the girls were all doing hornpipes and singing around the house over-excitedly:

'What shall we do with the drunken sailor?
What shall we do with the drunken sailor?
What shell we do with the drunken sailor,
Early in the morning?'

They were perfect little angels when there were visitors but when they had gone…!

Once the commotion had died down and the family had had dinner and the girls had gone to bed, Alfred and Louisa were left alone in the drawing room. Alfred picked up the novel he had been dipping into lately and then changing his mind, he put it down again.

Obviously troubled he said, "That Terence Duval! I had no idea he could be such an upstart! And he's our treasurer too!"

"Don't worry, dear," said Louisa. "It's just a sign of the times. He's obviously got Unitarian leanings the same as Jeremy has."

"Mmmm…" he pondered a moment. Then changing the subject somewhat abruptly, he said, "That book that you were loaned…You must have really got stuck into it to remember all that about the mulberry tree. I didn't realize there was so much to it…'the language of flowers,' that is. So when do you have to give the book back?"

"Oh, I don't. It was given to me…"

* * *

On that very same afternoon, Hugo, the organist, was cycling about in the country with Sally and Avril, two young choristers of about twenty. Hugo, being five years their senior and who was almost like an older brother to them, had agreed to escort them both out to explore the ruins at Rievaulx Abbey, which was about five miles over the river Rye. The three friends were test-driving their new bicycles on the way.

Hugo was a tall, rather ungainly fellow and a little effeminate. In fact, you wouldn't have thought he would have the innate sense of balance required to ride a bicycle. But he surprised himself and everyone else with his new purchase and held his own well. The two girls on the other hand were intuitively sporty types and quite robust.

It was a clear autumn day and the bare branches of the trees along the way looked strangely forlorn without their golden leaves to pay tribute to the unusually pale blue sky. They rode without mishap through the austere heart of the moorlands past a patchwork of fields and meandering stone walls. Then suddenly they came upon a sequestered valley which seemed almost like a lush oasis compared to everywhere else. They crossed over two hump-backed stone bridges spanning the river and then were presented with the awe-inspiring sight of Rievaulx Abbey in all its twelfth-century medieval glory.

It was a magnificent example of early English Gothic architecture. The chancel and the transept walls of the monastic buildings still stood at full height and the arches of the choir soared serenely heavenwards with flying buttresses supporting the vault.

The three young travelers parked their bikes and then wandered amongst the fallen masonry, very much in awe of the place. It had a feeling of timelessness about it or perhaps it was more an air of bygone reverence. Whatever it was, the sheer impact and stark beauty of the ruins left a deep impression on the threesome.

They soon found themselves upon the terrace, a huge half-mile expanse of lawn which overlooked the ruins in the valley. They sat themselves down on a picnic blanket and opened up a packed afternoon tea of banana cake that Avril had brought and shortbread and tea things that Sally had brought.

After a few moments of respectful silence surveying the scene, Avril suddenly had the urge to ask Hugo a question.

"How would you have liked to have been a twelfth-century Cistercian monk, Hugo?"

"Well," he said after some reflection, "I would have loved it I think. It would have been a good excuse to wear a frock! Except that the thick hairy cloth would have been itchy to wear," he said with a certain sense of repulsion.

"I can just picture you as a monk with a shaved head and everything," she continued.

The two girls giggled at the thought.

Then Hugo said, "At least I would have been a very learned monk and I would have known everything there was to know about music and art and literature. I think I would have been a composer and written Gregorian chants. You two would have been my servants and would have had to copy out all my manuscripts."

"Female servants in a monastery? You must be joking!" They laughed.

Hugo sniggered at the thought and absent-mindedly began plucking the petals off a daisy.

"This is nice banana cake, Avril," Sally commented. "What's the recipe?"

Avril had just got to the end of the list of ingredients when Hugo said, "Drat!" And threw his daisy down with feigned disdain.

"Oh!" said Sally. "So, who's your lady friend Hugo?"

"Tell us. We won't tell anyone," she teased.

"No, we won't tell," added Avril impishly.

In a fit of pique, Hugo playfully mussed up their hair and then picked another daisy. The girls readjusted their hair which they had both worn out loose today and then Avril suddenly remembered something.

"Did you know that they're putting on Gilbert and Sullivan's *Patience* down in York next week? We should all go."

"Yes. That's an idea," said Sally. "Why not? Do you want to chaperone us, Hugo?"

"Mmmm…" he said, his mind elsewhere. Avril went on, "It's supposed to be a take-off of Oscar Wilde's life…you know, the eccentric aesthete with his long hair and velvet breeches and his liking for sunflowers and peacock feathers."

"Really?" said Hugo, his interest at once aroused. "Sounds like fun. Can't say why I shouldn't accompany you. But you'll have to behave yourselves!"

He threw a bunch of daisies at them and the two girls laughed in feigned alarm.

"That's settled then," said Avril, picking daisies out of her hair. "We're all going to see *Patience.*"

Suddenly, Hugo had a mischievous idea.

"I would have thought that you would both prefer to go and see Oscar Wilde's play, *An Ideal Husband,* instead!" he said, holding up both hands as a shield and ducking behind it.

"Why you…beast!" they both exclaimed in mock horror and threw handful after handful of daisies at him with a fair force so that they ricocheted off his body like little bullets.

"You asked for that, Hugo!" they said.

"Oh, but I know you've both got broad shoulders." He grinned cheekily.

Three

By the following Wednesday night, the bells had been re-hung and now stood suspended in a circle from the reinforced framework inside the bell tower. The vicar had been very pleased with the result and was relieved to see that his bell tower was still standing. Where would he be without church bells and a tower to hang them in, indeed? The bell-ringers would be testing the tuning over the next few weeks and the vicar trusted that he would get a full report in this regard back from Louisa, his wife, who was lady captain of the bell-ringers. He knew that he could rely on her for any such matters relating to the running of the church. He trusted her implicitly in such things. Not like that young fool of a bell-ringer, James, who used to hang around one of the housemaids at the vicarage. He wouldn't trust him with a barge pole, at least not where she was concerned. He was glad he had since got rid of that Jezebel. Nothing but trouble, she was.

*Now, that Theodore fellow…*he thought vaguely.

He could see that he would have to keep an eye on him as a new parishioner and bell-ringer if he was making such an impression on his wife, what with all that flowery stuff in that book he had given her…

* * *

The long-drawn-out autumn sunset was drawing to a close and the sky changed imperceptibly through its various colors from blue to yellow to orange, tangerine and red, casting black silhouettes of the de-foliating trees and village chimney stacks against the distant horizon.

The scents of autumn flowers hung in the damp air and the muffled sounds of horses' hooves in the streets beyond the vicarage could be heard above the faint cries of paperboys selling their wares in the township while strident swarms of sparrows settled into the neighboring poplar trees for the night.

That Wednesday night, Theodore Bycroft arrived ten minutes early for bell ringing practice. He was awaiting the arrival of Louisa and lingered outside the belfry door because he had a gift for her. She arrived at five minutes to seven o'clock on the dot and was surprised to find him loitering outside the door. As soon as he saw her, he immediately took off his hat and gave a courteous little bow.

"Allow me, madam, to present you with this beautiful flower," he said, offering her his floral tribute. It was a beautiful white gardenia.

"Oh, thank you, Mr. Bycroft. But you shouldn't have really," she remonstrated.

"Not at all," he gushed. "You are just the sort of lady who deserves such treatment. And with me being a florist, it's no trouble at all to get you the very best."

Louisa blushed delightedly and ushered him into the bell ringing chamber. There, she daintily sniffed the flower's heavily scented perfume and admired its tender beauty before placing it very carefully inside her coat pocket and hanging up her coat.

Soon the other four bell-ringers arrived: James, Gareth, Charles and lastly Algie, who was on the tenor bell. Algie was an extremely big man but he had to be because the tenor bell weighed over a ton. He was a butcher…a tall (and wide) silent type. The other three were a wheelwright, teacher, and ironmonger respectively and all were from the village. Louisa introduced them all to Theodore, whom she explained was a semi-experienced bell-ringer who wished to sit in on Wednesday night practices for the time being.

"Perhaps you would like to do some 'call-changes', Mr. Bycroft and keep us on our toes," Louisa suggested. "And then later on perhaps you could swap with either James, Gareth or Charles and have a go on the ropes as well."

"Of course. But do please call me Theodore. Now that we are all bell-ringers together, let's use our first names. It's so much more friendly."

"Certainly, Theodore." Louisa smiled.

All was agreed and so the bell clappers were duly muffled with pieces of felt, the window louvres winched shut, the bell-ropes untied and the sallies held ready for action. The bells were always left in the 'up' position between use (that is, upside-down and resting in a position just off balance), to avoid any lengthy and often noisy raising of them before any ringing proper could begin. Louisa had always thought of them like this as resembling a cluster of baby birds in their nest with their mouths open.

The five bellringers then stood in their usual circle, each holding the colorful sallies at the end of the ropes firmly down before Theodore began by calling a 'round' from the sidelines. The bells rang out clearly and brightly from the treble to the tenor in sequence at perfectly spaced intervals. This in itself was some mean feat because the difference in weight of each bell meant that each one needed different speeds on both the downward hand stroke and on the upward backstroke to achieve evenly spaced rings. The sound was quite agreeable especially now that the bells had been re-cast.

"What about some 'doubles' next?" Louisa suggested.

There were no objections to this so off they went ringing their next sequence with Algie sounding every fifth note on the tenor with the exactitude of a metronome. The other four ringers performed the actual sequence which required a good measure of intellect and memorization. For this reason, the 'tenor-man' in a band was often considered by some bell-ringers around the country as having 'more brawn than brain'. But woe betide any bell-ringer here in Bingham who gave Algie any cheek! He was a butcher remember and he liked his pound of flesh.

Theodore called the changes before another short break and they changed from doing 'doubles' to another sequence whereby the tenor bell actually had to take part in the 'method' itself. That was when they ran into problems. Theodore called out, "Stand!" and the bells all came to a jarring halt. "Algie, you're running rather late and then early, old man," Theodore pointed out in his posh London accent.

"Er, sorry…I'll try that again. Didn't 'ear the changes you called."

"Oh, I can see I'll have to speak up," Theodore replied sardonically.

They tried again but after about five minutes it all turned to mud and resulted in chaos.

"Did you still not hear me, Algie?" Theodore asked disbelievingly.

The older man scowled:

"I think it's just as your voice is too soft for me bell," Algie corrected him. "Me 'earing's alright, it's just as your voice is too bloody soft!"

His face paled visibly at his own effrontery.

"Right-o gentlemen," said Louisa, taking charge. "Let's have Gareth calling the changes and Theodore, you ring Gareth's bell. How does that sound?" she asked sweetly.

The two men obediently changed places with Gareth calling out the changes in a deep sonorous voice. The ringing proved better, but still not perfect. This time it was Theodore who made the mistakes. The result was cacophonous. He was a little embarrassed, to say the least. Obviously, they would need more practice to perfect this 'partial peal' before Christmas. It was decided that Theodore would not take part in any ringing for Sunday services in the meantime until later next year. And Algie reluctantly agreed to Louisa's request of teaching the squire the ropes on the tenor bell in the New Year.

The practices continued in a similarly fractious vein over the next few weeks. However, as far as the floral tributes were concerned, they kept coming in abundance. In fact, Louisa was so intrigued with the white gardenia (which she discovered translated as 'you are lovely', from her little book), that the next Wednesday night she decided to repay the honor by giving Theodore a small bunch of violets from out of the rectory garden. She checked their meaning first of course, (which was 'modesty' according to her book), so she felt they would be quite a fitting reply. She felt as if she had been dancing on air for the past week. To think that such a handsome young man should take an interest in *her*! A married woman at that! She could not let such a dream of a man go unnoticed.

That night, Theodore's eyes lit up when she handed the violets to him at the belfry door, and he said:

"Why, thank you Louisa. How thoughtful. Wait on, I've got something for you too."

He reached inside his jacket and pulled out a beautiful white moth orchid flower.

"Oh, Theodore! That's beautiful! You shouldn't have. Thank you so much."

"You're welcome," he said. "It's so nice to face opposite a delectable lady when I'm pulling on a rope. The only problem is, sometimes I think it breaks my concentration!"

They both laughed and went inside to wait for the others.

By the following Wednesday, Louisa had discovered that the translation for a white orchid was 'you are beautiful'. Naturally she felt the need to reply to such a compliment now that she was in possession of a very good flower dictionary and had access to the greenhouse in the rectory back garden. Why *shouldn't* she reply? Becoming fascinated with the whole idea of conversing in the foreign language of flowers she whole-heartedly continued the conversation which had by now become a weekly ritual. The attraction of the secret code had captured her imagination.

That evening, she presented Theodore with her reply. It was a fern frond meaning 'I am fascinated'. Over the next few weeks, she received the following messages:

-A pale pink peony	:	*I am bashfully in love*
-A daisy	:	*She loves me, she loves me not*
-Forget-me-nots	:	*True love, forget-me-not*
-A gladioli flower	:	*I loved you at first sight*
-An acacia flower	:	*Secret love*

To which her respective replies were:

-Some sage leaves	:	*Domestic virtue*
-Morning glory	:	*Affection*
-Pansies	:	*You are in my thoughts*
-Periwinkles	:	*Friendship*
-Lemon verbena	:	*Enchantment*

Towards Christmas, Louisa was beginning to wonder where all this 'flower talk' was leading. However, soon other matters arose which caused the little flirtation to be put on hold for a while.

* * *

On the morning of Christmas Eve, Geraldine, Charlotte and Lucy were putting the final decorative touches to the freshly hewn Christmas tree that their father had provided for them. The smell of fresh pine pervaded the drawing room. A little extra tinsel here and another shiny bauble there made all the difference. Then all the presents had to be arranged 'just so' under the tree. Soon a postcard arrived to disrupt proceedings at the vicarage. It was from their eldest son, Thomas and the postcard was stamped and marked 'Saint Helena'.

"Saint Helena!" all the girls exclaimed in unison. "Where's *that?*"

"Well, don't just stand there. Go and check the atlas," Louisa suggested. Geraldine collected the atlas from out of the library and they all poured over it.

"There it is!" Charlotte announced. "Just over on the left hand side of Africa in the Atlantic Ocean! Good Lord, I wonder what he's doing there?"

"Well, let's read it and see," Louisa said.

She sat down in the drawing room surrounded by the three girls, while Alfred, who was sitting reading in his favorite antimacassared armchair, removed his reading glasses and listened attentively.

Louisa read aloud:

20th Nov, 1899.

"Dear Family,

How are you all? Well, here I am now based in St. Helena for a while. We just sailed in from Lisbon, Portugal after two weeks at sea. It's so nice to be somewhere relatively hot now (compared to England, I mean!) This is the place where Napoleon was incarcerated. I'm going to check out Longwood House where Napoleon stayed after I've explored the rest of the island. The cliffs are really steep here all over the place and the beaches are black and shingle just like home. Father, you'll be interested to know they have 'He' and 'She' cabbage trees here and even a native olive tree.

By the way, I suppose you've heard that war broke out a month ago in Africa with the Boers again. Cecil Rhodes wanted Dr. Jamieson to invade the Transvaal and overthrow President Kruger there. The invasion failed as you may have heard. We British are really in it up to our necks now. So, after five days here, we are off to Cape Town. We will be preventing supplies getting to the Boers in Pretoria and patrolling the coast all around the south of Africa. The Boers are said to have guns that outrange our armies', so the navel brigade is lucky to have twelve pounder guns with a similar range to the Boers.

To be honest, I'm quite looking forward to some action!

Love,

Thomas."

Lucy squealed and giggled excitedly. "Oh, doesn't he write small!"

"Yes, dear," Louisa explained. "That's so he can fit all what he has to say onto the back of the postcard." She got up and handed the postcard to Alfred who examined the postmark carefully through his spectacles.

"Well, that boy of ours is going to be in the thick of it all down there! I just hope he keeps his wits about him. He certainly takes after his grandfather, doesn't he, Louisa?"

"Yes, dear. He's really taken to the navy like a duck to water. But it looks like with war breaking out, he will be home later than we thought. I just hope he's alright out there…It's so far from home…Christmas isn't the same without him…At least Emma will be coming up from London this afternoon and Jeremy's coming up late tomorrow morning. So that will be nice."

Later that afternoon, Emma duly arrived by coach from York after a train trip up from London. She was thrilled to be home again because the nursing training in London had been her first big adventure away from home. Now she was back to be spoiled over Christmas. She carried with her a small posy of pink carnations which she had bought at the railway station for her mother. In fact, she was not unlike her mother in the looks department.

"Merry Christmas!" everyone chanted as she came through the door.

Rusty jumped up and down in excitement and everyone made a fuss of her. Then Louisa said:

"Oh, thank you for the posy, dear. It's lovely. Tell us all about London. And try some of my scrumptious mince pies…they're fresh out of the oven this morning."

"Oh yummy! I just *love* your mince pies! Is there any cream?" She reached out and took one anyway without cream, took a bite and then proceeded to give a report on events in London with her mouth full. "…Well, I'm sharing quarters with…three other girls…all the same age as me…at the hospital and we have…classes three days a week and practical work two days a week." She swallowed her mouthful of mince pie, brushed the crumbs away from her lips and continued, "I'm really enjoying it. Everyone is so friendly and helpful. And the patients! They're a real challenge! They are all so different. But I don't know how many times I've been told by some of the elderly ones, 'Never grow old!' Some of them look so ancient that you would expect that they should be already dead!"

Everybody laughed. Meanwhile, Rusty was looking at Emma in horror because she hadn't given him a little titbit. Unfortunately, Emma was too busy catching up with the news to notice. Rusty pawed her leg to let her know that she had forgotten him but she brushed him away.

"We got a postcard from your big brother," her father began. "He's on his way to Cape Town. The Boer War's started up again."

"Oh no!" said Emma. "I hope they don't want any extra nurses over there. Not that it would bother me just yet because I haven't finished training."

"Well, *we* wouldn't like to see you go either," chipped in Louisa. "It's bad enough having one child involved in a war, let alone two!"

"Don't worry, I wouldn't want to go anyway. All my friends are either here in Bingham or in London."

Louisa breathed a sigh of relief.

"Did you get my letter, Emma?" she asked. "The one with the pressed pansy in it?"

"Yes, I did, thank you, Mother." She paused suddenly and then said, "You know what I saw at the station today? A delivery boy carrying a big bunch of yellow roses off the train. I hope they're not for me! Fancy getting yellow roses on Christmas Eve of *all* days!"

"That sounds terrible," agreed Louisa.

"So how is it that you're back into 'saying it with flowers'?" asked Emma of her mother.

"Oh, there's a new bell-ringer in the village who's a florist and he's rekindled my interest in it." (She could feel herself blushing slightly.)

"Oh, really?" said Emma. "It's all the rage in London, I know that! I try and translate each new bunch of flowers that arrives for the patients."

They chatted on about life in the big city and how much Emma missed not having a piano to practice on during the past three months at the nurses' home. She was looking forward to limbering her fingers up on the piano in the drawing room with a few fast-paced Bach partitas and fugues. This she did with much enthusiasm and several mistakes until it was time for Louisa to supervise decorating the church for the evening service. Then it was home for a family dinner, an open house 'carols by candlelight' in the rectory drawing room at seven, bell ringing at ten o'clock and then the late service to celebrate the last Christmas Eve of the century. Louisa always enjoyed the 'carols by candlelight' at the vicarage because it not only gave anyone and everyone a chance to sing but she had the honor of listening to the inspiring voices of the church choir ringing out in her very own drawing room. Some of the young choristers had such pure angelic voices that it was quite a thrill for them all to hear them sing such old favorites as *Away in a Manager* and *Silent Night* completely unaccompanied.

For the late service, the church which had been recently redecorated inside with new wall-hangings, frescoes and mosaics, looked a sight to behold especially with the extra splash of color that the flowers now provided. Louisa and the ladies of the Guild had decorated the nave in strategic places with beautiful arrangements of red poinsettia (which translated as 'be of good cheer'), white lilies ('majesty and purity') and branches of green myrtle ('love, mirth and joy'). Hugo accompanied the choir on the organ and the vicar naturally gave a most thought-provoking sermon about the changing times they were living in and how one must hold on to one's religion as one's anchor in life.

* * *

Christmas Day dawned and there was a light snow falling over the village. The nine o'clock service was announced with a quarter peel on the bells which lasted nearly three-quarters of an hour, leaving the ringers feeling quite invigorated. Then Louisa had to dash inside the church to man the organ as Hugo had left for London for the next week. She noticed as she took her seat at the console that Theodore was seated amongst the congregation. Her performance immediately became self-conscious in his presence as she could sense his ardent admiration from afar.

After the service, the household at the vicarage was awash with excitement and expectancy. Jeremy was due home at eleven o'clock. He was an entomology student at Magdalen College, Oxford and the only one of the Picard children to follow their mother into bell ringing. When practicing ringing rounds at the Magdalen College bell tower, some of the non-ringing students would rib him and his fellow ringers. They believed that such repetitive actions suggested a great capacity for 'enjoying boredom'. Nevertheless, it was an activity which involved as much physical exertion as in rowing and once he got into change ringing, it would become much more of a challenge as a combination of music, mathematics and sport. However, what

Jeremy enjoyed most at the college was May Day. Every May the first, at six o'clock in the morning, the college's choristers would sing grace in Latin from the top of the bell tower and this would be followed by bell ringing, Morris dancing and punting on the Cherwell River together with a champagne breakfast. Naturally, the champagne breakfast was the biggest drawcard for Jeremy and his fellow students. Nothing was appreciated more than a good feed of bacon and eggs washed down with a little tipple or two of university brewed, sparkling elderberry wine.

However, brewing elderberry wine with his classmates was not the only intoxicating hobby that Jeremy had taken up during his sojourn at Oxford. He and a group of fellow students had taken to frequenting the numerous beer houses in Oxford and ogling the women there over a few drinks. There were no female students yet unchaperoned at the university, so naturally they were drawn to such watering holes out of curiosity at least. Jeremy found the 'come hither' looks of the prostitutes that visited these places quite fascinating, especially as he considered himself to be unattractive to the opposite sex, being merely an inexperienced, spotty and bespectacled young student and a vicar's son, at that.

The temptations of city life for a gauche young man such as Jeremy were almost too much to bear, although he did form an attachment to a young barmaid by the name of Nell at the Horse's Arms. Nell was quite an attractive wench with an ample cleavage and a cheeky smile, just a few years older than himself. He was pleased to discover that she had no aversion to insects of any kind whatsoever, as not even a saucy challenge with a live cockroach caught from off the bar and dangled enticingly above her cleavage would make her flinch. Jeremy was impressed with her fortitude. He doubted, however, whether such a model of 'female virtue' would have impressed his parents. Happily, they would never know the high jinks that he and his 'less than sober' colleagues got up to in these establishments.

Eleven o'clock soon arrived and Jeremy walked in the door laden with presents and luggage.

"Surprise, I'm here! Merry Christmas!" he called out. He was a lanky fellow, taller than his father, sandy-haired and being short-sighted, wore thick spectacles. Lucy, Charlotte, Geraldine, Emma and Rusty all rushed to the door with Louisa and Alfred not far behind.

"Merry Christmas!" they all chorused.

"Come on in, son," said his father. "Let me help you take all that luggage upstairs."

"Oh, thanks. Just be careful with that leather bag there, if you wouldn't mind though. It's got one of my specimens in it."

His father looked up questioningly.

"Oh, it's alright really. It's just a spider I've bought home to look after and study while I'm here as part of my thesis. It's one of those South American tarantulas."

"A *what?*" everyone chorused again.

"A tarantula. It's quite harmless really. It only eats crickets and the occasional mouse. It's just that it *looks* so horrible, being all big and hairy."

"Ughh!" his family all said together.

"Jeremy! How could you?" Louisa demanded. "I don't want anything of the sort in the house. And I certainly don't want you chasing the girls with that thing. Just take it outside right now…anywhere…just don't leave it in the house!"

Jeremy reluctantly took the leather bag outside and left it on the doorstep. Then he came back for a hot water bottle to keep the spider warm.

"Keep it away from my pigeons will you, Jeremy. I don't want it developing a taste for them instead of mice!" called out his father.

"Don't worry. I think he's going into a molt, so he's not hungry at the moment."

"Good."

With that, Jeremy made himself scarce outside with his awful arachnid and the four girls helped set the table in the dining room. There was still a light snow falling outside and through the morning mist could be heard the faint sounds of a Salvation Army Brass Band in the distance. They were playing *God Rest Ye Merry Gentlemen.*

Louisa paused in the kitchen and listened closely.

This would be the third Christmas in a row, she realized, that they would have celebrated without Thomas being present. She hoped it would be the last. Lost in her reverie, the back door suddenly burst open. It was Jeremy.

"Brr…it's getting worse out there! I think there's a storm brewing. And the weather cock on top the tower says the wind is coming from the north. Oh, everything's sorted out now, by the way."

"I should hope so," she replied. "Now, take your coat off and come and celebrate Christmas with us," she said, smiling forgivingly. She couldn't resist her last little dig as she led him into the drawing room, "You can talk to 'Incy Wincy Spider' later, when all the rain has gone…or should I say, snow?" She chuckled.

After the midday meal, everyone had had ample sufficiency of roast turkey and plum pudding and sat around in the drawing room, replete, to open their presents. Lucy ended up with the biggest pile and so had a grin from ear to ear. She especially liked the big teddy bear that her big brother, Jeremy had given her and hugged it to death. Jeremy ended up with the smallest pile amongst which was one of the new stylographic pens from his parents. He was always interested in new gadgetry and so spent the rest of the afternoon practicing his autograph. The three older girls received books, writing compendiums, hand mirrors, perfume sachets, lacy handkerchief sets, scrapbooks and suchlike.

Amongst Louisa's presents was a miniature Toby jug from Emma that for some reason reminded her of Thomas, and Alfred got a bird feeder gadget from Jeremy.

Several visitors braved the weather and dropped in to the vicarage during the afternoon with their Christmas greetings and chocolate almond bonbons. Rusty was always pleased to meet them if they were handing out bonbons but when the squire and his wife arrived with a packet of Christmas crackers, he was not so impressed. He hated those wretched things!

There was just one more Christmas service to go, evensong, and then Alfred and Louisa were looking forward to putting their feet up for a while.

Four

By now it was Boxing Day in the early evening. The blizzard that had been threatening on Christmas Day had now well and truly set in and everyone in the village had battened down their hatches. At the vicarage, the parlor windows rattled and shook and streamed with rain while outside the sky remained a doom-laden slate color. The wind was gusting up to gale force, dislodging branches from trees and creating havoc everywhere. Thankfully, the vicar had managed to feed and water his pigeons that morning and safely batten down the pigeon-house outside and Rusty was inside curled up cozily in front of the coal range in the rectory kitchen. He knew a good spot when he saw one.

The family spent an otherwise quiet evening together reading in the drawing room or playing with their presents and by ten o'clock everyone had gone to bed. Alfred and Louisa were both snuggled up in bed when at half-past eleven they were woken by a banging outside. It seemed to be coming from the church bell tower.

"Oh! Botheration!" Louisa grumbled. "That sounds like the internal door banging in the belfry. I'll have to get up and go and lock it."

"I'll go, dear," Alfred offered.

"No you stay here," she insisted. "It's my job as a key-holder to the bell tower to fix things like this."

"If you insist, but I really am quite willing, you know. I don't really like the thought of you out there all alone at this time of night…especially in this weather. I'll be waiting for you. Don't be too long," he cautioned.

She kissed him lightly on the cheek and grabbed her dressing gown and then donned her woolly coat over the top.

"See you soon," she said in a loud whisper and shuffled down to the back door. Here she put on her boots and ventured out into the night holding a lighted oil lamp before her. She struggled against the icy blast of the northerly gale and eventually reached the external door to the bell tower through the back gate. Her frozen fingers wrestled with the huge rusty key in the lock making a terrible din and she finally entered. She could still hear the internal door to the bell chamber banging insistently upstairs. It was as if she were being summoned.

"I'm coming, I'm coming," she called out, somewhat nettled.

Accordingly, she climbed the spiral steps and grappled with the offending door. No sooner was she standing alone in the bell chamber with the door shut securely behind her than she suddenly felt trapped.

There to her horror in the flickering of the lamplight she was confronted with the sight of a big black hairy thing the size of a dinner plate, rearing up on its hind legs at her. She screamed. It was encased in a glass box and there was a hot-water bottle propped up along one side of the box together with a pile of dirt.

"Oh my God!" she cried. "This is where Jeremy's keeping his tarantula…away from his father's pigeons! That boy will be the death ofme!"

She stopped to regain her composure and to get her breath back. When she had recovered sufficiently from the shock, she made a cursory inspection of the bells, the wheel-mountings and ropes. Satisfied that they were safe and secure, she then edged her way over to the opposite side of the tower as far away from the spider as possible and peered out through the window slats into the night. The snow and sleet was now pelting down unrelentingly outside. Then the wind began whipping around the tower with an even greater ferociousness. She drew her coat around herself more tightly and shivered with the cold.

Presently, in the eerie flickering of the lamplight she became aware of a certain presence…a presence other than the tarantula. The wind whistled ominously through the window slats. Through the raging tempest she imagined she could hear a faint wailing noise. At first, she thought she was mistaken but when she listened again, it was definitely the wailing of a woman. And it was becoming louder and louder.

Alarmed, Louisa spun around and was shocked at what she saw. There, hovering outside the window opposite was the hideous face of a haggard old woman with sunken eyes and long grey-white hair in a green cloak and she was staring at her. The repulsive specter was wailing remorselessly and wringing its bony hands through its tears. Its cadaverous features were vaguely reminiscent of someone she once knew.

She caught her breath and stood transfixed before the ghostly vision. All at once she recognized the face. It was that of her long-dead mother. She swallowed involuntarily, realizing then how Hamlet must have felt when he met face to face with his father's ghost. But what did it all mean?

In a flash, she recalled her mother's Irish ancestry. She had been a governess back in the mid-1800s. And this apparition before her was the epitome of an Irish banshee. But banshees normally attached themselves to families of noble birth. Did this mean then that there was some noble blood in her family tree? In which case she reasoned, someone must have been born on the wrong side of the blanket and she had now inherited a banshee through their bloodline.

She swallowed again and stared hard at the banshee. She struggled hard to remember what her Irish relatives had told her about the myths and legends of Ireland. Suddenly, she remembered. If a banshee were to reveal itself to someone, then this heralded a forthcoming death in the family.

"Oh no!" she almost choked. Shivers went down her spine. She stared wide-eyed at the banshee as the realization sank in. Immediately, the specter began to fade into oblivion almost as if it knew telepathically that the message had been received. The ululating stopped. Louisa stood for a moment, staring incredulously at the empty spot where the banshee had been hovering outside the window.

Struggling to contain herself, she drew her coat around herself more tightly and bolted for the door. The spider was now of no consequence. She rushed down the stairs in a frantic state almost forgetting to lock the intervening door. She battled to lock the outer door almost dropping the key in her nervous haste and was virtually blown through the back gate and in through the back door of the vicarage by the almighty power of the blizzard.

Five

No sooner had she locked the back door of the vicarage behind her than the telephone rang in the hall. By now, it was almost midnight. Her heart in her mouth, Louisa rushed to the phone.

"Who on earth could be phoning at this late hour?" she asked herself.

Just then, the cuckoo clock on the wall, punctual as usual, interrupted her train of thought with a jarring "Cuckoo! Cuckoo!" in a flurry of activity. She picked the receiver off the hook, her hands trembling uncontrollably.

"This is a toll call from Ireland. Will you take the charges?" an imperious voice asked.

"Y…yes," Louisa stammered.

There was a crackling on the telephone line and the cuckoo slid unobtrusively back into his cubbyhole, his little door slamming defiantly shut behind him. Then another more authoritative voice said:

"Is that Mrs. Louisa Picard of the Bingham Vicarage?"

"Y…yes. Who's speaking?"

"This is the Dublin Infirmary. We're just calling to say that your father, ex-Admiral Errol O'Donohue, has had a bad turn during the night. We don't expect him to last too much longer so you may like to come and see him within the next week or so if possible."

"Oh…" Louisa was struck dumb.

"Did you hear me Mrs. Picard?" (Crackle, crackle)…

"Yes…I'll be there as soon as possible. Thank you."

She shakily put the receiver back on the hook. For a moment, she stood rooted to the spot in shocked disbelief. Perhaps the banshee was right! There *must* be nobility in the family! Her husband would never believe her if she told him about what she had just seen in the bell tower. But she must tell him about her father, she realized. Alfred was a religious man and believed in things like miracles but she knew he didn't believe in anything mythological…or in ghosts, for that matter.

* * *

The next morning Louisa packed her bags which consisted of two large suitcases and a small wicker casket containing two of her husband's homing pigeons. Pigeon post would be faster than ordinary post, they reasoned, although slower than a phone call. But Alfred liked to make as much use of his little treasures as possible. He liked to see them get plenty of exercise. So, she placed the pigeon's casket inside a leather carry bag heated with two hot-water bottles. All of Alfred's pigeons were albinos as he liked to use them whenever he was officiating at gravesides or weddings for dramatic effect. Being white, they appeared to the everyday man-in-the street as a bevy of white doves signifying peace, purity and goodwill. They would take off in a glory of swirling white wings, circulate overhead for a time and then drop gently back to earth. The congregations would always marvel at the effect.

Louisa kissed Alfred and the children goodbye, realizing that Jeremy and Emma would most likely have gone back to Oxford and London upon her return. Luckily the blizzard had died down during the early hours of the morning and so the journey by horse and carriage through the snowdrifts to York would be less hazardous than it could have been otherwise.

She climbed aboard the carriage and waved goodbye as the carriage slowly pulled away from the curbside and the horses got into their stride. As the figures of her family receded into the distance, she soon became lost in thought with the events of the previous night running through her mind. How was her family connected to nobility and how could a ghost predict death? She was simultaneously both fascinated and horrified by the harrowing incident and by its grim portentousness. Soon she would be in Ireland where perhaps her Aunt Molly would enlighten her on the myths of Ireland.

She smiled to herself at the thought of Aunt Molly. 'Sweet Molly Malone' was how she always used to describe herself as a girl, so she would say. Then she would launch into a high-spirited rendition of:

'In Dublin's fair city…
Where the girls are so pretty…'

51

And whenever she passed a mirror, she would make a point of stopping to primp and preen. Louisa chuckled to herself and wondered if her dear old aunt was still the same or if she had changed much in the past five years since she had seen her. She reminisced upon her girlhood upbringing in Ireland and peered out the carriage window at the gently falling snow.

Before long she arrived in York and from here, she caught the train to Liverpool. On the train, the regular clatter of the wheels over the railway tracks caused her to drift off into a semi-sleep. Through the conglomeration of thoughts that crowded her mind, a solution of sorts arose in her subconscious. She would go and visit Madame Petrovsky, the famous spiritualist, while she was in Dublin. Perhaps she could throw light on her recent visitation in the belfry. She certainly needed some sort of reassurance and Madame Petrovsky could do that, she was certain. The parish of Bingham would never know of her meeting, she being a vicar's wife and so far from home. It might be considered sacrilege if they were to find out. But in spite of that, spiritualism was the 'in' thing at present. It had swept America like wildfire and now it was raging in Europe and the British Isles. The spiritualist movement had been publically discredited in the recent past after several charlatans had been discovered using trickery. However, a number of serious investigators believed there was definitely some truth behind the reports of genuine mediums. As long as she was discrete, Louisa reasoned, there would be no harm in it…in spite of what her husband might think!

Liverpool loomed on the horizon and she was soon aboard the passenger steamer bound for Dublin. It was a relatively quick eight-hour trip across the channel meandering around the decks and enjoying the sea air and then it was by horse and carriage to her hotel, the Excelsior, in Dublin. She would contact Aunt Molly tomorrow she decided, to arrange alternative accommodation with her, if at all possible. In the meantime, she busied herself unpacking in her hotel room and telephoning the infirmary about her father's condition.

From the news she received over the telephone, she decided to visit the hospital without delay. Being prepared for the worst, she folded up a big carpet bag and bundled it into her shoulder bag. She bought a posy of violets and forget-me-nots in the hotel foyer and then caught a horse-taxi up the hill to the infirmary.

There she was directed by the head nurse to her father who was on the third floor. She was given prior warning at the reception desk to expect the worst. Even so, when Louisa entered the large dormitory full of terminally ill old men, she was still not prepared for what it was that she saw.

Her father, a once fine upstanding Admiral of the British Navy and whom she once remembered as standing tall in his uniform fringed with gold epaulettes, shiny buttons and peaked hat, was now barely recognizable to her. He was but a mere shell of his former self. She found him lying in a crumpled heap upon his bed, barely able to speak and extremely weak. He was a cancer victim and the doctors blamed his condition upon his lifetime habit of smoking a pipe. The object of their ire lay incongruously amongst the paraphernalia of his bedside table as an enigmatic trophy to his renegade eccentricity. He himself liked to think of it more as an old friend keeping him company. The doctors had been treating him with quantities of laudanum as a pain killer and tranquillizer and also with a herbal remedy containing potassium iodide. However, medicine could only help so much and the end was now near.

"Father!" Louisa ventured, as she approached the bed. Her father looked up and smiled wanly.

"Is that you, Louisa?" he croaked hoarsely. "What's that you've got…flowers?"

"Yes. I thought they might cheer you up."

"Oh, thank you," he said and then began to cough uncontrollably.

The effort of speech was just too much for him. In fact, she had barely laid the posy on his bedside table than the coughing fit overcame him entirely. For a moment, she thought he wasn't going to come out of it and then he said:

"I thought you weren't going to come over, with me being here in Ireland amongst all your mother's relatives and you being back in England…You wouldn't like to pass me my pipe, would you?"

He was incorrigible, even at death's door. Not that he was allowed tobacco in here. He just liked the feel of his pipe between his teeth, a bit like a baby's pacifier. But he had barely got the words out when he was overcome by another coughing fit. In a few terrible moments, it was over and all was quiet. He didn't speak again. He had expired. His tired lungs had drawn their last breath.

Louisa had got there in the nick of time. She sat very still by the bedside and studied her father's face.

Instinctively, she took his hand and squeezed it. "Father," she said softly. "Can you hear me?" There was no reply.

"Father? Father…?" she asked, becoming alarmed.

Shortly, several nurses and a doctor were hovering about and drawing a curtain about the bed.

"I'm sorry, Mrs. Picard," the doctor said, after feeling the ex-Admiral's pulse. "Your father has passed away. We will send for the hospital chaplain immediately."

The last rites were said by the resident Irish Catholic chaplain and then one of the nurses suggested that Louisa clear her father's belongings. The staff disappeared and so in a daze Louisa cleared everything off the bedside table and emptied the little cupboard underneath of her father's personal effects into her carpet bag.

Presently she was back in her hotel room and telephoning her Aunt Molly to assist with funeral arrangements. They needed also to arrange to clear his household effects and put them up for auction together with his house which was in a very well-to-do area of Dublin, not far from her aunt's residence.

The funeral was three days later and by now Louisa was staying with her Aunt Molly and Uncle Jim. The funeral was held at a small Anglican church out of town and the grey drizzly weather suitably matched the somber mood of the congregation gathered there.

Rosemary (for remembrance) was thrown onto the coffin as it was laid in the ground and tears were shed by all Louisa's relatives…Aunt Molly and Uncle Jim, Aunt Mary and Uncle Albert, Aunt Jane and Uncle Toby and several cousins, nephews and nieces, too numerous to mention. Louisa couldn't help noticing that her well-preserved aunt, Aunt Molly, still looked beautiful even in grief. In fact, they could almost be mistaken for sisters…but only if Aunt Molly kept her black net veil pinned firmly over her face!

Louisa was the last of the O'Donohue line (until she married a Picard) and being an only child, she naturally stood to collect the entirety of her father's inheritance. Since her mother died when she was twelve, she and her father had been quite close, as even if he were at sea they would correspond by letter while Louisa would stay with Aunt Molly and her family. In fact, Louisa had even met her husband Alfred through her father. Her father had been visiting London as a naval lecturer and Alfred was a prospective naval cadet. However, the cadetship didn't quite eventuate as Alfred later bowed to family pressure to become a vicar. In the meantime, Admiral O'Donohue had invited the prospective naval cadets to a Navy Ball in London which Louisa just happened to be attending. And it was there that Louisa met her husband-to-be.

Her father had elected to live in Dublin upon his retirement as all his late wife's numerous relatives were there. He himself had been brought up in Torquay in the south of England and Louisa of course now had her own life up in the North Yorkshire Moors. As a widower, his effusive sister-in-law, Molly and the other relatives had taken him under their wing. He had enjoyed their company and all the social occasions and would have eventually liked to have married again. But now all that had been nipped in the bud. Now he was dead at the tender age of sixty-eight. And all because of a love affair with his pipe!

A few days passed and Louisa and Aunt Molly were having afternoon tea in her fine drawing room which opened out onto a balcony overlooking the city. They had been discussing family matters when Louisa suddenly asked:

"Aunt Molly…how much do you know about the myths and legends of Ireland?"

Aunt Molly looked up and with a twinkle in her eye, said, "Oh, you mean about the 'little folk' of Ireland, fairies and leprechauns…? Lots!"

"Have you ever seen one?"

"No, but your mother always used to say she had seen them down the back of the garden when she was a child."

"Really? Now that you say so, I do remember her talking to me about fairies," Louisa said. Then on a slightly different tack she asked, "So what can you tell me about ancestral ghosts and banshees?"

"Oh, not much I'm afraid. Except that banshees were supposed to attach themselves to the nobility…so that leaves us out. They were said to be always found around water and they would look absolutely grotesque and be wailing a lot. Their hair would be grey-white and they would usually be wearing a green cloak. They were said to appear on battle fields mourning the dead and washing the blood of the slain soldiers from their hands in the rivers nearby. To catch sight of a banshee was considered to be an omen forewarning of a death in the family. Of course, only the very fey would see them. To other lesser mortals they would be completely invisible."

"Really?"

"Why do you ask, my dear?"

"Oh, no reason really. I'm just interested…"

"You haven't seen one, have you?"

"A banshee?"

"Yes."

"Well, no…not exactly, I don't think…"

"I shouldn't think so. We're not connected to nobility…although I shouldn't doubt your mother thought so. Always a little bit of a social climber was our Bessie." She paused and said, "Oh sorry dear," tapping Louisa's hand. "I didn't mean to be rude. It's just that your mother Bessie always had very high aspirations for not only herself but for the rest of the family as well. I mean to say, she rose from being a coal-miner's daughter to being a governess and then when she married, she became an Admiral's wife. You can't do much better than that. The pity of it was that she died so young. She was only thirty-eight. Of course, all your aunts and uncles have done very well for themselves too. My Jim was a solicitor before he retired and both your Aunty Mary and Aunty Jane married well. Uncle Albert's still practicing medicine and Uncle Toby's a member of parliament."

Aunt Molly prattled on about the family history over the clink of her delicate bone china teacups while Louisa absorbed all the tittle-tattle, some of which she had heard before and some of which she had not. She had to mentally sift out the bits of information she didn't want and save the bits that she did. Such was the stream of information that flowed unceasingly from Aunt Molly's lips.

Finishing her tea, Louisa stood up and went to examine the family photographs arranged on the mantelpiece. The oldest ones there were only about fifteen years old as photography was still a relatively new science. But amongst the photographs she found a small miniature. It was a painted portrait of her parents on their wedding day. It was a very good likeness. She opened the locket around her neck and compared the portrait of her mother within against the one on the mantelpiece. Obviously, the same artist, she decided, to which Aunt Molly agreed upon closer inspection with her *pince-nez*.

"That reminds me," Louisa said. "I promised to write home to Alfred and the children. I hope you won't mind, Aunt Molly, if I write at your table here. I'll bring the pigeons out and release them from the balcony if that's all right."

"Not at all. Go ahead my dear. Be my guest."

With that, Louisa collected her writing equipment and then later the wicker casket while Aunt Molly cleared the tea things. She wrote two letters, one for each bird. She folded each letter up and then attached them both very carefully to each bird's leg with a metal clasp. Then with a quiet word in each bird's ear, she tossed them both into the air off the balcony.

They each took off with a battering of wings and flew high into the sky. She leaned over the balcony for some minutes and shaded her eyes as she watched them circling. Then they flew off in an east to north-easterly direction, instinctively knowing their whereabouts and their destination.

Louisa felt reassured that her family back in England was being kept up to date in the best practical way, considering her husband's penchant for his pigeons. But in the next few days she would be seeking reassurance for herself…from Madame Petrovsky…

* * *

Two days later, Louisa found herself seated in the sitting room of the great Madame Petrovsky. She carried out her calling from a small Georgian terraced house tucked around a corner from Merrion Square. The entranceway was decorated with a distinctive black and white painted door with brass knocker and fancy architrave and was crowned with an ornate semi-circular glass and wrought iron fanlight. Overhead, several quaint white wrought iron balconies were attached at the base of French doors set into a brick facade.

The room that Louisa had been ushered into, was on the first floor through a stone floored hallway and up a flight of steps. It was a young girl of about nineteen who had shown her in, Mrs. Petrovsky's secretary.

"You're early I think, Mrs. Picard. Madame is in preparation at present, so do make yourself at home on the settee there. She shouldn't be long."

She smiled graciously and modestly withdrew. Louisa smiled a tad apprehensively and took her place on the settee. The blinds had been drawn down and a white crocheted tablecloth was spread over a round table in the middle of the room. At the center of the table was a silver vase filled with white roses. Two sets of ornate candlestick holders carrying white lighted candles stood on either side of the flowers. Suspended over the table was a low-hung tiffany lamp edged with a long-tasseled fringe. It seemed to Louisa that there was only just enough clearance between the candle flames and the fringe for safety purposes.

Madame Petrovsky herself was seated at the table with her eyes closed. She seemed not to notice Louisa and held the tips of her steepled fingers together under her nose, almost as if she were praying. The flickering candlelight that played over her immobile features gave her a strangely ominous look. She sat there, serene and sibylline, her hooded eyes and hooked nose betraying nothing of her broodings in such an inscrutable sphinxlike pose. She was obviously in a deep state of meditation and nothing could disturb her. She wore a distinctive purple patterned silk shawl about her shoulders and her dark hair was drawn severely off her face into a bun. To soften the effect, two tiny ringlets curled around each ear beside a pair of hooped gold earrings.

Louisa shifted uneasily on the settee. There was a knock at the door and Madame Petrovsky suddenly awoke from her trance. She acknowledged Louisa with an apologetic smile and went to greet the four extra newcomers who were to make up the balance of the *séance*. She greeted them all cordially and then introduced everyone to each other. There was a man from the railways, a postman, a needlewoman and a teacher. Then with much fastidiousness she seated them one by one at the table in boy-girl sequence.

"Now ladies and gentlemen," she said with obvious satisfaction, "now that I have your undivided attention…" She cleared her throat, smiled encouragingly and continued in her mild eastern European accent.

"Do try to relax and take some deep breaths. It is very important for us all to be quiet and comfortable so it is not really necessary for us all to hold hands."

There was a slight pause as the little group of virtual strangers looked at each other self-consciously. Madame Petrovsky carried on.

"First of all, I have taken the telephone off the hook so we will not be disturbed. I have dimmed the light right down by drawing the blinds and as you can see, I have white candles and flowers here to attract the spirits. I will offer a prayer before we begin, to ask for protection and to ask that only positive spirits visit us here today. If you try and visualize a white light around the room, it will give you added protection. And deep breathing of course helps to raise the level of consciousness into the alpha state. I will attempt to introduce you each to at least one spirit in turn. So, close your eyes everybody and let us begin!"

Louisa sat as the others did, shoulders hunched, head bowed and eyes closed, waiting for something to happen. As the great medium began to call upon the spirits Louisa began to experience a few physical things change in the room…cool air blowing, strange noises, shivers down her spine and a tickling sense on her cheek. The first three participants spoke to their dear departed through the medium and then it was Louisa's turn.

"Who would you like to speak to Louisa, my dear?" asked Madame Petrovsky.

"My father, please, madame."

The medium nodded her assent and then called upon her spirit guide to present her with Errol O'Donohue, Louisa's recently deceased father. Nothing happened for a few minutes…so the medium called for him again. Presently, Louisa knew he was there. There was the unmistakable aroma of pipe tobacco permeating the air.

"Errol…do you have any messages for your daughter?"

There was a pause and then, "Yes."

"What is your message, sir?" the medium asked.

"Ask her where the devil she put my pipe!"

Louisa laughed. "Tell him it's quite safe. It's in my carpet bag and I'm taking it home with me," she said.

Her father seemed quite satisfied with this. Then he said through the medium, "Bessie's fine…still as beautiful as she was when I last saw her."

There was another pause and then he said through the medium again, "Tell Louisa to look after the children."

Then there was nothing. He had gone. Madame tried to get him back but it was hopeless, so she said:

"Is there anyone else you would like to speak to, Louisa?"

"My mother. Have a look at her portrait in my locket if it's any help," she offered.

"Thank you dear."

Madame then called upon Bessie O'Donohue through her spirit guide several times, but to no avail. Even the locket was of no help. It seemed that she was 'incommunicado' today.

"I'm sorry, Louisa. I can't reach her. Perhaps another day…"

"Oh, never mind. Thank you anyway, madame."

Disappointed, Louisa sat through the remainder of the *séance*. Still, she could always make another trip to Ireland sometime. But she was leaving for England tomorrow, so she wasn't sure when she would be back.

Bother! she thought to herself. *I wanted to ask Mother all sorts of things…about if it really was her that I saw through the belfry windows and about whether there was any noble blood in the family. But then of course, she might not have wanted to tell me anyway…*

She pondered the problem for a while and then attempted to focus her energy back upon the business at hand. When the rest of the *séance* was over Louisa made a point of asking Madame Petrovsky about banshees and how it was possible that they could foretell death.

"Oh, that's a difficult one, Louisa," she said. "Even I couldn't answer that one. You could try contacting the *Society for Psychical Research* in London, but I doubt even they could tell you. Banshees of course are supposed to be mythological ancestral ghosts, to my knowledge anyway. In which case, my answer to you would have to be 'I don't know'…"

None the wiser, Louisa was still glad that she had at least tried in her quest to uncover the truth. At least, she had made contact with her father and he seemed happy enough, so she was reassured to some degree. She thanked Madame Petrovsky for her services and walked out into the daylight, blinking at the comparative brightness of the grey Dublin day outside.

She was soon back in the bosom of Aunt Molly's household and packing again for the return trip to England the next day.

Six

It was an uneventful trip on the steamer from Dublin to Liverpool that 6th January. It was now 1900, but Louisa had not experienced much of a welcoming in of the New Year, singing *Auld Lang Syne* like other Irish folk. Her father had just passed away on 31st December, New Year's Eve and on the brink of a brand-new century, so she and her relatives had merely partaken of a quiet glass of wine or two and a few guinesses at home that evening as a mark of respect and to reminisce about old times.

Now she was on board the train bound for York over the freshly snow-ploughed tracks on the Yorkshire Moors and admiring the stark beauty of the desolate landscape under its fresh carpet of thick white snow.

Through the carriage windows she could see in the distance, mist-shrouded villages and bleak castle ruins dotting the countryside here and there huddled under their windswept blankets of snow. The whole district had been transformed into a white fairyland. It was the sort of winter scene that immediately brought to mind the music of Vivaldi's *Winter* from *The Four Seasons*.

There was a mysterious kind of serenity about the wintry panorama unfolding before her which perhaps echoed her state of mind. She was now an orphan of course, but yet still felt secure in the knowledge that her family lived on through the younger generation and that they would be waiting for her back in Bingham. There was still a sense of belonging in the warm bosom of her family there.

Inside the carriage all was silent apart from the inevitable background clatter of the train wheels. Seated opposite her a well-to-do middle-aged woman dozed, her head propped carefully against a white antimacassar, so as not to disturb her intricate coiffure. She wore masses of jewelry and a feathered hat lay across her knees like a large dead bird. And in the corridor outside, a man with mutton chop whiskers, probably her husband, stood restlessly smoking cigars. Louisa stared at the hat, the coiffure and the jewels and wondered absent-mindedly what type of business the husband might be fretting over to keep his wife in such luxury. She herself thought the jewelry rather too ostentatious to wear sleeping on a train. Any unscrupulous individual could quite easily snatch the jewels from her person and make off with them. Perhaps that was why the man in the corridor looked to be so on edge. Perhaps he was her bodyguard. Sinister connotations began to build involuntarily in Louisa's mind. She gazed out the window again, conjuring up all sorts of possible scenarios for this couple's relationship until the penetrating cold brought her up with a round turn. She drew her coat more comfortably about her and began to reminisce once more of her own parents' marriage and how they had met all those years ago.

Her mother, as a governess, had been employed by her father's uncle in London. They had met at an evening soiree at the uncle's house when her mother was singing an item. Her father had apparently stood at the piano turning the pages of the music for the accompanist and couldn't take his eyes off Bessie singing in her peacock-blue dress. They married a year later and then her father had become a naval midshipman in the Crimean War, the China Opium War and then later became involved in the bombardment of Alexandria in 1882. He was promoted to Admiral in 1890 but managed to take up the euphonium for a time in the Royal Navy Band. She used to love watching him entertain his grandchildren with his 'oom-pahs' as he practiced marching up and down his living room. It was a wonder he had enough 'puff' in him, all things considered.

Her mother had taught her the rudiments of the piano and singing while they were still based in London. But that didn't last long because she died of ptomaine poisoning after a summer picnic in Brighton. Louisa remembered the day well. In fact, she and her father were lucky to have survived themselves. They had been as sick as dogs. It was the pickled pork that did it…pig's trotters!

Louisa was then transferred as a young girl of twelve to live with her Aunt Molly and Uncle Jim in Ireland. Her father would come and stay whenever he had leave but by now had taken up his dreadful pipe-smoking habit. She remembered with a smile how she used to tease him by hiding his pipe. It used to get him so irritated! She chuckled at the memories. She and her six cousins would often get up to mischief but they didn't get away with too much…not with Aunt Molly at the helm. Uncle Jim was a more retiring sort and did as he was told by 'she who must be obeyed'. He was always told in the nicest possible way, of course.

As the train approached York, Louisa got to thinking about her meeting with Madame Petrovsky. She was still puzzled about the banshee and several unanswered questions still plagued her mind. Why had she not seen a banshee prior to her mother's death from ptomaine poisoning, she wondered? Perhaps Louisa herself was not sensitive enough or 'fey' enough to be able to see one at the tender age of twelve? Or perhaps a banshee was unable to materialize until after its owner's death? Or then again, perhaps her mother had not been of noble blood? This latter, Louisa realized was the most likely answer. But then why had she been able to see the banshee in the belfry?

She struggled with all these nebulous issues as the whistle blew and they pulled into the station. Suddenly, as the brakes squealed into action and steam puffed and billowed high above the windows, her memory was given a similar jolt.

"I've forgotten to write to Thomas!" she exclaimed, putting her hand up to her mouth. "I must write and tell him about his grandfather as soon as I get home."

The woman opposite awoke with a start and the man with the mutton chops was suddenly at her side helping her up. They smiled fleetingly at Louisa before making a rapid exit. Louisa peered out for them when she finally alighted on the platform with her two suitcases and empty wicker pigeon casket, but the mysterious couple was nowhere to be seen.

Doors slammed and a whistle blew somewhere in the distance while Louisa waited for assistance on the platform. The train shuddered, then shuddered again and began to move. She cast her eyes around searching for a porter through the crowd when suddenly a handsome young man in uniform materialized at her side. "Where to, ma'am?" he asked politely.

"A horse and carriage to Bingham, thank you," she answered.

The porter slung the wicker casket over his shoulder by its straps, lifted a suitcase in each hand, flashed a winning smile and said:

"Follow me, ma'am."

Louisa followed him obediently along the platform, subconsciously appraising his manly gait from behind. For some strange reason, she suddenly found herself thinking of Theodore again. She was sure that he must have heard through the parish grapevine of her urgent visit to Ireland to see her ailing father. Distractedly, she wondered if he would still be offering her flowers from out of his garden at the next rehearsal. Secretly, she hoped he would.

64

Seven

Louisa arrived back in Bingham via horse and carriage from York in the late evening of 7th January. By now, Jeremy was back in Oxford and Emma was back in London. Her three youngest children, Geraldine, Charlotte and Lucy were all back at the church school in the village. She was embraced at the front door by her husband Alfred and the three girls.

Rusty's tail was wagging frantically at the sight of her. "Welcome home!" they all said. "We got your pigeon post just before Jeremy and Emma left, so we're all up to date."

"Oh good. Now, how about a nice cup of tea and some supper for your mother?"

The girls scuttled off to the kitchen with Rusty while Louisa and Alfred retired to the drawing room.

"So how are you, my dear…after the funeral I mean? Did you have a good trip? I hope you gave my apologies to say that I was unable to attend at such short notice?"

"Of course, dear. Yes, everything went smoothly and Father is now at rest. All the aunts and uncles and cousins and nephews are fine."

"Ah, that's good," Alfred said, making himself comfortable in his favorite armchair. "You know what, Louisa?" he queried, picking up his spectacles.

"No, what?"

"I didn't realize how deucedly difficult it is these days to write a decent sermon. I've just spent the last three days in my den trying to figure out a memorable punchline for my next sermon. Talk about nerve-racking!" Then he said, "I must show you this novel I've been reading lately. It's called *Stephen Remarx* by an author called Adderley…" He paused and looked up at her over the rim of his spectacles saying, "I'll read you an excerpt from it here…He talks about some workmen laughing at their mate who goes to church every Sunday and he says, quote…'like a little girl, to listen to a sky pilot yarning about the stars and cherrybims.'" He paused for effect and removed his spectacles to look at her. "Now that just about sums it up these days, doesn't it? I'm just another 'sky pilot' of course, nothing more than an idle fellow talking a lot of waffle in their eyes…"

Louisa looked at him blankly.

Presently he said, "You know Louisa, I'm inclined to agree with that poet, Mathew Arnold with his lament about the conflict between the old and the new world…

> *'Wandering between two worlds, one dead,*
> *The other powerless to be born,*
> *With nowhere yet to rest my head,*
> *Like these, on earth I wait forlorn.'"*

He paused and then said, "He's talking about the old Carthusians of course and the new leaders of Western progress."

Impressed, Louisa said, "You should put that in your next sermon, Alfred."

"Mmmm…perhaps I will."

"Wasn't it Arthur Roberts who published several volumes of his sermons?"

"Yes," he said. "Seventeen, to be exact."

"Well, there you are then," she said significantly.

"Oh, one day maybe," he said vaguely. Then changing the subject, he said, "I went to visit Mrs. Philpot just after you left. You know, the one who came down with typhus fever. Well, you wouldn't believe it, but old farmer Giles asked me to refuse to administer the Sacrament to her, just because she had killed a fox out on the moors with one of the hunting parties. Can you believe the cheek of the man!" he said incredulously. "I'm all for animals' rights myself but that was going just too far!"

Louisa giggled and then asked, "How are your pigeons, dear?"

"Oh, fine. The two that flew back from Ireland have settled down well. That reminds me…you will be pleased to know that Jeremy has removed his tarantula from the belfry and taken it back to Oxford with him."

"Oh, thank goodness for that!" she exclaimed, relieved.

"It's just that he said he knew of someone who kept their pigeons in the belfry."

"Really? Deaf ones, I'll bet!"

"Yes. Quite," he agreed.

"Oh, and by the way, you will be sorry to hear that we have lost a couple more tenants on the glebe…"

"Oh…" she said, disappointed. "Oh well, it's lucky that I'll be collecting on my inheritance soon…"

Just then, the girls entered into the drawing room laden with tea things, Rusty trotting hopefully behind. Geraldine cranked up the gramophone in the corner and some quaint honky-tonk piano sounded in the background.

"Oh, I could *murder* for a cup of tea!" exclaimed Louisa, looking parched and gratefully accepting her tea and pikelets from Charlotte. Irritated slightly by the juke-box-like music coming from the gramophone, she said, "And what I wouldn't do to hear Enrico Caruso, the famous tenor, give us a recording on gramophone! He's been approached to do it, I hear. I just *love* tenors!"

Alfred looked at her obliquely over the top of his teacup and said jokingly, "Just as well everyone you know is a baritone then…apart from me, that is!"

Louisa guffawed and picked up a pikelet.

"You're no tenor dear…just a baritone in tight trousers who likes to play Bach's *Air on a G string* on the fiddle!"

They all laughed and the music slowed to a throaty moan and then took off again in a sudden flight of fancy at a higher pitch as Geraldine's laughter made her lose control of the crank.

* * *

The next day Louisa was back into the swing of running the vicarage, helping out at the rectory reading room and keeping in touch with the Ladies' Guild. She made a point of writing to her eldest son, Thomas, that day and telling him of his grandfather's recent death. On the postscript, she purposely gave some motherly advice against smoking. She worried about him being so far away, even though he was quite grown up now. She did try not to be too much of a 'Jewish mother' to her children, but they all seemed to be growing up so fast.

* * *

Wednesday night soon approached and Louisa was looking forward to some new bell ringing sequences and of course, meeting up with her gallant admirer. She was curious to see whether he might bring her any more flowers. Not that she would ever contemplate getting too involved with Theodore, because obviously she had a husband. Her husband would go berserk if anything serious came of this little flirtation, she knew, but she was interested to see just how far she could go without causing any trouble. She enjoyed the flattery and attention as well. Her beauty would not last forever and why shouldn't she be appreciated by other men if they found her attractive, she reasoned. Besides, her husband hardly ever gave her flowers…

She arrived at the belfry door just before seven as usual to unlock and there, dependable as ever, stood her faithful admirer waiting patiently.

"Why Louisa! How especially charming you look this evening! The trip away obviously did you good."

"Oh, thank you, Theodore." She blushed.

"Sorry to hear about your father, but I brought you this to cheer you up."

He handed her a perfectly formed scarlet ranunculus which he had grown in his hothouse.

"Oh, thank you, Theodore, you shouldn't have."

"Oh yes, I should. It says from me to you, 'You are radiantly charming,'" he said, flashing her an urbane smile.

"Oh, that's lovely Theodore," she said, quite flushed. "I can see I will have to return the compliment next Wednesday."

Louisa hurriedly tucked the flower in her coat pocket as the other bell-ringers were now arriving.

"Glad you're back, Louisa," said big Algie. "We've been missing the treble bell. It hasn't been quite the same without you, has it you lot?" he said, flippantly.

James, Gareth and Charles all looked inanely at each other and then somewhat grimly at Theodore (who had been taking Louisa's place in her absence). With a certain amount of tactlessness, they agreed that they had indeed missed Louisa's presence. Theodore visibly cringed like some shrinking violet and turned almost as red as the ranunculus he had just brought Louisa. The others glared at him.

"Oh, never mind," said Louisa, unfurling the ropes. "I'm back now. Who wants to call the changes? Theodore? Right, let's go!"

They rang the bells down from their upside-down position in order from treble to tenor and then Theodore began. Louisa let him call the changes all evening because from the amount of tension in the air right from the start, she thought she might have a mutiny on her hands otherwise. It was a very serious business, was bell ringing.

Thankfully, by the end of the practice, the other four ringers were a little less disgruntled and Theodore had returned to his normal color. Louisa's renewed presence had certainly defused any potential problems for the foreseeable future. She breathed a sigh of relief at the end of the practice and thanked them for keeping the home fires burning while she had been away. As she explained, no one was indispensable, not even she.

"See you all next week!" she called out as she locked the outside door.

* * *

The following Wednesday evening, Louisa spent some time pondering upon which flower she should take in reply to Theodore's ranunculus. She roamed casually amongst the plants in the greenhouse at the vicarage and let her mind drift free. It was so relaxing to just potter in the garden and communicate with nature, even inside a greenhouse. A flowering quince stood at the southern end of the building where it was warmer and the tree had begun flowering two months early. Its flowers were a beautiful rose-pink.

"Just the thing," thought Louisa. "It looks beautiful. That's just what Theodore needs at the moment…something to cheer him up after having to put up with all the flak he's been getting lately from Algie and co."

She was quite *au fait* with the meanings of the various flowers now because she had been studying her dictionary while she was away.

So, what if it means 'temptation', she thought. *He's a lovely man and he deserves it. And he is tempting too.* She giggled to herself.

She picked a sprig of the flowering quince and tucked it inside the pocket of her coat which was hanging inside the scullery. Just then her husband appeared and asked, "Where have you been Louisa? I was looking for you."

"Oh, just down in the greenhouse."

"What's that you've got there? My flowering quince? I'm trying to let that thing get ahead. Why did you have to go and cut it?"

"I'm just taking a cutting along to bell ringing practice."

"What for?"

"The florist is interested in it…this particular color."

"Hrumph! Let him grow his *own* flowering quinces, damn it! He's a florist, isn't he?"

The vicar took this as a mortal offence as his garden was his pride and joy. Louisa cringed imperceptibly.

"It will grow back, dear," she said consolingly.

Disgruntled, her husband ignored the remark and said:

"Where's that book I was reading, do you know?"

"Geraldine had it last. You might have to ask her."

The vicar looked around helplessly while Louisa donned her coat, gave her husband a conciliatory kiss and walked across the church grounds to the bell tower, her trophy in her pocket. There, Theodore was waiting at the mutually appointed time. His face lit up when he saw her.

"I've got a little present for you, Theodore," Louisa said, smiling.

"Oh, have you my dear?" he said, sounding interested.

She gave him the sprig of flowering quince and he was at once overjoyed.

"Louisa, how sweet of you. Now here is something from me to you."

He reached inside his coat and pulled out a single daffodil.

"It says, 'You are the only one.'"

She gasped in surprise and took a step backwards.

"Thank you, Theodore, but you shouldn't be telling me these things!"

"How can I not?" he asked. "It's the truth."

They looked at each other for a moment, searching each other's eyes and then hastily went indoors. They were soon brought down to earth by the arrival of the other bell-ringers.

This time Louisa had Theodore call the changes for the first hour only and then swapped him over onto Gareth's bell. They rang out some rudimentary rounds so that Theodore wouldn't be out of his depth too soon.

"That was great, everyone," Louisa said when they had finished. "Next week we're having the squire come and visit us to try his hand on the tenor bell. So, we must all remember to help him along and give him our due consideration. The worst thing we could do would be to put him offside."

"Quite right," everyone agreed.

"Don't worry. I'll sort him out," said Algie, twisting the end of his rope.

"That would be great," said Louisa, slightly disconcerted.

* * *

Another week rolled by and Louisa again began asking herself what sort of offering she should take to her 'suitor'. As long as her husband was out on his rounds whenever she picked anything, he should be none the wiser that she was giving away any cuttings, she thought. She scoured the depths of the greenhouse and found some maidenhair tucked shyly away in a corner.

"Perfect!" she thought. "Perfect, because maidenhair translates as 'discretion'."

She picked a small frond and tucked it in her coat pocket. She just hoped it wouldn't wilt too much in the interim.

Again, at the rendezvous that evening, Theodore was waiting. Louisa presented him with the fern frond which was slightly the worse for wear, to which his reply was a single red rose and two jonquils. Louisa swooned slightly, quite overcome.

"You know what the red rose says, don't you, Louisa…? 'Passionate love,'" he said softly in a confidential manner. "The jonquils say 'I desire a return of affection.'" He looked at her meaningfully and drew closer. She could feel his warm breath on her face. Her heart was pounding. What was she to do? Their lips drew closer but she tore herself away. They must have forgotten how long they had been lingering in the doorway because suddenly Algie appeared. Louisa hurriedly unlocked the door and let him in. James, Gareth and Charles soon followed and then lastly the squire.

Once inside, Louisa pulled herself together and announced, "Welcome everyone…and to the squire. Thank you for coming along, sir."

"It's an honor, to be sure, my lady," he said. "I can't wait to get started and get these biceps pumping power into those ropes."

"Right-o, folks," Louisa said. "Theodore…" she blushed self-consciously, "if you wouldn't mind sitting the first half out and we will have the squire calling the changes. Thanks."

Everyone did as they were bid and the resulting sound was quite acceptable. She couldn't help noticing however, that both she and Theodore were being closely watched by the big man on the tenor bell.

Next, it was the squire's turn on Algie's tenor bell.

Algie handed the sally over to the squire and instructed him on how to control the rope. At first, the squire was all of a dither.

"It's the gout in my big toe playing up," he complained. "I don't know why it has to play up now. It's that fine cellar of mine, you see. You must come and visit and sample some of my wine someday," he said to Algie, softening him up.

"Why, thank you Squire," said Algie. "Now let me show you again."

They finally sorted things out together once the squire's posture and the position of his feet had been corrected.

"Now I will show you how to retard the bell slightly to allow another bell to ring before it and then how to speed it up to ring in front of another bell," Algie went on. "Good!" he said, once this had been perfected. The squire had cottoned on well. "Now, the one thing that you must *not* do, Squire, is retard the bell too much. If you do that, the stay on the wheel up top is likely to hit the slider hard and if the slider snaps, the bell will turn over again in another revolution and wind the rope up in the process. If you keep hanging onto the rope you could be hoisted into the air, you see. And you don't want that, do you?"

"Er, no…" said the squire, letting go of the rope.

"Good. We're ready to play some rounds now, Louisa," he announced.

The squire was looking a little the worse for wear with all this unused-to exercise he was getting with his arms up in the air. His great frame was not accustomed to such exertion.

"Right-o. Rounds it is, everyone. Treble to tenor in sequence. Off we go!"

Louisa started off pulling on the treble bell, all the other bells sounding in sequence with the squire pulling on the tenor bell at the end of each round. This went on for a good half hour non-stop. By this time, the squire was really getting a sweat up. Each time the squire reached up to pull on the rope, his trousers would slip a little further down from around his wide girth. By the time the half hour was up, his trousers had very gently slipped to the floor and revealed a surprisingly disproportionate pair of spindle shanks. This set everyone a-titter and the round turned to mud. The squire was most embarrassed needless to say, pulled his trousers back up and disappeared from the ringing chamber, most indignant.

"Why didn't someone tell me to wear tight trousers?" he called out as he left.

When he had gone, uncontrollable laughter broke out. "We've really gone and done it now!" said Louisa. "I doubt if he will ever come back."

During the week that followed, Louisa tried to avoid the squire at all costs. She also worried vaguely about how much Algie had seen at the belfry door. He obviously suspected something. Not that she and Theodore had done anything wrong…

Before the next Wednesday night's practice was due, Louisa roamed up and down the greenhouse in the vicarage gardens.

What can I give Theodore this time? She mused. *He knows how I feel about him and yet…*Suddenly she spied exactly what she wanted. A yellow tulip ('hopeless love') and a poppy ('consolation'). *Spot on!* She thought delightedly. She picked the two flowers and put them in her coat pocket. *Surely Theodore must know that this just can't go on? I hope he gets the message with these*, she thought.

That evening Theodore was waiting for her as usual but before she could give him her offering, he thrust under her nose some penny royal, a scarlet pimpernel and a spider flower.

"These are for you, Louisa, my love. They are saying to you in the sincerest possible way, 'escape to a lover's secret meeting; elope with me.'" He bent over her so that they were very close and she could see and feel his smoldering eyes piercing into hers. His lips looked moist and inviting.

"Theodore!" she gasped. "I'm a married woman…to a vicar! I can't just…"

Her thoughts were in a whirl. How could she even *think* of elopement? It could only lead to divorce. Think of the disgrace and scandal it would create in the village! Not to mention the consequential loss of her children.

That didn't even bear thinking about!

He kissed her gently on the mouth and then taking the keys from her, unlocked the door and they went in.

Louisa was still hot and bothered when Algie and the other three ringers arrived. She sensed suspicion in Algie, but then again, perhaps it was just her own sense of guilt making itself felt. Meanwhile, Theodore kept giving her simmering looks all through the whole practice which quite put her off her stride. All things considered; the practice did not go well. The timing went wrong and mistakes were made throughout…no matter who called the changes. Everyone went home disgruntled and dissatisfied. It must have sounded a mess to anyone that was listening. The squire hadn't turned up which was probably just as well. Perhaps he was still being tailored for new trousers.

Before Louisa locked up however, Theodore met her in the stairwell dressed in his great-coat. He leaned one hand against the wall above her head and said plaintively:

"Won't you be my Jersey lily…? Or should I say, Guernsey lily?"

"Your Lillie Langtry? The Prince of Wales's mistress?"

"Yes, but *my* mistress? I'll be your sweet prince."

"Oh!" said Louisa, her heart pounding once more.

"Or to quote Milton's immortal words about a lady-love," he went on,

'To sport with Amaryllis in the shade,
Or with the tangles of Neaera's hair…'

He lightly touched her hair with his fingers and stroked the side of her face. He smiled wantonly at her.

Louisa froze. And yet she was fascinated by this man.

This beautiful masculine creature who spoke so eloquently and in such a circumlocutory manner. She was mesmerized by him. He was an Adonis in the truest sense. He lifted her hand and kissed it. The perfume of all the flowers in her pocket suddenly made her feel heady in that confined space. She dashed out the door for some fresh air, Theodore following closely behind.

She locked the door in the moonlight and then suddenly when she least expected it, Theodore had scooped her into his arms and was kissing her passionately and longingly on the lips. Louisa swooned and fell back in his arms, succumbing helplessly to his passionate desire.

At that same moment, an upstairs curtain in the vicarage opposite flicked unheeded to one side…

Eight

It dawned crisp and cold the next day with the snowdrifts outside beginning to thaw quite quickly now and the promise of spring in the air. The crocuses were just showing their pretty heads along the riverbank and the birds were singing more vociferously than usual. It was 14th February, Valentine's Day…the anniversary of the execution of that ancient saint who died all in the name of love. At the vicarage, the three Picard girls, Geraldine, Charlotte and Lucy had all risen early in wait for the morning post. Lucy was quite volatile and excited and was dancing around chanting:

"Who will be my valentine? Who will be my valentine?" and making faces at herself in the hall mirror.

Rusty was right behind her, jumping up at the mirror and thinking it was great fun. Charlotte on the other hand was touchy and quick-tempered while Geraldine was quiet and withdrawn. Louisa herself was dreading the arrival of the morning post. She just hoped and prayed she would not receive a valentine from you-know-who. She would be devastated if she did. She didn't dare to imagine what would happen if she did.

There was a *'thunk'* at the front door as the dreaded mail arrived and slipped through the metal slot. Lucy and the dog both raced to the front door to see who could get there first and then after a giggling scramble, Lucy held three letters up triumphantly.

"One for Charlotte, one for Mama and one for all of us," she crowed.

She ran into the dining room and placed her collection in a pile on the table. Charlotte's eyes shone with anticipation.

"Oh, let me open mine," exclaimed Charlotte, grabbing the letter that was addressed to her. She fumbled with the envelope, tore it open and pulled out a rather plain-looking card with a hand-painted water color of a young girl playing with a hoop. She opened it and read silently, her pursed lips gradually betraying her mask of sangfroid:

'Tis all in vain your simpering looks
You never can incline,
With all your bustles, stays and curls,
To find a valentine.'

Her mouth dropped open in dismay and she stood there motionless, the card dropping to her side.

"What is it, darling?" her mother asked. "Let me read it."

Louisa pried the card from her daughter's hand, took one look and said, "Oh, Charlotte! Someone's sent you one of those 'pennydreadfuls!' How mean! Now who could that have been?"

Charlotte, whose mouth had been turning down further and further, looked at her with sudden realization.

"I know who it was, Mama! It was Peggy Olverstein from my class at school. She's always giving me cheek and pulling my hair and calling me 'carrot-top'! I bet it was her! I *hate* her! I *hate* her!"

"Well then. Don't worry about it," said her mother. "Just put it in the rubbish and forget about it. She will get her come-uppance, no doubt. Just pretend you never received it in the first place."

Charlotte did as she was told and stomped into the kitchen, muttering to herself and screwing up the card as she went. Rusty, thinking that food was in the offering, followed her out expectantly.

"Now, let's see what else we have here," Louisa said with some trepidation. She was much relieved when she recognized the handwriting on each of the other two letters.

"This one's from your father to me," she announced happily, picking one of the letters up.

She opened the envelope with a paper knife and inside was an exquisite perfumed valentine of embossed lacy paper and gold trim. She opened the card and all at once it became a three-dimensional pop-up of a carriage full of flowers. The verse read:

'When cupid calls,
We must obey
And so, I send
My love today.'

"Oh, that's beautiful! Here, have a sniff, Geraldine. I wonder where your father is. Oh yes, he's gone out early on his rounds this morning, hasn't he? Well, I'll just put this on the mantelpiece and then open this other letter from Thomas."

She rose to place the valentine in the other room and by the time she had got back, the three girls were pouring over Thomas's letter on the dining room table. Lucy was kneeling on a chair and leaning over Geraldine's shoulder so that she could see his writing better. Louisa drew up a chair and said, "Thank you, Geraldine…"

Geraldine obediently gave her the letter to read while the three girls re-positioned themselves around her with the dog underfoot. She read aloud:

"Dear Family,

29th Jan 1900.

I was sorry to hear about Grandpa's death and sorry I couldn't be at the funeral. Don't worry, Mother, I can't stand the smell of tobacco, so I shan't be taking up the 'habit'. I'm writing from Cape Town today. They're starting to use St. Helena (where I've just come from) for holding Boer prisoners now. We've been checking passing ships' papers and searching ships in international waters as we've patrolled down the West-African coast.

Only four days ago there was a battle at Graspan down here where about 400 of the naval brigade from HMS Doris, Powerful and Monarch were used as infantry against the Boers. This is the first time this has happened…so far! Personally, I think I'd rather keep my feet planted firmly on deck!

We had a nice Christmas dinner on board ship, but there's nothing like your cooking, Mother!

Love to you all,
Thomas."

"That was a short letter," said Lucy rather pointedly.

"Well, I expect he's very busy dear," said her mother.

"If the naval brigade are being used as infantry, things must be getting pretty serious."

"Oh," said Lucy, sticking her finger in her mouth.

Louisa sat there for a moment in reflection. Then rising suddenly, she said:

"Now let's not all get morbid thoughts. Your grandfather went to war and he came back and so will Thomas…just you see. Now off you go girls and make sure your rooms are tidy before you go to school."

The three girls lingered about the table a little longer and then went on their way.

* * *

Not far away on the other side of the village, the florist, Theodore Bycroft, was preparing to go into the village to open up his shop for the morning. He usually left at about 8:30 and walked along the river bank road to work. However, this morning he left a little later than usual.

At eight thirty, there was a mail delivery through his front door slot. There was just the one letter and he bent down to retrieve it off the floor. He turned the letter over and examined the handwriting to see if he could recognize it, but it was written in a beautiful calligraphic script. He did however notice that the letter gave off a particularly strong perfume. Intrigued, he opened it carefully. Inside was an exceptionally elaborate valentine and it appeared to have been hand-made. The surround was of lace and embossed gilt paper and the center consisted of a silk tassel attached to a stiff paper lid. He pulled the tassel and removed the lid to find a cobweb effect of netting over some pressed blue hyacinths set against white satin with a tiny silver-papered mirror and a verse of poetry. The verse read:

'Good valentine, be kind to me
In dreams, let me my true-love see.'

Fascinated, he placed and replaced the paper lid several times, catching a whiff of the scent and catching sight of himself in the tiny silver mirror each time as he did so.

"Now who could have sent me this?" he wondered. "Louisa? Hyacinths…? I doubt she would have sent flowers as mundane as hyacinths…Not *now*. On second thoughts, hyacinths *do* stand for 'constancy'. But I would have expected something more like a rose from Louisa…especially on Valentine's Day. Or on the other hand, nothing at all…because of course, I sent her nothing, but only because I have a good sense of propriety towards a married woman on such an auspicious day. But *Hyacinths…?*"

He turned around and around with his hand up to his chin, pondering the question.

"So why should she send me hyacinths, if it were her?"

Baffled, he turned around again in the opposite direction and peered dubiously up at the ceiling. Holding that pose, he absent-mindedly tweaked his moustache as if it might somehow be the key to the riddle.

Suddenly, it came to him…the myth of the ancient Greeks. Hyacinthus was a handsome and athletic Spartan youth with a beautiful body and tightly curled hair. Apollo, the sun-God had fallen in love with him and occasionally descended to earth in his chariot to engage in athletic sports like discus throwing. However, Zephyrus, the west wind, also loved Hyacinthus and became insanely jealous. He blew a gale which caused the discus to fly off course and it struck Hyacinthus dead. The blood of the beautiful youth was then changed into a hyacinth plant, with the coiled petals and leaves resembling Hyacinthus's curly hair.

*Hmmm…*he wondered. *Could this by any means be from someone in my cricket team from down in London? I wonder…?*

He looked at the envelope again and it was indeed postmarked 'London 12th Feb 1900.'

"Interesting! Very interesting and intriguing, I must say…A prank perhaps for a florist getting a taste of his own medicine on Valentine's Day…or perhaps something a little bit more…'personal'?"

He placed the card and the envelope on his kitchen table and still puzzled, went off to work.

* * *

That same evening back at the vicarage, Louisa was preparing for bed. She was brushing her long lustrous auburn locks in front of the mirror at her dressing room table. A dozen beautiful red roses stood in a silver vase at one end and several bottles of perfume at the other.

Alfred was already in bed reading by the light of a dimmed bedside gaslamp. He was reading one of his botany books. Presently, he looked up and said, oblivious to her unveiled beauty:

"I say, Louisa, this is interesting stuff. According to ancient Egyptian hieroglyphics and Chinese manuscripts, priests and physicians were distilling the essential oils from plants and using them thousands of years before Christ to heal the sick. They are the oldest form of medicine and cosmetic known to man. And there are 188 references to oils in the Bible."

"Really?" she said, pulling her brush through her hair and speaking to his reflection in the mirror.

"Yes. In fact, rose oil is supposed to be the most desirable and expensive oil in the world. It takes thirty roses to make just one drop of rose oil and sixty thousand roses to make an ounce."

"Incredible!" she said. "In that case," she said looking at him slyly, "perhaps you should have given me the perfume instead of those roses there…"

Nine

Louisa ruminated much upon what her husband had told her the previous night about just how precious roses were. She had no doubt that they were indeed the 'Queen of Flowers'. Simply to smell their exquisite fragrance was immensely uplifting to one's spirit. But as she rambled wistfully through the grounds of the vicarage her thoughts were inexorably drawn back to her admirer, Theodore.

Perhaps I've been too hard on him, she thought. *Perhaps I should have acknowledged Valentine's Day after all and sent him a small token of my esteem. That would not necessarily mean that I would be about to accept his advances of course. But just a little something would let him know that I'm thinking of him and that I care.*

Preoccupied, she drifted into the greenhouse and looked in on the pigeons cooing in their loft as she passed. The way they all sat in pairs gently preening each other and cooing made her think they really did look like a lot of white lovey-doves today, or was it just her mood?

"The last thing I want is for Theodore to leave our little band of bell-ringers. I like him and I like to see his handsome face opposite me in the bell chamber when I'm pulling on the ropes."

Meandering amongst the greenery, she mulled over in her mind what to do when her attention was suddenly attracted to the southern corner of the greenhouse.

There, hanging pendulously down on the branches of the flowering quince were several plump greenish-yellow fruit.

"It couldn't be…could it?" she asked herself as she approached. "Why yes…these quinces are well and truly ripe…! But of course," she reasoned, "…the tree started flowering in mid-winter instead of early spring because it's so hot in here and it's on the south side. Well, I think I'll just have to pick them and make some jelly while the going's good. Perhaps I'll even give Theodore a pot. Just the thing!"

With renewed enthusiasm, she picked all the ripe quinces and placed them carefully into a wicker flower basket that happened to be nearby.

This is a great idea, she thought, *especially as I know that the flowering quince belongs to the rose family. That's quite significant in itself really, now that I know all about rose oil. It's not as if I would be giving Theodore actual roses...just something that's related to roses. And it's not as if I'd be giving him the quince flowers themselves which mean 'temptation' this time. I would merely be giving him something made from the fruits of the flowers...quince jelly, which when made to Aunt Molly's delicious recipe is 'temptation' itself!*

She congratulated herself upon her fine powers of deduction and gathered up the basket of fruit to take into the kitchen. She placed the fruit on the table, donned her apron and scurried around in the top drawer for her favorite recipe.

"Ah! Here it is!" she said triumphantly. "*Aunt Molly's Quince Jelly 1872.*"

The listed ingredients were:

3lbs quinces (prepared weight)
8 cups sugar
1–2 tbsp. freshly squeezed lemons (if necessary)
water (approximately 2 pints)
6 x 8oz sterilized jelly jars

She already had some lemons, so began by sterilizing the jars and rubbing the quinces down briskly with a towel to remove the down off their skin. Then she cut the quinces in half and removed the core and seeds. She tied the core and seeds together in a piece of cheesecloth and put them to one side. Then placing the fruit and seed bundle in a large stock pot, she covered this with water by about one inch so that the quinces were floating slightly. Next, she covered this with a lid, brought everything to the boil and simmered for about thirty minutes until the quinces could be easily pierced with a metal skewer. The aroma that filled the kitchen was divine...a sort of pineappley perfume.

"No wonder quinces are called 'room deodorizers'," she mused.

She mashed the soft fruit while it was still cooking in the pot and pressed the seed bundle gently to extract the pectin. Then when the pulp was tender, she strained everything through another piece of cheesecloth and reserved the liquid juice.

Next, she checked her recipe and measured out six cups of the liquid juice and returned it and the seed bundle to the pot. She added the sugar, stirring all the time until it had dissolved, then squeezed the bag of seeds until the liquid juice thickened.

After 25 minutes, the liquid had not quite jelled in the pot so she added a tablespoon of lemon juice and cooked another five minutes. She checked the consistency of the jelly by drizzling a little bit of it off the wooden spoon and onto a cold plate.

Perfect, she thought. *Now all I have to do is ladle the jelly into the jars and pop their little cheesecloth tops on.*

This she did and then stood her six little masterpieces on the bench, all dressed in their cheesecloth tops and tied up with string. As an afterthought, she returned to the greenhouse to pick a small bunch of blue periwinkles which she placed in a small jar of water on the kitchen windowsill.

Lucy was the first to arrive home from school (being in the primary section), so when she arrived home, Louisa said:

"Lucy dear…would you mind running a little errand for me?"

"Now?"

"Yes, please dear. Just take one of these pots of quince jelly around to Mr. Bycroft's florist shop in the village will you, dear? Say it's from Mrs. Picard and give him this little bunch of periwinkles too will you, dear?"

"Yes, alright. Can I take my skipping rope? It's just upstairs."

"Yes, alright. Off you go. Just remember to skip on the footpath and not on the road. And mind the puddles," she warned.

Lucy ran upstairs and then presently came down into the kitchen again with her skipping rope.

"I'll be back soon, Mama!" she called out to her mother who was by now in the drawing room playing the piano. Lucy ran off out the front gate to the familiar tinkle of 'Country Gardens' wafting after her all down the lane as she went.

Louisa was well satisfied with her afternoon's work in the kitchen and as the music flowed effortlessly from her fingertips, her thoughts were on Theodore.

"Blue periwinkle is perfect. 'Friendship and happy memories', is what they mean. I'm sure Theodore will understand…"

Ten

After school the next day Lucy came racing home and asked her mother:

"Mama…will you take me ice-skating down on the duck pond today?"

"Oh, but Lucy, the ice is melting now dear."

"Papa took us all ice-skating when you were at your Aunt Molly's. Can't we go? Please, please?"

"Well alright," Louisa reneged, "seeing as you did that errand for me yesterday. But we won't be going skating. We will just go looking for snowdrops there under the trees and see how many we can find."

"Can we take Rusty?"

"Yes, I'm sure he would love to come."

Excited at the prospect of an outing, Lucy called Rusty who was equally as excited. They donned their galoshes and walked about a quarter of a mile down the hill on the northern side of the village where they navigated their way down a slope strewn with huge limestone boulders. The path down to the duck pond was slippery and there were puddles of melting ice and snow everywhere. Across the valley under the lowering skies, they were able to catch a glimpse of the old smelt mill ruins where lead used to be extracted in the olden days from the old mineshafts that still dotted the high dales of the surrounding moors. Two black-faced shaggy sheep stood quietly grazing on the hillside opposite, their distant bleating as if in homage to the spring thaw.

Louisa and Lucy paused to catch their breath and listened to the shrill cries of a startled lapwing as it circled its newly built nest, warning off the intruders. They continued down the slope to a small secluded pond which was hidden in the shadows of the surrounding hills and bordered by a grove of bare-branched willow trees. There were still patches of ice on the surface of the pond and the damp ground crackled underfoot as they crunched their way through some icy patches where the pale sun was unable to reach.

The further down into the depths of the valley they went, the more the damp air stifled their voices. There were no echoes at all down here from the surrounding hills. It was as if they were now cut off from the outside world and entombed in a small microcosm of Jules Verne's reckoning. Holding hands for mutual support in this seemingly inhospitable environment, they crunched their way over the patchy ground, their breath billowing out in small clouds in front of them as they went.

Cautiously they approached the water's edge, following in Rusty's footsteps over the uncertain ground and stood still to absorb the dismal atmosphere which enveloped the place.

The sodden grey air clung solemnly to the depths of the valley with a tenacity that created a certain sense of impending doom. All manner of oppressive thoughts began to cloud Louisa's mind. Through the haze she could almost imagine the diaphanous tableau of the Lady of Shallot floating eerily past in her briar-covered barge, her fair hair floating feebly amongst the lily-pads as she drifted inexorably downriver to her death. Except that this was a pond, not a river. She cancelled that thought for a moment to re-establish her bearings.

There was a small marble plinth at one end of the duck pond with a life-size statue of a lady pouring water into the pond. And nearby at the water's edge were several broken-down wicker chairs that had been placed there for the benefit of tired skaters. In fact, one chair lay upturned in the shallows and another was even floating on a piece of ice out in the middle of the pond.

It was a quiet deserted spot but they could hear tell-tale sounds of a woodpecker drilling and tapping at a tree trunk nearby. They noticed a couple of robins careering past after Rusty disturbed them with his sniffing about in the undergrowth. Rusty suddenly started to yap excitedly and point with a great show of bravado.

"Oh no! Don't say he's found a hedgehog!" they both said together, raising their eyes heavenwards.

They looked at each other in exasperation and then began their own search. It was too early yet to look for mushrooms but they did find quite a substantial crop of snowdrops growing under the trees. They picked as many as they could until it suddenly appeared to grow dark.

They looked up to see that a huge black cloud had gathered overhead. The temperature dropped suddenly while at the same time a flock of crows flapped and cawed disruptively from the branches of a dead tree beyond the pond. Their watchful silence had broken. Over to the north a sickly pale green sunlight filtered down through an opening in the clouds and the crackle of thunder overhead announced the arrival of a storm. All at once, Rusty stood there shaking like a leaf. Big heavy drops of rain began to fall. Mother and daughter wrapped their coats around them more tightly and prepared to make for home.

Just then, Louisa stopped dead in her tracks. Through the curtain of falling rain and skeletal trees, she could just make out beside the statue, evidence of a second figure. Its features were becoming more and more discernible the longer she peered at it. It was a woman in a long green cloak with long straggly hair and a sunken face.

"Oh, no!" she gasped. "Not the banshee!"

She grabbed Lucy and held her tightly to her breast.

The old woman by the statue began wailing and wringing her hands. Then she placed her hands under the statue's vessel as if washing something off them. Louisa was trembling and asked Lucy in a shaky voice, "Lucy…how many people do you see over there by the statue?"

"None. Just the statue. Why?"

"Good. Never you mind. Now come along! Don't let go of my hand!"

They raced through the teaming rain with no umbrella, Rusty hard on their heels. They began wending their way back through the boulders and up the slope. A short burst of hailstones pelted down, hindering their progress. Lucy slipped when she lost her footing and Louisa had to haul her back up the slope with both hands. When they got to the top of the hill, breathless, the hail suddenly stopped and they were able to stand in the rain and check their bearings. Louisa dared to look back now but the banshee had vanished. Shivers ran down her spine. The chill in the air seemed to heighten the sensation.

Presently, they arrived back at the vicarage dripping wet, windblown and disheveled. The snowdrops that they had collected bowed their heads, quite waterlogged with their burden of raindrops. Strangely enough, as soon as Louisa reached out for the front door knob, the rain stopped. Evidently, it was just another of those localized quirky 'spring showers' that they had got caught up in. However, they could still hear the faint grumblings of distant thunder as they changed their clothes and dried the dog.

Lucy arranged the snowdrops into two separate vases over the sink in the scullery while Louisa began to prepare the dinner. But before she could put her mind at ease Louisa had to make an urgent visit to the rectory library.

"I *must* check up on the local history here," she muttered to herself. "There has to be some sort of explanation."

It was not long before she found what she was looking for. It was an old and slightly worn volume with yellowed pages but the binding still held it together well. She looked up the index to check out whether any battles had been fought upon the Yorkshire Moors. But she discovered that the only battle that had ever been fought close to Bingham was *The Battle of Marston Moor*, which was fought on 2nd July 1644 and that was six miles west of York. Charles I's men had surrendered to the Roundheads under Oliver Cromwell. Six thousand men had been slain…

* * *

That night during dinner, Louisa was unusually quiet…

Eleven

Everyone slept late the next morning at the vicarage because it was Saturday. Breakfast was a rolling buffet at the breakfast room table on a first come, first served basis. The three girls sparred lightly with each other over what they were each going to do this weekend while Alfred sat eating his breakfast and Louisa supervised the toast and the porridge over the coal-range. Once the girls had finished breakfast, they withdrew to tidy their rooms and the day's post arrived at the front door.

Alfred heard the mail drop onto the floor, so got up and went to collect it. There was just the one letter and it was for Louisa. He delivered it to Louisa who was still bent over the coal-range making toast and then he sat back at the table again to pour himself another cup of tea.

"For me? Thank you, dear," Louisa said.

She nervously fingered the letter. It was slightly perfumed and she wondered if Alfred had noticed. On tenterhooks, she turned with her back to Alfred and opened the letter. It was a hand-written note from Theodore Bycroft. And at the top of the page as a letterhead was a single pressed iris petal and a single pressed rose-pink astilbe frond.

"Oh…'a message for you; I'll be waiting,'" she mentally translated. It read,

'My dearest Louisa,
Thank you for your kind gift.
I must see you soon, my darling. Please will you
meet me at 8:30am tomorrow morning at the belfry
before you begin your bell ringing. Please be discrete.
Fondest love,
Theodore.'

She had only just finished reading the note when the telephone rang.

"I'll get it," said Louisa, thinking that it might be Theodore perchance.

She briskly screwed up the note and dispatched it promptly into the rubbish bin. (Unfortunately, in her nervous haste, it missed and landed conspicuously on the floor.) She breezed out airily into the hallway with an innocent air and picked up the receiver.

"Hello?" she said…"Emma! How lovely to hear from you…Who? Your beau? Of course! You're both welcome to stay…We'll put him up in the spare room…"

She spoke for a good fifteen minutes and as she did so, Alfred noticed the faint smell of toast burning. He got up from the table and rescued two pieces of half blackened toast from the hinged bread holder which had been left inadvertently hanging over the flame and then noticed the screwed-up ball of paper by the rubbish bin on the floor. He stooped to pick it up, unscrewed it curiously and began to read.

By the time he had finished reading it, he was absolutely fuming.

"How dare he!" he seethed. "Who the hell is this Theodore fellow anyway? It's got to be that damned florist! Damn him! I'll show that flowery bastard a thing or two. How dare he interfere with my wife!"

He clenched and unclenched his fists and ground his teeth, the adrenalin pumping fiercely through his veins. The small prominent blue vein on his forehead pumped voraciously. Louisa chatted on, unaware that she had caused a fuss and Alfred pocketed the note carefully and sat down again at the table on the pretext of re-reading the morning paper.

"To hell with the toast! I don't want any more anyway. It's that bastard Bycroft I'm worried about!" he fumed silently, furiously turning the pages and ripping one. He made a monumental effort to contain his anger as Louisa flounced back into the room, quite bubbly and overcome.

"Oh, Alfred. Great news! Emma's coming up next week…with her beau! His name's John, he's a solicitor and they're going to stay for a week. We'll put John in the spare room. He plays the piano, so we can have a soiree one evening. I'm so delighted that we will have another young man in the house…even if it's only for a week!"

She prattled on and Alfred grunted his approval from behind the cover of the newspaper, allegedly preoccupied with the daily news.

How could she? he asked himself…*carry on with another man behind my back? Surely, she must know how foolish she's being? He must be a good five years younger than her but that's beside the point!*

He flapped the newspaper noisily in irritation and cleared his throat. The extent of his outrage could be gauged by the altered timbre of his vocal cords. Louisa, seemingly oblivious of his annoyance, was now fussing about in the kitchen and rationalizing her thoughts:

I can't meet Theodore tomorrow morning. Not now. It's such an inopportune time. Especially now that I have Emma and John to prepare for. It will be so exciting to see them. Besides, I'll probably see Theodore either in the congregation after bell ringing tomorrow or at next Wednesday night's practice.

Alfred in the meantime had other plans. He *himself* had decided to meet Theodore at the rendezvous tomorrow morning. But he resolved to say absolutely nothing to his wife.

* * *

That evening, Theodore Bycroft was sitting in his drawing room in his favorite easy chair with his feet up, casually dressed in his quilted smoking jacket. He raised another glass of celebratory brandy to his lips and drank appreciatively through his perfectly coiffed mustache. It served him as a filter on many an occasion, but not tonight, because this was his best brandy. He swallowed the draught and then to savor the piquancy, sucked on his moustache as he relished every last drop. He held his crystal glass aloft to the light and admired the amber tincture of this precious dram which he held in such high esteem.

It had been a hard day's work digging that old stump out of the front garden that afternoon. He was lucky to have had some help from the curate who was a neighbor and who just happened to be passing by. They had enjoyed a brandy together once the job was done and then the curate had left.

Now Theodore was relaxing after a hot bath and lamb chops for dinner. He was looking forward to meeting his beloved on the morrow…

Twelve

The Sabbath dawned and the vicar rose early. He had business to attend to…that is, he had a rendezvous to keep. He left his wife in bed at 6:30, dressed and then strode restlessly about the kitchen psyching himself up for a confrontation in the belfry.

Then at 7:30 before anyone else came down to breakfast he grimly lifted the keys to the bell tower off the rack in the scullery and purposely strode outside across the frosty lawn towards the back gate. He noiselessly opened the gate and went through, absent-mindedly reading the noticeboard which he had nailed to it some time ago as he clicked the latch.

"MAN-TRAPS ARE SET AT NIGHT IN THESE GROUNDS," it said.

(This he had placed there as a deterrent to the village lads who came around to the back of the rectory courting their two housemaids after the trouble they had had last year.) Vague thoughts of planting further notices elsewhere crossed his mind. The keys jangled almost nervously in his pocket as he crossed the grounds towards the tower.

He let himself in the outside door, leaving it ajar and then quietly climbed the spiral wooden staircase to the internal door of the belfry. The faint tapping of his footsteps resounded staccato in the hollow of the stairwell as he went. Unlocking the internal door, he left this also ajar and entered the bell chamber. He peered curiously through the window slats at the waking world outside and then took the last flight up the spiral staircase to the roof. Here he offered the soft morning breeze wafting through the battlements a chance to clear his mind. He stayed a few moments, staring vacantly at the weather cock as if it might be able to supply him with answers and then went softly down the two flights of stairs again to lie in wait for his quarry. It would be a good hour's wait sitting on the bench in the ringing chamber but he didn't mind waiting. He needed the time alone to sort out his thoughts and feelings and what he was going to say to this 'devious cad'. His thoughts were spitting hellfire and brimstone, of which he was most unaccustomed and he found it difficult to think as a rational man. He leaned forward and put his head in his hands.

"Oh, God!" he prayed. "Let this be over with quickly!"

Before long, he heard footsteps. Then he heard a voice call out in the open doorway, "Louisa, is that you?"

The vicar stood up.

"It's me…her husband."

The florist, who was by now well inside the bell ringing chamber, took a step back in surprise. The vicar held up the crumpled note under the florist's eyes.

"Just what is the meaning of this, my man?" he asked, his eyes flashing vehemently. "You wrote this, did you not…to my wife, I believe. I have it as evidence against you."

"Y…you what?" stammered the florist, taken aback.

"Just keep away from my wife, you understand?"

The vicar looked so full of hatred and venom that the florist found himself involuntarily backing up the spiral staircase. It was hard for him to believe that this man, a man of the cloth, could become so possessed. It was as if the devil himself had taken him over.

"But, sir," the florist said, "your wife gave me some of her quince jelly. It was delicious. I only just tried it this morning."

"Damn the jam! What about the rest of your incriminating note and the flower petals, eh? What do you say about those?"

"Oh, it's just the language of flowers, sir," stammered the florist lamely.

The vicar held the crumpled note before him in both hands with arms outstretched as if it were some kind of crucifix and forced the florist back against the wall in the bell chamber.

"Flowers! Hah!"

The florist stood rigid with his back plastered against the wall while the vicar stormed circling around him, eyeing him intently like some snarling wild dog about to attack. To the florist, he looked a complete anachronism with his white 'dog collar' around his neck. Likewise, the tarnished crucifix upon his chest completely contradicted his usual pre-eminence. Sweat was pouring off the florist's brow and his mouth was dry. He daren't move.

Suddenly, there was an almighty crash and a muffled clanging that rent the air. This was followed by a second, less clamorous thump. Then there was silence…

* * *

In a few moments, blood began spiraling down the bell rope of the tenor bell through the hole in the floor. It was somehow gruesomely reminiscent of a barber's shop pole from out of the Dark Ages.

Then came the sound of footsteps on the cobbled pathway outside.

Shortly afterwards, someone else approached from downstairs. There was a shriek and then a frenzied clattering of footsteps up the staircase. It was Louisa.

"Algie! What are you do…Aghhhhhhhhh!!!" she screamed.

She had just spotted Theodore lying on his back, motionless with one hand laid upon his chest. There was a slight bruise on his head. Then, as if that wasn't enough, Algie was pointing agitatedly to the other body under the bell. Louisa approached it cautiously from the other side. Pained recognition slowly registered on her face as she stared at the grisly sight.

"Aghhhhhhhh!!!" she screamed again, tearing herself away in horror.

There, lying crushed beneath the tenor bell (which weighed over a ton), was the broken body of her husband. She could see even in her own distressed state, that the bell must have somehow turned over on him. It would have taken very little to tip it over from being left in the 'up' position.

Louisa, in utter shock, began to tremble and shake uncontrollably. She was distraught and on the brink of collapse. Algie tried to comfort her but she was sobbing inconsolably.

"Alfred…Theodore…both dead!" she wailed.

That was when James, Gareth and Charles arrived on the scene.

Needless to say, there was no bell ringing that day to call the people to church.

The Sunday service was cancelled.

Thirteen

By ten past nine that morning the village constable, Constable Kenny and his assistant had arrived and a doctor, Dr. Peabody, was at hand. One of the victims was pronounced dead. That was the vicar, due to being crushed under a ton or more of weight. The florist was found to be still breathing although he had a knock on the head, the contusion perhaps setting off some brain damage. Dr. Peabody was in attendance upon him upstairs while the constable set up his proceedings on the ground floor of the bell tower.

The crumpled note had been salvaged from the vicar's still tightly gripped hand under the bell and kept as evidence for future use. Louisa in the meantime had been escorted home by the constable's assistant, Addison, to allow her to recover from the shock in more comfortable surroundings. The curate's wife, Betty, had arrived and was soon at Louisa's side to comfort her and her three daughters.

Meanwhile the police had some unsolved questions to answer. Obviously from the evidence of the note, they suspected a romantic liaison between the florist and the vicar's wife. But the question was whether the vicar was pushed and why there was so little injury to the florist.

The only motive they could think of so far was of the vicar wanting revenge upon the florist for meddling with his wife. Then again, Algie was under suspicion too and had been detained for questioning along with the other three ringers.

"At what time, Mr.…?" the constable began.

"Riverton," Algie volunteered.

"At what time, Mr. Riverton, did you arrive at the bell tower?" Constable Kenny asked.

"Twenty to nine, sir."

"That's a rather early hour wouldn't you say, Mr. Riverton, when the appointed time for bell ringing to start on a Sunday morning is normally nine o'clock?"

"Oh, I was up early this morning, sir, to check on the blocks of ice that arrived in my butchery last evening. I had to check how much they had melted overnight in the brine because I've never had ice installed before. My meat's always been salted before. And so, seeing as I finished there just before eight thirty this morning, I came by here early too."

"Did you see or hear anything suspicious?"

"I heard some shouting coming from the bell tower as I approached, sir."

"The vicar's wife, Mrs. Picard, says she found you in the belfry with the two bodies when she arrived. Is that correct, Mr. Riverton?"

"Yes, sir."

"Did you have any personal grudge against either the vicar, the Reverend Picard, or against the florist, Mr. Bycroft?"

"N…n…no, sir," Algie stammered.

"Thank you, Mr. Riverton. You may go now, but we will be in touch with you further if necessary."

James, Gareth and Charles were not given quite so much of the third degree but they collaborated Algie's apparent dislike of the florist during bell ringing practices. They were not sure if this was merely a 'professional' disdain of Theodore's bell ringing or if the dislike went deeper and was more personal, they said. The three ringers were then dismissed and Constable Kenny then began to form a hypothesis which he put before his assistant.

"Let's say that the florist pushed the vicar under the bell. Then the big butcher fellow killed the florist because of his dislike for him and to pay him back for killing the vicar," he mused, thinking aloud so that Addison might benefit from his ponderings.

He walked around and around the bell ringing chamber with one hand up to his chin and the other buried deep in his coat pocket. He was obviously deep in thought, so Addison kept a respectful silence. Upstairs, workmen were busily preparing to remove the crushed corpse while the florist was very soon to be taken to the City Hospital in York. All the evidence from the scene upstairs had been noted and now it was just a matter of cleaning up the mess.

At 2:30 in the afternoon, Louisa herself was questioned by Constable Kenny and his assistant in the drawing room of the vicarage. Louisa was sitting on the couch in a tear-stained state sipping tea from a bone china teacup. She offered the two policemen some refreshments but they declined. They sat down opposite her and placed their helmets almost apologetically on the floor beside them. The constable cleared his throat and then addressed her very matter-of-factly.

"Mrs. Picard…" he began. "I am sorry to have to inform you of this on such a sad occasion, but I have here in my possession, a note…a note of a rather delicate nature, I'm afraid."

Louisa wriggled uncomfortably in her seat.

"It hints at a liaison," he continued, "between yourself and Mr. Theodore Bycroft, the florist. Do you admit to being a party to this?"

"I, er, well, we…it was a light-hearted flirtation," she said, dismissing it with a wave of her hand. "Nothing more."

She blew her nose on a lace-trimmed handkerchief which had the initial 'L' embroidered daintily in pale blue in one corner.

"Are you sure?" he inquired.

"Oh, well, more of an intrigue, an infatuation I suppose one might call it."

"Do you suppose that your husband had a right to be jealous?"

"N…no, not really. Nothing happened that was of any consequence, really."

"Mrs. Picard…" the constable paused and looked at her intently. "Would you consider that your husband Alfred was a violent man?"

Louisa's back straightened significantly and she looked at him steadily.

"No, definitely not, sir."

The constable breathed more easily.

"Oh. And one more thing, Mrs. Picard. Did you see the butcher push anyone in the tower?"

"No, sir."

"Well, thank you for your co-operation, Mrs. Picard. That will be all for now, thank you."

The two policemen scooped up their helmets and showed themselves out.

Constable Kenny and his assistant strolled back to their makeshift office on the ground floor of the belfry. They corroborated the evidence together as they went on their way.

"It looks to me," said the constable, "that the vicar had a good motive to kill the florist. But the strange thing is that the florist had hardly a mark on him. That slight bruise looks more like where he may have fallen against the scaffolding of the bell supports. But we shall have to see what all the medical evidence points to after the hospital report. Alternatively, the vicar may have accidently tripped and fallen under the bell or he was pushed by the florist in self-defense. Or, the butcher pushed the florist into the scaffolding who then knocked the vicar under the bell. There are just so many combinations and permutations!"

"You have it down to a fine art, sir," replied his assistant with some admiration.

"Experience, Addison," he said touching his nose with one finger. "It all comes with experience."

* * *

Meanwhile, Louisa sat alone with her thoughts in the drawing room while Betty cleared the tea things. The three girls were still in the breakfast room where they had remained puffy-eyed and drinking tea during Louisa's interview with the police.

Louisa realized that her husband must have somehow found the note yesterday and gone to avenge himself on Theodore and then come to blows over her. The tragedy was that she had almost lost them *both*…her faithful loving husband and her ardent admirer. Now there was the added indignity of a scandal in the village…of which she was innocent. It would all be public conjecture and tittle-tattle, she knew. How was she going to cope? She was not only an orphan now but also a widow! She dabbed her eyes with the corner of her handkerchief as one by one her three daughters drifted back into the room to comfort her.

"At least I still have my children," she said reassuringly as she hugged them all. *And my inheritance*, she reflected mutely as an afterthought.

The girls arranged themselves on the armchairs around their mother quietly weeping and sniffing their support. Louisa smiled at them bravely. Then an impromptu thought crossed her mind which caused her to reproach herself:

What a pity I hadn't got around to giving Theodore a striped carnation as a refusal and a columbine as a sign of folly sooner. Then perhaps none of this would have happened! How could I have been so remiss!

She was struck with remorse and blew her nose again. Then pulling herself together for the sake of the children, she put on a brave face and looked fondly at her little Lucy who was sitting beside her. Suddenly, she wondered if the banshee down by the pond had anything to do with all this. She shuddered at the thought. Her children were her main concern now.

98

Suddenly, Lucy piped up with, "Mama…has Papa gone to heaven now?"

"Yes dear," Louisa replied. "And we will all be saying goodbye to him properly in three days' time. We'll give him a lovely send-off with his white pigeons. I know he would love that…"

Fourteen

Louisa went around in a daze over the next few days or so. She was able to contact both Jeremy in Oxford and Emma in London by telephone after much ado and tell them the bad news. They were both horrified of course and promised to attend their father's funeral on Wednesday 22nd at ten o'clock at the Bingham parish church. The curate had been 'marvelous' she told them and both he and his wife Betty had everything organized, including a stand-in vicar, the Reverend McAlister from a neighboring village.

Louisa balked at the idea of having to tell Thomas who was still in Cape Town, of his father's death by letter. After much deliberation, she finally decided that it was her duty to tell him the bad news. However, she cautioned him in her letter by adding a postscript:

"Do not feel that you must come home. We would all love to see you but by the time you arrived back, you would have missed the funeral. I am sure we will cope somehow. I quite appreciate the fact that your country needs you more in Africa, so do not feel bad if you don't make it home just yet. Your homecoming will be all the sweeter when the time is right.

Best wishes,
Your loving mother."

Louisa sealed the letter and placed it on the sideboard in the dining room ready for posting. Just then, the doorbell rang. It was the squire.

"How are you ma'am?" he asked. "I am so sorry to hear about the terrible accident with your husband. Terrible! Now is there anything I can do? I thought perhaps I could stand in for you on the treble bell for the next little while…you know, to keep the bells ringing, like."

"Oh, that would be lovely, Squire," she said. "That's very kind of you. Are you sure you will be able to manage it? It's quite different from the tenor bell…you won't have to heave on it so much."

"No, I'll be fine thanks. As long as I wear tight trousers, everything will be fine…just you see!"

They both laughed and Louisa invited him in for tea and scones in the conservatory. Betty had very kindly brought over a big batch of freshly made scones in case any visitors popped in.

"Mmmm…these are delicious!" said the squire most appreciatively. "She's very efficient, is that Betty."

"Yes, she's been a godsend," agreed Louisa, "organizing the flowers and the food and everything else. I don't know what I would have done without her."

"That's what friends are for," said the squire, relaxing into his chair. "To rally around in times of crisis."

"Yes," agreed Louisa, sipping her tea and peering through the profusion of hanging greenery. She had just caught sight of someone riding a bicycle up the path outside.

"Why, it's Hugo," she said surprised and went to greet him.

"Hello Mrs. Picard," he said, propping his bicycle up on its foot stand. "So sorry to hear about the vicar. I've brought you these," he said and presented her with a bunch of red, yellow and orange poppies from out of his bicycle pack. "I thought they might cheer you up."

"Thank you, Hugo. Do sit down and join us. I'll just put these in some water." She went out and returned shortly with the brightly bobbing poppies arranged somewhat higgledy-piggledy in a cobalt blue stained-glass vase. The two men were chatting about which organ music the vicar would have liked to have played at his funeral.

"Now then, Hugo…I don't think 'Ring Out, Wild Bells' would be quite appropriate in this case under the circumstances," the squire said pompously. He swallowed another mouthful of his tea and said, "What about something like 'There is a Green Hill Far Away'?" Then turning to Louisa, he asked, "Mrs. Picard…what was the vicar's favorite hymn?"

She hesitated slightly as she placed the vase of flowers on the table and replied:

"Oh, 'Abide with Me.' I think he quite liked that one for funerals."

"There you are, Hugo…from the horse's mouth."

They chatted on some more until all the scones but one had disappeared from the plate and then shortly afterwards, the two men departed, leaving Louisa and her girls to their own devices.

* * *

The appointed hour of ten o'clock drew nigh the next day for the Reverend Picard's funeral. Lilies, white roses and weeping willow branches decorated the church.

Louisa thought she had never seen the church look so beautiful. Her two elder children, Jeremy and Emma had arrived (including Emma's beau, John) and also several of her relatives from Ireland, Aunt Molly and Uncle Jim, Aunt Mary and Uncle Albert, Aunt Jane and Uncle Toby and three or four of her cousins. Louisa was dressed in obligatory black and wore a fine black veil over her face which hid her features from view. This time, she and Aunt Molly (who wore a similar veil), really did look like sisters.

The Reverend McAlister conducted the service and Hugo accompanied the congregation's singing of 'Abide with Me' beautifully on the organ. The casket itself was laden with lilies and white roses and after the eulogies Louisa and the children all went forward to kiss their husband and father a final goodbye. All the children were a great support to Louisa, especially when the pallbearers (of whom Jeremy and John were two), carried the coffin out of the church and into the graveyard. When it was time to lower the casket into the grave outside, sprigs of rosemary were thrown onto the coffin. Jeremy performed the honors and released all of Alfred's white pigeons into the sky. They flapped heavenwards and then put on a breathtaking display swirling overhead in a wide arc before gently fluttering back to earth. Alfred had always thought that releasing the pigeons like this symbolized the release of the spirit from the deceased.

If he had been physically present, Louisa knew that Alfred would have been impressed. Little Lucy had the final word however, by calling out goodbye to the birds as they circled overhead.

* * *

At that moment in the village, there was a telephone call at the Bingham Police Station. The policeman on duty, Sergeant Jorgenson, lifted the receiver.

"Hello, is that the Bingham Police?" a voice asked.

"Yes. Bingham Police here. Sergeant Jorgenson speaking."

"Oh. This is Dr. Roosevelt from the City Hospital in York. Is Constable Kenny there?"

"No, he's at a funeral at this moment."

"Oh. Could you give him a message, do you think?"

"Certainly."

"Just to say that the florist from Bingham who is in our care at the moment, Mr. Theodore Bycroft, has awoken from his comatose state. He began making progress in the early hours this morning and is now quite lucid. Amazing really. We didn't think he was going to make it. But Constable Kenny needs to know as he will probably want to continue his investigations I should think."

"Certainly Doctor. I will report to Constable Kenny as soon as possible."

Sergeant Jorgenson replaced the receiver, buttoned his coat and collected his helmet. He leaned around the door of his office and said, "Back soon, Sarg. Urgent business down at the vicarage." And then he left.

* * *

By now, the gathering at the graveside was beginning to gravitate towards the vicarage. Louisa thanked the reverend for his kind words at the service and then stood silently with her children at the graveside for a few moments. They were still stunned at what had happened and just seemed to be silently going through the motions. Then they too made their way slowly through the church grounds and into the vicarage.

Betty, the curate's wife, with the assistance of the Ladies' Guild, had organized a splendid morning tea which was set out in the drawing room and the conservatory. There were cucumber sandwiches, cheese straws, aspic molds, cold meats, savory puffs, butterfly cakes, Madeira cake, trifle and scones with strawberry jam and cream. It looked delicious. As everyone drifted in, tea was poured for them and the sibilant conversation grew gradually louder and louder, especially once the squire arrived on the scene as he had a very domineering presence.

Presently, the doorbell rang at the front door. "I'll get it," said the curate.

On the doorstep stood Sergeant Jorgenson. "Er, Sergeant Jorgenson at your service, sir. Is Constable Kenny in there, by any means? I have a message for him."

"Of course. Won't you come in?"

"Er, no thank you, sir. I'll stay right here if you don't mind," he said, straightening himself up and with the chin strap of his helmet catching his jaw.

The curate presently returned with Constable Kenny who looked a little surprised to see his sergeant standing there in the doorway.

"I've just had a report from the City Hospital in York, Constable, that Mr. Theodore Bycroft, the florist, has made a recovery. I just heard about fifteen minutes ago. He is alive and well. So, he's all yours now if you need to continue investigations."

"Marvelous!" said Constable Kenny. "I'll be on my way as soon as I've finished my cup of tea. Thank you, sir."

The sergeant clicked his heels together and departed. The curate who had been hovering over the constable's shoulder all the while, turned gleefully to the constable and said:

"That's wonderful news! Who said they didn't believe in miracles?"

He swung around in a most sprightly manner and made for the part of the crowd inside that was thickest and chanted capriciously:

"The florist has risen! The florist has risen!"

As he raved on in his sing-song voice, he waved a half-eaten piece of savory puff in one hand in time to his words over the heads of the crowd as if he were conducting an imaginary orchestra with the little titbit. The constable left him to his delirious pontifications, gulped his tea and excused himself from the gathering.

Meanwhile, the story was now out and the room was buzzing with the news. Above it all, the squire was heard to mutter distastefully:

"What's all this about a 'resurrection'? It's not even *Easter* yet!"

Louisa, who had been in the kitchen, returned in due course carrying another pot of tea. When she heard the news, she exclaimed:

"Oh, that's *wonderful* news!" and stood smiling brightly at everyone around her.

However, Eleanor Duval and Betty, the curate's wife, who were standing nearby were obviously not quite of the same opinion. They both raised one eyebrow each, gave each other dubious looks and simultaneously bit into their cucumber sandwiches…

Fifteen

At four o'clock that same day Constable Kenny arrived by horse and carriage at the City Hospital in York. Theodore Bycroft was propped up in bed with several pillows and was looking out the window of a private room where he had been taken for the purposes of the forthcoming interview. The room was bare except for a glass of water by his bedside and the obligatory bell-pull at the other side of the bed.

"Good afternoon, Mr. Bycroft," said the constable, shaking his hand. "Constable Kenny at your service. Glad to see you have made a recovery."

"Thank you, sir," said Theodore with a slight lisp.

The constable pulled up a chair that was parked just outside the doorway.

"Now, I have a few questions to ask you if you don't mind, Mr. Bycroft, now that you're feeling better."

"Not at all, sir."

"Were you or are you on friendly terms with the vicar's wife, Mrs. Picard?"

"Yes, sir. We are both bell ringers at the Bingham Anglican Church."

"So I understand…" said the constable, appreciably. He went on, "I have in my possession, Mr. Bycroft, a note in which you may recognize your handwriting."

He pulled the note out of his pocket and showed it to Theodore.

"Y…yes. That is my handwriting."

"So you admit to having written this note to Mrs. Picard arranging a rendezvous for Sunday, 17th February, at 8:30 am at the belfry?"

"Yes, sir."

"Did the rendezvous ever take place?"

"No, sir. The vicar was there instead."

The constable nodded.

"Was there a confrontation in the tower?"

"Yes, sir."

"Can you tell me exactly what happened?"

"The vicar was threatening me and he walked backwards into the slider of the tenor bell. He tripped over it and knocked the bell away from its stay. Then he fell under the bell and it turned over on top of him. It was horrible. Blood everywhere!"

The constable nodded again and continued, "How were you yourself injured?"

"I think I must have fainted."

"Really?"

"Yes, well, I hadn't been feeling quite myself that morning anyway. I had had a bit much to drink the night before after digging a huge stump out of my front garden. The curate pitched in and we managed to get it out. He stayed for a brandy afterwards but then when he had gone, I must have overdone it. So the next morning I had a slight hangover and dealt with it by taking a 'hair of the dog' before going to the tower. On hindsight, I probably wasn't in the best of condition in which to be meeting a lady."

"Yes, Mr. Bycroft," agreed the constable. "Probably not."

Then leaning back in his chair, the constable said: "So you fainted at the sight of the vicar being crushed under the bell or you fainted because you had a hangover?"

"I don't know, sir. Both probably."

"And you ended up with a bump on your head which knocked you out."

"Yes. I must have fallen against the oak scaffolding, I would say."

"Very interesting." The constable paused and then asked, "Did you see the butcher, Algernon Riverton, at any time that day?"

"No, sir."

"Or hear anything strange while you were in the tower with the vicar?"

"No, sir."

"Did the butcher harbor any ill-will towards you?"

Theodore gave a half smile. "Er yes. I got the impression he thought I was a first-class twit actually…but only as far as my bell ringing went. I have been a little 'rusty' lately but I'm not as stupid as he likes to make out."

"Ah, I see," said the constable stroking his chin. "A little professional jealousy perhaps?"

"I suppose so," agreed the florist. "But don't ask me anything about what happened straight after the accident because I can't remember a thing…only that I woke up in a strange room in a hospital bed. They said it was two o'clock in the morning when I first started to come around. But my legs are still a bit wobbly."

"Well thank you, Mr. Bycroft," said the constable standing up. "You have been most helpful. I wish you a speedy and total recovery."

They shook hands and the constable departed.

That all sounds quite plausible to me, thought the constable as he made his way towards his carriage. *All I need now is to corroborate his story with the curate…assuming that the curate has regained his sense of sobriety by now.*

With one bound, he was aboard the carriage bound for Bingham, confident that the mystery was now very close to resolution.

Meanwhile, now that the constable had gone Theodore had a sudden afterthought:

I've never fainted after a hangover followed by a 'hair of the dog' before. Why this time? Could it have been the sight of the vicar being squashed to a pulp that did it…or something else? I did feel strange that morning…kind of queasy. Perhaps it was something I'd eaten that morning? Strange…the only thing different I had for breakfast was that quince jelly that Louisa gave me…

Suddenly, he sat bolt upright. Surely Louisa wouldn't willfully try to poison him in order to discourage his advances? He was horror-struck at the thought. The very idea was ludicrous! That he could even suspect such a thing was abhorrent to him. He shuddered at the thought. But seeds of doubt were now sown in his mind.

* * *

In the interim, Louisa had been entertaining her relatives at the vicarage now that the rest of the funeral gathering had departed and was getting to know John, Emma's beau from London. He was a quiet and studious young man and rather shy, Louisa thought. She decided to draw him out of his shell a little and said:

"I'm sorry you had to meet the family in such sorry circumstances, John. Poor Alfred…he would have liked to meet you." She paused regretfully, reflecting upon her husband's recent death. Then changing the subject, she said, "Fancy you being a solicitor! Tell me how you met our Emma."

"Well, I was in hospital, ma'am," he said diffidently.

"Really? Go on," she said.

"Yes. Well I had shingles and Emma was one of my nurses."

"Really?"

There was an awkward pause in the conversation so Emma came to his rescue and said, "Yes. Shingles is quite rare in someone of John's age. The pain was as bad as appendicitis, but the doctors knew it wasn't that because of the rash and blisters that showed up first. I had to give him morphine for the pain." Then turning to him she said, "But you're alright now, aren't you John?"

"Oh yes. I'm really fine now. I don't know if it was the morphine or the nursing that worked best. Probably the nursing…" he said, glancing shyly at Emma.

Emma smiled and changing the subject, said, "Did you know that John used to row for Cambridge University?"

"Really?" said Louisa, turning towards John. "Our Jeremy's at Oxford, your old rival's." Then leaning over towards Jeremy, she said, "Glad you didn't bring your spider with you this time Jeremy!"

"Not at all, Mother. I've left him in very good hands at the moment. But he's quite friendly really."

"Not around me, he's not!" she exclaimed, shuddering.

Nervous tittering went around the room and the mutual agreement was unanimous.

* * *

Later that evening Aunt Molly and Uncle Jim who were also staying at the vicarage were having supper in the drawing room with Louisa.

"We had a lovely trip across on the train Louisa, didn't we Jim?" Aunt Molly was saying. "I just love this time of year with the early spring lambs and crocuses and snowdrops in the fields. It's so nice to get away. A pity it had to be in such sad circumstances. Poor Alfred. Such a waste."

"Yes, Auntie. I don't know how I shall manage," said Louisa.

"Nonsense dear. You'll cope. You have all your lovely children around you and a very fine curate to help run things. I'm sure you'll be alright dear. It won't be long before Thomas gets back from overseas either. The time will just fly, I'm sure. And that young man of Emma's seems a nice lad, doesn't he?"

They chatted on oblivious of the time and then Uncle Jim rose and excused himself to go to bed. (Uncle Jim and Aunt Molly had been designated the 'spare' spare room next to John's.) When he had withdrawn, Aunt Molly eased closer to Louisa on the settee and took her hand.

"You know, Louisa, I don't know whether I should tell you this," she said confidentially. "But coming across Marston Moor on the train yesterday, I was looking out the window to the north and I had this strange sensation. I don't know if I was dreaming or what but I got this peculiar idea that I may not see you again. Silly of me really, I suppose because I am getting on a bit…seventy-two I'll be in six months' time."

Louisa looked at her aunt reproachfully.

"Oh, I shouldn't have said anything, should I?" said Aunt Molly. "I'm just a silly old aunt going a bit potty," she said, tapping Louisa's hand. "Now don't you worry. Just forget I said anything, there's a good girl." She smiled at her encouragingly and then got up from the settee. "I must away to bed, Louisa. It's past my bedtime. See you in the morning."

"Goodnight, Auntie," said Louisa.

Sixteen

Three days later, Theodore Bycroft was released from the hospital and allowed to go home. He had made an extremely rapid recovery and his lisp had disappeared but now he needed to walk with the aid of a walking stick. His right leg was slightly gammy but was improving all the time. He arrived back in Bingham on the evening of Friday 24th and limped gamely up to his front door. As he did so, he was not unaware of the curious stares of his neighbors.

He went indoors, locked the door behind him and removed his hat and coat. One of the first things he did was to go into the kitchen, open the pantry and find that quince jelly that Louisa had given him.

"I don't want to insult her cooking," he said to himself, "but you can never be too careful."

He found the offending comestibles, lifted the cheesecloth cover and sniffed it with a scrutinous air. Unable to make an instant analysis, he cursed frustratedly and then shamelessly tipped the contents of the jar down the sink.

"So much for that!" he said and went to pour himself a brandy.

* * *

Over the next few weeks Theodore was able to go back to work at his florist shop on a part-time basis, his trustworthy assistant doing the lion's share of the work. However, he found over the coming weeks and months that as a relative newcomer to Bingham, even though the police had stressed to the local newspapers that the whole unfortunate incident had been a series of accidents, he was treated with increasing suspicion by the villagers. He was not considered to be so much a 'marriage wrecker' as 'the one who pushed the vicar under the bell.'

Algie Riverton on the other hand was treated with a little more civility by the villagers because he was a local. Three generations of Rivertons had lived in Bingham before him, and there was no known motive for Algie himself, to be rid of the vicar. Hence, Algie was absolved from the crime in the villagers' minds, but Theodore was not.

Theodore later came to spend less and less time at his florist shop in Bingham and more and more time in London on other business. The local gossip was that he now had another romantic liaison with a young lady in London.

In fact, word had it that Hugo, in his travels, had spied Theodore in the National Gallery in London pointing out the intricacies of a Monet painting to some innocent young *ingénue*. She was hanging on his every word while he stood there lecturing about the meaning of waterlilies and suchlike whilst at the same time stabbing knowledgeably at them in the air with his walking stick. If the truth be known, it was almost too good a scene in itself to be passed up by any artist worth his salt. If caught on canvas, this little spectacle could perhaps have been effectively entitled 'Teacher and Pupil' as a painting within a painting. Theodore was so unmistakably photogenic and the young lady…well, she was delectable. She was petite, blonde and about twenty-five.

Hugo kept out of sight but managed to overhear Theodore explaining to the young lady:

"Now then Frieda, the subtleties of modern impressionism show these Monet waterlilies here (meaning 'purity of heart') in *quite* a different light, ephemeral really, from the pink roses (meaning 'happiness') over there in that early renaissance Botticelli…But then, good art has a certain rhetoric of its own really…"

Hugo gulped and was just glad that Louisa wasn't there to witness this little scene. In fact, he wished he hadn't witnessed it either. His heart gave a thump and he pranced mincingly up and down behind an arras, stealing green-eyed glances at his crippled heart-throb. He was feeling just a teensy bit jealous.

"Just who *is* this 'other woman'?" he asked himself. "He's wasted on her…"

* * *

A few weeks later, Gareth, one of the Bingham bell ringers, was visiting the Chelsea Flower Show in London during late spring and happened upon Theodore taking tea with a young lady in one of the pavilions. Quite a dish she was, he noticed…petite with blonde hair, about twenty-five…*although her attention did seem to be wandering*, he thought. Perhaps she was not overly fond of handsome gentlemen with gammy legs? He wasn't sure, but as soon as he approached them, she excused herself and left. Gareth was a little taken aback. He did not normally have that sort of effect on women.

In spite of this, he greeted Theodore amiably and the two of them discussed the show and the idiosyncrasies of the fairer sex, amongst other things. From the way that Theodore was speaking, Gareth got the impression that he was a dab hand with the ladies. Or then again, was this all a ruse perhaps?

Theodore chatted on and then being in his element, reverted back to the subject of flowers, upon which he was an expert. Gareth received a not unwelcome lecture on the meanings of flowers and how Theodore thought there should be an official flower emblem set up for all the bell ringers of England.

"What about a cowslip?" Gareth volunteered. "You know, Shakespeare…'Where the bee sucks there suck I, in a cowslip's bell I lie.'" he quoted.

"Yes, but a cowslip translates as 'pensiveness'," said Theodore. "Not quite appropriate I shouldn't think in describing bells or bell-ringers. I was thinking more along the lines of bluebells. They are a native spring wildflower as well established and prevalent here in England as the art of bell ringing itself. Bluebells are also known as wild hyacinths and translate as 'constancy'. There is nothing more constant than the sound of bells ringing out over the English countryside on a Sunday morning."

"Hmmm…very true," agreed Gareth, being a dye-in-the-wool bell-ringer himself.

Theodore sat there pondering the worth of this fanciful idea while Gareth waited expectantly for more pearls of wisdom. A red-headed woman with a broad Scottish accent brushed past their table inadvertently bumping Theodore's chair which made him spill some of his tea. She prattled on to her companion, oblivious of her blunder, leaving Theodore open-mouthed to mop up the mess. He was just wringing out a handkerchief full of warm tea over the table centerpiece when he suddenly stopped, startled.

"On second thoughts, maybe bluebells aren't such a good choice. I just remembered that the Scottish name for the bluebell is 'Dead Men's Bell.' It is said that if you ever hear the ring of a bluebell, you are hearing your own death knell…"

The two men eyed each other abruptly. In truth for Theodore, such a bald misstatement seemed dangerously close to the realms of credibility. Except he doubted that his hearing was that acute. Suddenly bluebells seemed to be not such a good idea. Could it be that the vicar had heard bluebells ring before his death? Theodore shunned the thought because it was too late now. No one would ever know. It was mere superstition after all…Gareth averted his eyes with some awkwardness and took another sip of his tea. Charitably, he changed the subject around to women again, for which Theodore was grateful.

* * *

By chance in June, Hugo once more ran across Theodore in London at a certain gentleman's club. This time Theodore was alone.

Strange, Hugo thought, *for such a handsome man to be so alone.* He peered ruminatively at Theodore from across the crowded room. Then with much alacrity he was struck with the thought, *Now's my chance to make his proper acquaintance…*

Seventeen

One week had passed since the vicar's funeral and Jeremy Picard had by now returned to Oxford. Louisa's aunts and uncles and cousins had likewise since departed for Ireland. However, Emma and her beau, John, were still at the vicarage for just one more day.

Despite her underlying melancholy, Louisa could not help noticing that John appeared to be overly nervous that day. He would drop his knife and fork at breakfast whenever she spoke to him and seemed unusually distracted. Before the day was out, she discovered what was bothering him. It was after dinner when Emma was out of the room that he broached the subject with her.

They were in the drawing room together when he blurted out:

"Mrs. Picard. I wondered if I might ask you for Emma's hand."

Louisa looked up in shocked surprise. "Oh, this is all very sudden, John."

"Yes, but we're in love and we've known each other seven months."

"Oh…" She considered a little longer and then said without further ado, "Of course you may, John. I'd be delighted. The whole family would be delighted…even Alfred, if he were still here."

"Oh, that's marvelous Mrs. Picard. Thank you so much. I will go and tell Emma immediately."

He rushed out of the room to tell Emma the good news and they were soon all gathered together in the drawing room with Geraldine, Charlotte and Lucy as well.

"Open some champagne from the wine cellar, Geraldine dear and we will celebrate," said her mother. "It's so nice to be able to celebrate some good news isn't it?"

Geraldine returned with an 1895 vintage of Portuguese sparkling rose, as they had no French champagne and filled six wineglasses while Charlotte passed them around. Lucy was not forgotten and was allowed half a glass as it was a special occasion.

"Here's to Emma and John upon their engagement," Louisa said proudly and raised her glass in a toast. "And here's to absent friends and family," she said, her eyes a little teary. Then she smiled bravely and said, "We wish you both all the very best of luck, Emma and John."

"To Emma and John," everyone chanted as one.

The effervescence of the 'pink champagne' helped to add a certain something to the atmosphere but the merriment was still tinged with sadness. Louisa was only just getting used to the idea that she would never see her husband again. She missed him terribly. She hadn't sung a note around the house all week which was quite understandable but also quite out of character. Instead, whenever she found herself becoming depressed and miserable, she would sit at the piano and play incessantly until it became quite irritating to the rest of the household.

Then there was Theodore, whom she feared she had lost. Neither of them had contacted the other since that dreadful day. Besides, she had already heard gossip in the village that she and Theodore had conspired against her husband. It was ludicrous. She…an accomplice to murder? Let alone the idea that others considered her to be a 'scarlet woman'!

Yes, Louisa was miserable alright. She longed to go back to Ireland and see Madame Petrovsky and perhaps see things from a different perspective. It would be nice to just get away from Bingham for a while.

Perhaps I would be able to talk to Alfred through Madame, she would think hopefully. *Then again*, she realized, *I can't go. I've got too many parish duties here…the three girls to look after, the dog and the pigeons to feed. I can't go and that's all there is to it*, she would tell herself resignedly.

She did not relish the idea of being a widow…especially a gossiped-about widow and a vicar's one at that.

* * *

The next morning at breakfast, Louisa was feeling particularly morbid and fractious. Seeing that her husband wasn't at the table she rather recklessly raised the subject of spiritualism.

"Have you ever spoken to the dead, John?" she asked.

Emma gave her a disapproving look and shook her head, but she carried on regardless.

"It's all the rage now you know, spiritualism. It's the new parlor craze. I wouldn't be surprised if there are a few mediums in London who are very good. Forget about table-turnings and ectoplasm and poltergeists. I mean the genuine article, the real McCoy."

Her prospective son-in-law was immediately caught off balance and stammered:

"N…no, Mrs. Picard. I can't say that I have ever…"

"You should. You never know which of your forebears you might meet. A great-great-great-great step grandfather who was a pirate perhaps or even someone who was a lady-in-waiting to Queen Anne. It's a new world out there."

"Y…yes, ma'am. I'm sure you're right," John stammered awkwardly.

John and Emma looked at each other across the breakfast table as if to say, 'What's got into her today?' They both shrugged and looked blank.

Relentlessly, Louisa prodded him:

"Let me know if you find someone who's good down there in London John, and I'll come and visit."

"Yes ma'am."

By now, John was starting to get the jitters. Who was this strange woman whose daughter he was about to marry? She was really acting rather weirdly this morning. Without realizing it he dropped his knife and fork back onto his plate. Unawares, he carried on raising the imaginary scrambled eggs on toast up to his lips and opened his mouth. Biting on thin air made him realize his mistake.

Something must have set her off to get her talking like this, he thought. *I just hope it wasn't me.*

* * *

By mid-morning, Emma and John had departed for London; Emma back to the nursing school and John back to his solicitor's job. Now there was just Louisa and her three girls left at the vicarage. The girls went to school for the day and Louisa spent the day helping in the rectory reading room and conferring with the curate and the ladies of the Guild. But she was not happy. She felt sad and lonely as if she were being gradually ostracized by the villagers. She wished Alfred was still alive to help her cope but that could not be.

Lucy soon arrived home from school to lighten her burden skipping up the pathway to the front door.

Straight away she could tell that her mother was down-in-the-dumps, so she took pity on her.

"Mama," she said, rolling up her skipping rope. "I have to tell you something. Come into the breakfast room."

Curious, Louisa followed her and together they sat down at the breakfast room table. Then Lucy began, "You know that day when you asked me to take the quince jelly around to Mr. Bycroft's shop?"

"Yes, I remember…"

"Well, before I went, remember you went to play the piano and I went upstairs to get my skipping rope?"

"Yes…"

"Well, I got that nasty medicine out of Grandpapa's stuff at the bottom of your wardrobe and emptied it all on top of the jelly that I took around to Mr. Bycroft's."

"You did *what*?" exclaimed Louisa.

Lucy took a deep breath and began again.

"I tasted the jelly first and then licked the spoon until it was clean. It was so clean I could see myself upside-down in the front of the spoon. It tasted very nice, Mama," she said, looking all the more earnestly at her mother as her mother backed further and further away from her in anticipatory horror. "Then I mixed the medicine into the jelly because it hadn't set properly and then I put the little cover back on, tied it up with the string again and took it to Mr. Bycroft."

"Lucy! How *could* you!"

Lucy cringed, looking suitably guilty.

"Why did you do a thing like that?"

Lucy wriggled uncomfortably and said, "'Cause I saw Mr. Bycroft kissing you outside the bell tower that night when I was looking out my bedroom window at the moon."

Louisa gasped.

"I didn't like him, Mama. I thought he was going to take you away from us."

"Oh Lucy! That's terrible! You could have killed the poor man! What did you do with the bottle?"

"I put it back in the carpet bag later on."

"Stay here," said Louisa, "and don't move!"

She raced upstairs and rummaged through the old carpet bag at the bottom of her wardrobe. She found three medicine bottles, one of which was empty. On the label it said:

'Laudanum: Tincture of Opium'

"Oh my God!" said Louisa exasperatedly and raced downstairs with it. "Lucy!" she said, in no uncertain terms. "You were lucky Mr. Bycroft didn't die! This medicine is very dangerous and is meant to be taken only in very small doses according to a doctor's orders. You are a very naughty girl!"

Lucy screwed up her face and began to cry.

"Oh dear," Louisa said. "I know you didn't mean to poison Mr. Bycroft, but you mustn't play with other people's medicines. I suppose I should have thrown it out long ago, to be honest."

She soothed her daughter down and said:

"There, there, dear. I know you only did it to protect me."

She cuddled Lucy until she was quiet and then said, "Just don't breathe a word of this to anyone…not to Charlotte or Geraldine or Emma or Jeremy or Thomas or even John. No one…ever. Alright?"

Lucy nodded and went quietly upstairs to her room.

Eighteen

Nearly a year passed by and it was now the day before Valentine's Day, 13th February 1901. The whole of England had been in mourning because Queen Victoria had died the previous month on 22nd January. She was 81 when she died and had reigned for over sixty years. Tokens of grief were everywhere in Bingham on the day of her funeral. Shop fronts were draped in black entwined with purple and flags were flown at half-mast. The curate had conducted a memorial service at the church and the villagers had marched up to the town hall accompanied by funeral music to lay floral wreaths at the foot of the flagpole there.

As for Louisa, she was coping with the fact that her mother was dead, her father was dead, her husband was dead, her would-be-lover was 'as if' dead (as she had not seen or heard from him since that fatal day last year) and now her beloved Queen was dead. She seemed to be becoming more and more abstracted and self-absorbed as time went on and seemed to be cutting herself off from the real world. She still went through the motions of attending the Ladies' Guild, bell ringing twice a week, running the rectory reading room, but it was if she were only half there. Mentally she was somewhere else. Her piteous state had become more noticeable to both Emma and Jeremy over the past year when they had come to visit. Needless to say, Louisa had not entered the bell chamber in the tower for the past year, for obvious reasons. It would have been too distressing for her. She only went as far as locking the intervening door.

As far as Emma was concerned, it looked as if she would be having a long engagement while she waited to finish her nursing studies. Jeremy on the other hand was due to graduate next year in entomology at Oxford.

Suddenly the telephone rang in the hallway of the vicarage raising Louisa from her reverie. She lifted the receiver off the hook.

"Hello?" she said.

"Mrs. Picard?"

“Yes.”

“It’s Hugo here. I was just wondering if you wouldn’t mind filling in for me on the church organ from Sunday on for a few days. It’s just that I’ve got a visitor coming to stay from London at short notice.”

“That’s quite alright Hugo. Certainly. I’ll be there. Don’t worry, I’d be delighted.”

“Thanks, Mrs. Picard.”

She hung up and absent-mindedly went to look out the windows of the conservatory. It was quite gusty outside and it looked like it was going to get worse by the look of it. She sighed. The weather had been so depressing lately.

There was a *thunk* by the front door. Thinking it must be the postman, she went to investigate. Sure, enough there was some mail. A couple of bills and a postcard. The postcard was postmarked, ‘Maputo, Mozambique.’

“Girls! Girls!” she called. “We’ve got another postcard from Thomas!”

Geraldine, Charlotte and Lucy soon came running and they crowded around their mother at the kitchen table. Once they were settled, she said:

“Listen to this…

10th Jan 1901.

Dear Family,

How are you all? I’ll be very surprised if you get this by the end of February because we are stationed at the mouth of the Limpopo River in Mozambique and the mail will probably go via the Suez Canal. The navy is still experimenting with wireless telegraphy between Dalagoa Bay and Durban (250 miles) since we had that success last April over the 50-mile range. (Not bad considering the army rejected all the equipment in the first place!)

Did you know that Cecil Rhodes’s father was a clergyman? He made his fortune in diamonds before becoming Prime Minister of the Cape Colony. Perhaps there’s hope for me yet!

Love,
Thomas.

P.S. I’m coming home in mid-March. I’m really looking forward to it!!!”

"Oh! That's wonderful news!" they all chorused.

"I wonder if he will have a beard or mustache when he gets home." Lucy giggled.

"Of course, he won't, Lucy…not in the navy. They make you shave them off," said Louisa.

The two older girls giggled behind their hands. "Right-o, off to school with you all," Louisa said.

"Don't be late and take your coats today. It doesn't look very nice outside."

* * *

That evening the stormy weather had worsened. It had become a howling gale. Geraldine, who had been reading aloud from *Martin Chuzzlewit* to her sisters in the drawing room, finally gave up, complaining, "I can't concentrate with that wind blowing so much out there. I think I shall just go to bed, if that's alright, Mother."

"That sounds like a good idea to me, dear. It's a terrible night tonight."

Geraldine folded the book on her lap and withdrew, followed by her two sisters.

"Goodnight, Mama."

"Goodnight, girls. I'll see you in the morning."

By the time Louisa got to bed, it was ten o'clock. But she lay awake a long time before she could get to sleep. She was just about to drop off when she heard something banging. Her eyes shot open. It was the intermediary door in the tower.

"Oh, no!" thought Louisa "I *hate* having to shut that door. Especially at night when it's blowing. Perhaps I'll just stay here and let it bang."

She lay there for a while half asleep, anticipating every 'bang' and being jolted awake with each successive one. Finally conceding defeat, she muttered with annoyance and hauled herself out of bed. She wrapped up warm in her dressing gown and woolly coat and ventured downstairs. She collected the keys and oil lamp from the scullery and donned her outdoor boots. Then she courageously opened the back door to face the elements.

She was buffeted about by the squalling wind all across the grounds to the tower and then once she had unlocked the outer door, was blown unceremoniously inside the ringing chamber. Once inside, she shut the outer door and leaned with her back against it and her lamp held high. The banging was definitely coming from the door upstairs. Taking a deep breath, she gingerly climbed the spiral steps. She reached the top step and then poked her head around the offending door. The wind blasted her full in the face from the window slats opposite.

At that same moment, there was a low growl of thunder overhead and it started to rain heavily. A sudden chill filled the tower. Suddenly, in the lamplight she was confronted with the dreaded and accursed specter which she so abhorred. It was hanging in mid-air, hideously staring at her through its unseeing eyes. Lightning flickered across its necrotic features and it began its obscene obsessive-compulsive ritual. This time it was blood that was being wrung from between its bony fingers. It began to open its toothless mouth in a wicked caterwaul…

Louisa screamed.

"Oh my God! Oh my God!" she yelled and fled down the stairs forgetting to lock the door. She tripped on the bottom step of the spiral staircase but managed to regain her balance just in the nick of time. She was spooked out of her wits. This time she knew the banshee was calling for her.

"Oh God! Oh God! She's after me!" she cried as she tore through the teeming wind and rain. "It's all my fault. Alfred's death…flirting with Theodore…leaving dangerous medicines around!"

She sobbed loudly as she navigated the rest of the way back through the rain to the vicarage back door. Just as she reached out for the door handle, she suddenly remembered her father's words at Madame Petrovsky's:

"Look after the children."

"Oh my God! The children! The children!" she cried.

She dashed upstairs in a state of utter panic still dripping wet and sobbing. She reached the two doors of the girls' bedrooms and with much trepidation, peered in. Lucy was sound asleep in her room and Charlotte and Geraldine in theirs.

Reassured for the moment, Louisa dashed downstairs through the kitchen and dining room, sobbing more quietly now and wiping her nose on her wet coat-sleeve. Lightning flashed and two dead rosebuds dropped onto the paper doily from the flower arrangement on the dining room table. In the distance, thunder rumbled low and menacingly. She looked in at the piano in the drawing room and then had a change of mind.

Intent on what she was now doing, Louisa dashed out the front door of the vicarage with her lamp held high and ventured back into the fury of the storm. She bolted across the grounds towards the main door of the church and let herself in. She caught her breath for a moment and then ran down between the two sets of oak pews towards the organ console. She threw herself upon the seat and began to pull out all the stops. She desperately wanted to purge her guilt upon the organ. Thunder clapped about her and so in a contest of wills, she played louder in a torrent of cascading notes emulating the Dies Irae from Verdi's *Requiem*. The organ pipes were not only vibrating to the wrath of the Last Judgement in the *Requiem* but also to the passion of her playing and the power of the thunderbolts from the firmament above.

The acoustics of the empty church amplified the sound so that the thunderbolts exploded like the deafening cannon-shots of Tchaikovsky's *1812*. Lightning began to lick hungrily around the church windows.

Suddenly, the main door to the church burst open with a bang. A man stood there dripping wet. He held a walking stick in his right hand. Lightning flashed again and lit up his face. It was Theodore Bycroft who had returned. Thunder boomed overhead once more. He stood there for a moment, confused and unsure of himself. He expected to see Hugo at the organ. He scrutinized the impassioned figure of the organist under the lamp-lit console from where he was standing at the far end of the church. It was definitely a woman.

Kaleidoscopic flashes leapt eerily around the chancel under the lamplight like some harbinger of evil as she flourished her arms over the keyboards.

Realizing that the organ was electric, he suddenly yelled out:

"Stop!!!"

But she couldn't hear him because of the noise. Taking things into his own hands, he suddenly launched himself like a cannonball from the back of the church but the hindrance of his limp meant that he could only stagger madly down the center aisle. He threw himself at Louisa and their bodies connected. Simultaneously, a tumultuous thunderbolt sounded directly overhead and a flash of blue lightning illuminated their impact. There was a crackle of electricity in the air and a pervasive smell of smoke.

Their two bodies fell apart like a collapsed spring…Louisa's onto the lower keyboard and Theodore's onto the floor on his back with his walking stick still in his hand. A long-drawn-out dissonant chord sounded on the organ which slowly became lost to nature's own orchestration. It was as if it were giving voice to Louisa's last breath.

Scattered on the ground lay the flowers that Theodore had brought from London. But they never reached their intended recipient. They were blue hyacinths…as blue as a Mediterranean sky…

* * *

Not ten minutes later, the three young Picard girls arrived and stood peering in from the church doorway. All three were soaked to the skin and were standing huddled together shivering in their clinging wet nightdresses.

All three were crying…

Nineteen

It was nearly midnight and Hugo looked anxiously at his fob-watch.

"Where the dickens is Theodore?" he asked himself. "He was supposed to have been here for supper over two hours ago! Obviously, he has been held up in all this atrocious weather, I'd say."

He dimmed the gaslight in the living room of his upstairs flat overlooking the River Rye and once again admired the artistry of his own handiwork sitting on the mantelpiece. It was a valentine for Theodore made up as a paper puzzle purse. On the outside, he had painted a big red heart with a bluebird of happiness in each corner trailing part of a long blue swirling ribbon in each of their beaks. As you folded and unfolded the puzzle purse, the verse read:

'My love is like a cabbage
Divided into two
The leaves I give to others
But the heart I give to you!'

He was longing to give it to him. *This* time he would personally present Theodore with the valentine and reveal his true feelings at last. An anonymous card in the post like last year would never do. Surely their friendship had developed now beyond *that*? In fact, he had not seen Theodore for a whole month since he was down in London last on 12th January to celebrate Theodore's thirty sixth birthday. He wished Theodore didn't have to spend so much time in London.

"But," he sighed, "this is the way it has to be."

It was such a pity that Theodore was now lame he thought, but then on the other hand, would Theodore ever have looked at him (even as a friend), if he were not lame? He doubted it. He felt very honored to have someone such as Theodore take notice of him at all...a callow and spindly looking youth by comparison. Although he did have some compensating features…a certain 'charm' even if he did say so himself.

He had met up with Theodore at a particular gentleman's club last summer after attending a cricket match at Lords to see the 'Black Prince of Cricket', Ranjit Sinhji, demolish the French. England won and being typically patriotic, they found themselves having a celebratory drink together afterwards at the same table.

Theodore much regretted his own inability to play at the crease now and tended to drown his sorrows in brandy. He also bemoaned the fact that he was less attractive to the ladies about town, now that he relied more and more heavily on his walking stick. Losing the likes of young Frieda to a more robust rival two months previously, had really irked him. Hugo had provided that much needed sympathetic ear to all his troubles and Hugo's reward was the freedom to dress up as flamboyantly as he liked now that he was away from his home town. Theodore in turn, enjoyed the flattery of his attentions and so Hugo's visits to London became more frequent.

This Friday night Theodore had decided upon a special one-off visit to Bingham to sort out his business affairs and Hugo had very kindly offered to put him up at his flat. This suited Theodore because he would be away from the prying eyes of his nosy neighbors…now that he was considered *persona non grata* in the village. What he was not aware of however, was the intensity of Hugo's feelings towards him. What he *did* know, was that he needed all the friends he could get, so he gratefully accepted the offer and even brought flowers as a thank-you gift. But he had no idea the weather was going to be so bad. It got worse on the train up to York and by the time he was aboard the horse and carriage from there to Bingham it had become a howling gale.

He was running late for supper with Hugo in his flat but then what made him even later was the fact that as the coach was passing the Bingham church, he could hear something strange above the crash of the thunder. It was the organ. Someone was playing that electric organ in the middle of a thunder storm! It had to be Hugo! He urgently asked the driver to stop, paid his fare, grabbed his suitcase and flowers and made a dash through the storm as fast as he could up the church steps…

* * *

Valentine's Day, Saturday, 14th February, dawned the next day amid much mayhem at the Bingham Police Station. It had been a terrible start to the day after a horrible stormy night. Just after midnight the curate had dashed out to the station in the middle of the thunderstorm to say that the three Picard girls were in distress at the vicarage.

Geraldine Picard had just telephoned him and was almost incoherent. Eventually he was able to extract from her the fact that her mother and the former florist, Mr. Theodore Bycroft, were lying dead at the foot of the organ console in the church chancel. Hurriedly, he had told her to get off the phone in case of a lightning strike and promised to contact the police immediately on foot.

Constable Kenny and his faithful assistant, Addison, were thus on the scene in under fifteen minutes. Dr. Peabody was also called out to assist. The curate attended the grisly scene as well while his wife, Betty, attended to the girls who were beside themselves with grief at the vicarage.

"What a catastrophe!" the constable exclaimed when he first set eyes upon the victims. "Definitely a lightning strike I would say, Addison. Just keep away from that organ and that brass-studded walking stick!"

They removed their mackintoshes and shook the raindrops off between the pews. Then Dr. Peabody eyed the bodies briefly and his body language confirmed the constable's guess.

"Bloody dangerous!" he said. "That's what some of these new-fangled contraptions are! Bloody dangerous!" He happened to notice the curate cringe, so he said at once, "Oh, excuse me, Curate, for swearing in church. But whose idea was it to install an electric organ anyway?"

"Oh, the vicar's, sir. He and the squire arranged it," said the curate, somewhat embarrassed.

"Hrmphh!" said Dr. Peabody obviously unimpressed. He raised his eyes heavenwards and then coughed rather disparagingly. Then he said, turning to the policemen, "Well, Constable, I'll have a look at these two for you."

So saying, he noted the shredded clothing and the blown off shoes and stepped gingerly over the spread-eagled body of the florist and bent down to feel his cheek.

"Still warm," he said.

Thunder rumbled overhead. Then he said ruminatively, "I wonder what the devil they were doing in the church together at this time of night anyway…"

Suddenly, the doctor was taken completely unawares as Theodore's arm jerked unexpectedly at an odd angle and nearly struck the doctor in the face. Dr. Peabody had to make a quick side-step. Forgetting his p's and q's he suddenly yelled:

"Jesus! This chap's still alive! He's obviously just been very badly stunned I'd say!"

"Look out! There goes the lady too! She's coming around!" yelled one of the policemen.

Louisa's head rolled to one side and gazed unblinkingly at the doctor. One side of her face was etched with fine blood vessels and capillaries that stood out like a road map.

"Quick, get some water and smelling salts!" yelled the doctor. "They're partially paralyzed, but hopefully it will wear off."

* * *

By morning, the storm had abated and the news had travelled throughout most of the village…that the vicar's widow, Mrs. Picard and her paramour, Mr. Theodore Bycroft, had been found together in the church at midnight…seared by lightning. Some said that they had been found locked in a deadly embrace, others that they were found in various stages of undress. There was much speculation and gossip amongst the villagers as to the goings on…and in the house of God, at that!

Betty, the curate's wife, just happened to be in Algie's butcher's shop that morning just as Hugo stepped in to buy two pieces of choice steak for himself and his yet-to-arrive guest.

"I just *knew* that fireworks would explode sooner or later," said Betty to Algie as he passed her sausages over the counter. "That Louisa Picard was a right little 'butter wouldn't melt in your mouth' type. And *now* look what's happened. Caught in her own trap I'd say. And that Theodore Bycroft! He was no better. Tarred with the same brush. I mean to say, what did they think they were playing at, canoodling at midnight and in a *church* of *all* places! I say they both got their just deserts! God obviously had the last word and struck them both down with a lightning bolt. Good riddance to them, *I* say."

She tucked the sausages and then the sweetbreads into her shopping basket, paid her money and then strutted out the door with a self-righteous air, full of

129

her own importance. Even Algie was left quite taken aback at this out-and-out backstabbing while Hugo stood there like a stunned mullet with his mouth agape.

It couldn't be, could it? he asked himself...*True, that Theodore had still been seeing Louisa on the side? His Theodore...the one he loved? And he had been struck by lightning? And Louisa?*

He couldn't believe it.

"Can I help you, Hugo?" asked Algie presently.

"Er...yes...er...no...er, that is, I'll have two pieces of rump steak please..." he said very hesitantly. Then plucking up courage, he asked, "Is it true what the curate's wife just said then? About Louisa Picard and Theodore Bycroft?"

"Apparently so. They were struck by lightning in the church last night. God only knows what they were doing there together and at *that* time of night too! And in the middle of a thunderstorm at that. Sounds crazy to me."

"Oh!" Hugo swallowed and felt a lump rising in his throat. "That's terrible!"

He was almost choking with raw emotion. So, Theodore had spent the night with someone else...his ex-lady friend...while he, Hugo, had spent the night alone, worried sick about him and his whereabouts. Never mind that Theodore had got himself injured in the process, but Hugo felt quite hurt that any consideration for himself had been quite obviously cast aside.

Why didn't he telephone me, Hugo asked himself, *to at least warn me and put me out of my misery? And what in heaven's name am I going to do with two pieces of prime rump steak now?*

"There you are, Hugo," Algie said as he passed the steak over the counter. "Have you got guests tonight then?"

Hugo went a sudden shade of scarlet and then just as suddenly, as white as a sheet. He was starting to feel faint so he just said, "Oh, I don't feel very well all of a sudden. How much was that?"

"Two shillings."

He paid his money and with his head almost bursting, ran out of the shop.

Oh my God! Theodore's been struck by lightning! he yelled to himself in his head. *I can't believe it! What am I going to do?*

He rushed home on the brink of tears and slammed the front door behind him. The draught that was created blew Theodore's card off the mantelpiece.

"How can people be so wrong about things?" he sobbed, releasing a pent-up flood of tears. "Theodore belongs to *me*, not Louisa."

He threw himself in his favorite armchair, pulled out a handkerchief and drowned himself in his misery.

* * *

The police by now had established Louisa's movements during the previous night. The three Picard girls had advised them that they had heard someone playing the church organ above the sound of the storm just before midnight. They had gone to look for their mother in her bedroom but she was not there. They had called out for her and searched every room of the house, but she was nowhere to be found so they ventured outside in a panic hoping to find her at the organ in the church. They were just minutes too late, for when they arrived the playing had ceased and their mother was lying stunned across the keyboard with Mr. Bycroft likewise at her feet.

What Constable Kenny wanted to know was what Theodore Bycroft, of *all* people, was doing there of *all* places and at *that* time of night? Obviously, some sort of illicit early Valentine's Day greeting from what they knew of the history of the case. Perhaps the flame between the two paramours had re-ignited due to the dawning of Valentine's Day again? But why did they decide to rendezvous in the church? Because there would be less likelihood of discovery of their smoldering secret love in such a place? They were protected by meeting under the cover of darkness but why did Louisa advertise the fact that she was there to all and sundry with her organ playing? Perhaps it was some sort of musical catharsis to their (unconsummated?) love that she thought no one else would hear above the noise of the storm? And apart from that, was Louisa conscious of the fact that she was in a potentially dangerous situation or was she blissfully unaware?

Constable Kenny found himself wrestling with all these as yet unanswered questions. He needed more information. Notices were posted around the village asking for any reported sightings of either party during the period in question. A certain coach driver eventually fronted up to say that he had picked up a passenger by the name of Bycroft who was travelling from York to Bingham on that Friday night. His final destination was to be 14^A Bishop's Court but just before midnight, the passenger had suddenly asked to be dropped off at the church instead. The coachman had obliged and noticed that the passenger used a walking stick and carried a suitcase and flowers.

Constable Kenny followed up the lead and soon found himself knocking on Hugo's front door on Sunday morning. (The church service had once again been cancelled out of respect for the ex-vicar's widow.) Hugo answered the door wrapped in his multi-colored velvet smoking jacket worn over his bicycle breeches.

"Morning Mr. Blanchard," said Constable Kenny. "Bingham Police. Do you mind if I and my assistant, Addison, come in?"

"No, sir, not at all. Come in and take a seat," he said. "We have reason to believe, Mr. Blanchard, that Mr. Theodore Bycroft was on his way here on Friday evening, the night of the thunderstorm. Is that correct?"

"Yes, sir. He was coming up from London to stay for the weekend."

"Thank you, Mr. Blanchard. We just needed confirmation of that from a second source other than the coach driver." He paused and looked at Addison. "Very interesting, Addison. We've got all the information we need now. Those blue hyacinths that we found on Bycroft…they mean 'constancy' according to my wife's flower dictionary…The poor sop obviously still hadn't got over Mrs. Picard, I'd say. And their late-night Valentine's rendezvous got nipped in the bud." He then turned to Hugo and smiled saying, "Thank you Mr. Blanchard, you have been very helpful. We will see ourselves out."

He paused at the doorway, turned and said, "Oh, by the way, both Mrs. Picard and Mr. Bycroft are comfortable and in hospital now."

He smiled again and they left leaving Hugo standing in the middle of his living room staring incredulously out the window.

"Blue hyacinths…? He *did* say blue hyacinths, didn't he?" he asked himself. "They were for *me*. They're *our* flowers…Theodore's and mine. He *loves* me! He must have stopped at the church for some reason first (to pray perhaps or to repent his sins perhaps?) and then run in to Louisa by chance. She *does* live right next door to the church so I suppose it's quite feasible she could have been checking things were alright during the storm. Oh, this is *great* news! Theodore was going to give me flowers…our special favorites. How sweet of him!"

He gazed sentimentally out the window at the gently falling snow and said aloud, "Stupid coppers. They don't know true love when they see it staring them in the face! If only the rest of the village knew how much I love that man…that would *really* get the gossip-mongers going. May God save him!"

Twenty

Thomas Picard inhaled deeply on his treasured tobacco and stared thoughtfully out to sea. Lost in reverie, he leaned on the ship's railings and dreamed about his four full days leave soon to commence in Cairo. He was aboard a British cargo ship bound for the Suez Canal and excited at the prospect of a spot of sightseeing on the way home to England.

He exhaled slowly and dreamed of floating down the Nile aboard an Arab dhow under full sail and illuminated by a tangerine desert sunset. He was becoming captivated by the power of his own imagination. There was nothing more romantic in his eyes than something as exotic as this. His prospective home-coming combined with romantic anticipation caused him to reminisce so that he was not surprised when a song that his sister Geraldine used to sing suddenly came to mind. She was a budding soprano who showed much promise…

> *'On wings of song far roaming*
> *With thee, my sister, I glide*
> *Where the gay flowers are blooming*
> *On banks by the Ganges tide.*
>
> *Oh there in a garden of roses*
> *While moonbeams calmly shine*
> *The lotus flower uncloses*
> *Her eye to gaze on thine.*
> *The lotus flower uncloses*
> *Her eye to gaze on thine.'*

Not that the Ganges runs through Egypt of course, because it runs through India. But there were bound to be lotus flowers in Egypt opening their sacred white petals up to the sky, he mused. He dreamed on and vaguely wondered what Mendelssohn's plaintive song would sound like if played solo on the French horn, as he was a French horn player himself and played in the Navy Band.

His thoughts carried him away to what the caliber of Egyptian brass bands might be compared to the English, and whether their uniforms might be robes, or coats and trousers when he suddenly had a recollection. Verdi's opera *Aida* had been commissioned by the Viceroy of Egypt for the opening of the Suez Canal some thirty years ago. Strangely enough, he had heard that Verdi himself had only recently passed away just five days after Queen Victoria on 27th January of that same year, 1901, in Milan. Apparently, he had a state funeral of even greater proportions than his famous opera.

Thomas took another drag on his cigarette. He still couldn't quite believe that his own father was dead. And that the accident that had killed him had happened over a year ago. He knew that his mother would have taken it very hard but knew also that his brother and sisters would have rallied around her with the utmost support.

"I suppose I'll be the head of the household for the time that I'm home," he mused. He paused reflectively. "Dammit, if I'm going to set a good example, I'm going to have to give up on these deuced cigarettes…at least temporarily…before I disgrace myself in my mother's presence. She would have a fit if she knew I haven't given them up yet…but there's always tomorrow."

He squinted against the sun at the big plume of steam puffing out of the ship's funnel and watched it as it faded away into the blue of the sky. He was a well-built young fellow, just like his sea-going grandfather and had somehow inherited the same swashbuckling air. He was quite well tanned now from his world travels and was looking forward to a second consecutive summer at home.

The strong heat of the spring sun beat down on the ship's deck and a lone seagull hovered motionlessly on an up draught over the ship's bow. As the ship veered further north-west around the tip of Somalia into the Gulf of Aden, the first mate, a weather-beaten looking sort of chap, went up to Thomas and leaned on the rail. He pointed northwards towards Yemen fifty miles away or so in the distance and said, "Now, *that's* one place we're not bloody landing today, lad. Just three months ago a band of land-lubbing pirates…Bedouin, they were massacred the crew of a yacht that got stranded not far from Mukalla on the Yemini coast. Bloodthirsty bastards! Of course, they looted all they could get as well. Poor buggers didn't stand a chance!"

No more barbaric than the Boers, I'm sure, Thomas thought to himself, reflecting quizzically as he inhaled on the last of his cigarette. He threw the stub overboard, blew the smoke upwards and grinned.

"Pretty dangerous place, huh?"

"I'd say so, son. Take these waters for instance. Laden with sharks they are. And the coastline up here has reefs which can rip open a ship's belly like a saw. See those grim-looking promontories out there? They're volcanic cones. Extinct, we hope, but you never can tell. If we ran aground on a submerged reef or got wrecked against one of those steep cliffs, we would be goners!"

"Thanks for the vote of confidence."

"Not at all, son, not at all. Just thank your lucky stars that you and I are bound for good old Mother England!"

With that, the seaman went on his way, leaving Thomas to contemplate his words in silence. He didn't like to deflate the man's ego by telling him he had seen all this before during his five years in the navy, although briefly.

Two days later they passed Jeddah on the Arabian coast. At the same time, Thomas noticed a number of dhows crossing from the Philistine to the Phoenician coast laden with black people.

"Pilgrims," said the first mate significantly as if in answer to his unasked question. "They're coming back from Mecca. Ramadan's just finished so they're on their way home. They're the lucky ones I'd say. A lot of them snuff out in the Arabian Desert and a lot of the ones that are left get sold into slavery."

"Really?"

"In fact, a lot of slave agents pose as missionaries.

They escort the pilgrims towards Mecca and lure them into a trap with slave traders over there."

"That's terrible!"

"Yes, but what is worse is that the police over there turn a blind eye as the traders are *licensed*, would you believe?"

Thomas stood rooted to the spot. He couldn't understand why slavery was so rife in these parts.

"But then again," the seaman went on, "a lot of poor young girls may even *prefer* slavery with its relatively carefree existence in luxury compared to a free life of poverty in the desert."

He went about his business again leaving Thomas staring out towards Jeddah, beyond which Mecca was fifty miles inland, and wondering about the shipwrecks he could see in the harbor there with his binoculars. Were they the wrecked dhows of pilgrims or pirates or smugglers or slavers? He was beginning to wonder about these barbarous lands.

* * *

In the late afternoon, they arrived at Suez where one other ship was unloading cargo. It was a barren featureless landscape except for a few stucco out-houses that lay scattered along the nearest bank. The Sinai desert lay stretched out on the other side for one hundred miles. A gong sounded outside on the nearest bank where the sentries proclaimed each hour between smoking their communal hookah in the guardhouse.

Several huge black men roused themselves from slumber atop the bales at the custom house, ready for action. Seagulls launched themselves off the roofs in a flickering ribbon of grey and white and whirled expectantly overhead.

Thomas collected his bags, swung them over his shoulder, thanked the captain and was soon off astride a donkey towards Cairo accompanied by a couple of muleteers and their train. As they approached the city Thomas became acutely aware of the ubiquitous fly and mosquito, the date palms everywhere and the smell of molasses wafting across from the sugar factories along the Nile.

The city of a Thousand Minarets became suddenly silhouetted against the orange skyline, surrounded by its perennial cloud of dust as they approached. Soon they could hear faint musical chanting of the muezzins' voices raised above the city as they called their fellow man to prayer from atop the minarets. The voices from the sky seemed to Thomas like a chorus of spirit voices. In fact, somehow, they seemed more befitting in calling the faithful to prayer than the clang and jingle of his own English church bells. But he already knew what his mother would have to say about *that*!

They continued on through the maze of narrow city streets past the tall and narrow latticed houses with their attached balconies. Upon the rooftop terrace of one home, a lady veiled in black stood surrounded by a cloud of gathering pigeons. Thomas's mother again crossed his mind except that he had never seen her dressed in black quite like that and his father's pigeons were completely white.

As the night drew in, Thomas noticed that the people in the streets were carrying small lanterns to help light their way. He was soon dropped off at a likely looking hotel for English tourists, paid the muleteers their piasters together with a few cigarettes and went in.

* * *

Next morning, Thomas was up bright and early to take in the sights. Luckily all the hotel staff spoke at least a little English and they had arranged for a dragoman (native tour guide) to be at the disposal of each of their European visitors. Thus, Thomas was introduced in the lobby to El Mahib who was dressed in a uniform of long baggy trousers, striped waistcoat and red tarboosh upon his head. He bowed low saying his salaams and then drew himself up to his full height. He was a very proud looking Egyptian of about forty with brown crinkly skin, intelligent brown eyes and very white teeth. In the center of his forehead was a bluish mark which Thomas found out later was not a tattoo but hard discolored skin from making constant obeisances to Allah with slightly too much enthusiasm. Around his waist hung a small teapot of water for ceremonial washing before prayer and also a tiny brass amulet in the shape of a hand. This stood for the five precepts of Islam; faith, prayer, pilgrimage, fasting and charity.

"Effendi, I will interpret for you and be your guide. Please allow me to take you firstly to the bazaars. You will like."

"Why, thank you El Mahib. First rate! I'd be delighted. I'll be right behind you," Thomas said, grinning enthusiastically and hoisting a small knapsack over one shoulder.

They went outside and flagged down a passing gharry (a small horse-drawn carriage), which happened to be empty, climbed aboard and trotted through the waking narrow streets. People in Cairo tended to be up at dawn with the call of the muezzin and to retire at noon in the heat of the day. Then they would venture out again in the cool air of evening. As they passed through the labyrinth of streets and alleyways, they passed public fountains where heavily veiled women were filling enormous earthenware jars and carrying them on their heads.

The driver stopped at a pre-arranged spot in what was now called Old Cairo (formerly Babylon) and the dragoman and the young Englishman alighted. Here at one of the numerous bazaars, the streets were roofed with matting draped over long rafters and shafts of dusty sunbeams lit up the shifting crowds below. Vociferous shopkeepers peddled their wares while others sat cross-legged with lotions and potions spread out on rugs before them, smoking their pipes in silence and scrutinizing their prospective customers through the growing haze. Into the bustling fray charged the dragoman followed not far behind by his young employer. Thomas knew he would have to keep a strict eye on him if he were not to become lost.

As they jostled their way through the ebbing and flowing crowds they passed other dragomen in their distinctive uniforms, barefooted Egyptian farmers in their blue shirts and red skullcaps, Greeks in white tunics, swarthy Bedouin in their flowing garments and white turbans, and English men in palm-leaf hats and knickerbockers. There were veiled women in black, riding on decorative donkeys, dervishes, Abyssinians, Arabs, beggars with every imaginable deformity, serpent charmers, apothecaries, in fact, every variety of humanity in every imaginable shade of complexion. A small herd of goats trotted by adding their bleating to the din of camel bells ringing, troupes of wandering musicians wailing and the incessant bargaining of the shopkeepers. Aromas of coffee, spice, fruit, garlic and cooking oil greeted their nostrils as they wandered past merchants selling lemonade, sherbet, oranges, dates, sugarcane and dried fish and the like. Whenever there was any haggling going on, the merchants could be seen eagerly obliging their customers with complimentary puffs on their hookahs and endless cups of strong Turkish coffee.

They turned a corner into another alleyway where there were several shops selling only the one commodity such as brassware, or carpets, or slippers or sweetmeats. This meant that with more competition between sellers, prices tended to be better for the customer. Thomas bought a few souvenirs from a brassware shop and perfume shop for his family and from there they found their way down another alleyway where they discovered a small open air coffee house.

"Ah…perfect!" enthused the dragoman. "Effendi, you would like coffee perhaps?" he asked with typical Oriental politeness.

"Thank you, El Mahib. To tell the truth, I *am* getting a little parched. I could drink anything at the moment as long as it's wet!"

They sat themselves down on a divan enjoying the fresher breeze and waited for their coffee to arrive. It was Turkish-style, strong, with sediment still in the cup and served in egg-cupful sized coffee cups. Anything more than this size would have been too over-heating if drunk all at once in these climes.

Just then, a procession of harem women returning from the bath and borne along by donkeys with decorated hindquarters passed them by. Their attendant eunuchs beat back the throng as they passed.

Thomas stared openly at them as they continued on their way. He was certain that those eunuchs would make superb castrati, perhaps even better than the famed Farinelli, but he doubted whether any of them would get the opportunity to sing such music here. In fact, he doubted very much whether he would get the opportunity to hear one of them even speak to him. Thomas's startled reaction to the passing procession prompted El Mahib to comment:

"Things are very different here, Effendi, compared to England you know. We Muslims *buy* our wives here (provided they have sufficient dowry of course!)" He chuckled.

"Yes, so I believe. Do arranged marriages actually work?"

"Yes, from my experience. Love matches are considered frivolous here. Muslim women are trained from childhood to please men, you know. But the Koran forbids more than four wives…any more, and they become concubines, that is, domestic servants or slaves to the other wives."

Thomas balked.

"Personally, I don't think I could handle any more than one wife myself."

The dragoman laughed and took another sip of his coffee.

"I'm just sorry I can't take you to visit inside a harem. However, I did hear of one unauthorized gentleman who was very short, who managed to enter a harem in disguise. He had to get rid of his moustache first of course!"

"Really?"

"Yes, and then there was the case of the male tourist who visited the blind muezzins at the top of their minarets. From there, he could see right into the forbidden precincts of the harems on the terraced houses below. When the muezzins were alerted to his little ploy, they mistakenly chased each other down the spiral stairs of one of the minarets and stabbed each other to death."

"That's terrible!"

"Yes. Terrible but true. Most of the muezzins are blind, but to make up for it they have very powerful resonant voices that carry well."

"Their voices are truly amazing!"

Thomas took another sip of his coffee and wondered whether a retired eunuch might be able to get a job as a castrati muezzin in his old age. On reflection, he thought not, as their voices would be too high and wouldn't carry as well. But it was possible that they were less likely to be blind, he thought. At least, they wouldn't be tempted to spy on the harem women on the terraces below, he mused, even if they were blind! He played with his coffee cup and then asked, "So, what about love? Do the women here ever dream of love…in a place where she has to *share* her husband with many others?" He paused. "I have four sisters, you understand…"

"Of course. But it works both ways. For instance, consider the famous love story of 'The Madman' by Qays. The daughter of a very powerful sheik falls in love with a poet. But she is forced to marry someone else because of family and social pressures. In despair, he roams the hills and deserts and goes slowly mad. Then there is the case of the medieval king in Yemen who when his city was taken by the enemy, is said to have poisoned himself when he saw his concubines forced by the victors to dance and sing in public on the city wall. It is taboo in the Koran for women to dance for men. Traditionally, women only dance and play music to entertain each other in the harem."

"Oh."

"Speaking of which, let me take you to the Convent of Howling Dervishes this afternoon and you will see some real religious dancing and singing to Arabic music. Today is Friday, the Mohammedan Sabbath, so the timing will be perfect."

"Fantastic! I would love to go…But do they really *howl* in a convent?" he asked incredulously.

"You must judge for yourself. Seeing and hearing is believing. But first, I will show you some of Cairo's beautiful mosques."

"Oh yes. I'd love to see inside some of those buildings. They all look like they're straight out of the *Arabian Nights*."

They left the bazaar and flagged down another passing gharry. They travelled through the hurly-burly of the narrow streets of Old Cairo passing several painted frescoes on houses with colored Arabic script in vermillion and ultramarine, advertising the fact that the inhabitants had made the pilgrimage to Mecca. The mosques they visited were beautiful examples of Saracenic art with richly ornamented domes sculptured in arabesque patterns, minarets of variegated red and white or black and white marble and porticoes and tombs richly ornamented with similar tracery and sculpture. They visited the great Citadel of Muhammad Ali, the beautiful but dilapidated Mosque of Sultan Hassan (where El Mahib was called to prayer at noon), and the Mehemet Ali mosque in the hills overlooking all of Cairo. From the platform here, they had a superb view over the city with its cupolas and minarets, the pyramids at Giza and Sakkarah, the Delta dotted with villages and palm trees, and the sparkling Nile River itself, speckled with white sails.

By two o'clock, they were back in Old Cairo at the Convent of Howling Dervishes.

A group of about fifty wild-looking dervishes of various ages were squatted at one end of the hall while a party of English people was seated on chairs at the other end as spectators, wondering whether they should behave as if in church and looking suitably uncomfortable. In fact, they were mortally ashamed of their feet. Those who had forgotten to bring slippers had their feet wrapped up in pocket handkerchiefs. El Mahib always carried a spare pair with him for just such occasions as this, so Thomas was spared any added embarrassment.

A group of musicians then arrived with two trumpets, two lutes, a one-stringed fiddle, a tambourine, two drums and a single mugwiz. (This latter was a two-pronged flute type instrument with a double-reeded mouthpiece.) Thomas was intrigued to see that the fiddle player moved the instrument itself while the bow in fact was kept quite still and immobile. His father would have liked to have seen this indigenous fiddle, he thought. Although he couldn't have imagined his father ever playing one of these things as it would not have been versatile enough for his liking.

Presently the lead dervish (whose long grey beard looked like it had been dyed with henna), arranged all the others shoulder to shoulder in a circle with himself at the center. Softly he began chanting the words, "Allah! Allah! Allah!"

One by one the others took up the chant, both their heads and voices rising and falling in time to the melismatic music. After some minutes of this where several notes were intoned for just one syllable, the whole circle eventually began rocking madly to and fro as the leader accelerated the pace while the voices rose to a hoarse scream. Only the trumpets were audible above the din. Every now and then a dervish would convulsively spring up three feet above the heads of the others while others would fling their heads violently backwards. As the frenzy mounted, some shrieked, some groaned and a few others staggered out of the circle writhing and shrieking at the spectator's feet. Then the leader clapped his hands and the dancing stopped. Most of the dancers sat where they had stood, some kept on swaying and muttering to themselves and one was laid out stiff and straight in a fit.

"Can nothing be done for that fellow there?" Thomas whispered urgently to his dragoman.

"He is struck by Mahammad," said the dragoman.

Just then, the leader went over and knelt by the stricken man, touched him on the shoulder and whispered something in his ear. After a few tense minutes, the man struggled to his feet and was led away by his comrades.

There was a murmur of relief from everyone and a simultaneous rising of the spectators. Thomas came away impressed but convinced that this was not a style of dancing that he would like to take up. A slow fox-trot or a waltz, preferably in the arms of a charming and beautiful young lady, would be much more to his liking. For the life of him, he couldn't think of any dances in England which held anything remotely like 'religious significance' as here in Egypt. Morris dancing? No, he knew that had pagan origins. As for the singing, his Celtic roots meant that his musical ear was quite unattuned to this strange roulade of melismatic music, extempore verse and hand clapping to which he had just been subject to listen. But as El Mahib explained to him later, the dervishes with their dancing and singing were undergoing a type of 'spiritual cleansing' in the presence of Allah. However, Thomas found it rather difficult to come to terms with that concept, coming from a completely alien culture.

Later in the afternoon Thomas and his dragoman took a side trip by gharry up the Champs Elysees of Cairo, Shubra Road. It was a beautiful drive up to the Viceroy's Summer Palace, the street being lined with giant sycamore figs arching overhead like a long green tunnel and interspersed with acacias along the way. The palace gardens were resplendent with citrus, bananas, pomegranates, oleanders and roses. But what took Thomas's breath away was the size of the poinsettia flowers. They were huge…twenty-two inches across…far bigger than those grown in England. If only his father could have seen them…

* * *

It seemed that everywhere in Egypt that Thomas travelled, there was always something to remind him of home. On his second day, there he and El Mahib were crossing the Nile from Cairo aboard a dahabiya to connect with a camel caravan to Giza. The dahabiya was like an Oxford University barge, (which would have been much to his brother Jeremy's liking), shallow and flat-bottomed and adapted for sailing with two masts. It was early spring so the Nile was still very low in spite of the fact that the Aswan Dam had been built just two years earlier. But there on the shores of the Nile growing amongst the date palms, tamarisks and eucalyptus was a grove of mulberry trees…just like the one at home in their front garden! He wished he owned a box brownie camera so that he could prove it to all his family back home! Instead, he made a point of picking a few leaves and pressing them in his log book.

"Effendi…what a pity you are going home so soon.

Next week…if you like plants and flowers, that is, is the 'Scent of Spring Festival'. All the feluccas and dahabiyas are decked out with flowers and then they float down the Nile. Beautiful! A shame you will miss it. Many unattached young English ladies attend the picnics on the river bank…always chaperoned, of course."

"Oh…then perhaps I should extend my stay?"

"I would be delighted, I'm sure."

"Thank you, El Mahib, but I fear I must refuse. I have family duties back in England. I would love to stay longer but I have already arranged my passage for the day after tomorrow."

"Well, you must come back to Egypt again some time. Bring your family."

"Thank you, El Mahib."

* * *

About twenty camels were waiting couched in a circle at the caravanserai and batting their beautiful long eyelashes against the prevailing wind-borne sands. Thomas and the dragoman were soon sitting astride their beasts of burden and gently swaying from side to side as they were carried across one of the three Cities of the Dead towards Giza seven miles away where the Sphinx and the pyramids lay.

That day, Thomas learnt a lot about 'Egyptology' from El Mahib and how hieroglyphics came to be deciphered from the Rosetta Stone by Champollion back in 1822. His father would have been fascinated by all this, he thought. El Mahib was very knowledgeable and lucid, and besides discussing the peculiarities of two-dimensional Egyptian art, kept Thomas amused with his numerous stories, one of which was a true 'ghost' story.

Apparently, a couple of ecclesiastical researchers had been searching for ancient manuscripts in the catacombs of one of the old Coptic churches which happened to be decorated with some rather grisly statues of Egyptian gods. They were scared out of their wits by the roaring of what turned out to be none other than old Fatima's lost donkey which had wandered into the tomb. (The Coptic church, he explained, was similar to Greek Orthodox except that the Copts have their own Pope, known as the Patriarch of Alexandria.)

At Giza, they scaled the heights of the great pyramid and explored its tunnels, emerging at the end of the day somewhat begrimed and bleary-eyed like a pair of newly exhumed walking artefacts. But it was the Sphinx that really took Thomas's fancy. It sat there, crouched like a huge watchdog in the sand, looking forever east as if for some dawn not yet risen.

* * *

Unaccustomed muscles being rather sore by the next day, the two travelers decided to indulge themselves on the hundred-mile trip to Alexandria and back in the relative comfort of modern rail. (Thomas could not help noticing that the women all sat in the back carriages of the train, while he and El Mahib travelled first class. His mother and four sisters would not have been impressed.)

Alexandria appealed to Thomas because of its illustrious history. It was where Cleopatra had committed suicide, where Alexander the Great was buried, where the great fire-powered lighthouse, one of the seven wonders of the world had once stood, (now gone due to an earthquake), and where the great Library (now gone due to fire), had once stood. Of course, Cleopatra's Needles were also no longer there. One now stood sentinel by the Thames in England and the other in Central Park, New York. In fact, once he arrived in Alexandria, he was a little disappointed because all the points of interest were now no longer to be seen!

Approaching Alexandria in the train, Thomas gazed out at the birdlife feeding in the Delta while the dragoman gave a running commentary.

"As you can see, Effendi, there may be egrets and ibis out there but there are no more papyrus swamps, hippopotamuses, crocodiles, ostriches, lions or antelopes. They have all gone. There are still a few crocodiles much further up the Nile, but even they are being hunted for ladies' handbags now. Camels of course were introduced to Egypt much later than the pyramids by the Persians, so that is why we saw no pictures of them in the pyramids. The same with the water buffalo. They were introduced by the Mamelukes. But of course, the shadufs you see out there to raise water have been around for eons."

The sight of seagulls again announced the fact that they had now arrived beside the seaside. Even though it was a very warm outside, Muslims were reluctant to bathe in public the dragoman said because of their 'morality'. It was exceptionally difficult for women in their robes to bathe as they had to wear long black cloaks reaching down to their ankles as well as their veils.

Thomas was in two minds whether to go for a swim as the water looked very tempting. However, modesty bothered him more than morality as he had no bathing costume with him. Hence the two travelers resigned themselves to sitting sweltering under a date palm admiring the allure of the water. It was tantalizingly close and yet so far. The natural air conditioning that the sea breeze provided seemed not quite enough. Thomas loosened his collar and stared out to sea in the vague direction of home. The only one of his family daring enough to entertain the idea of a public dip in the Mediterranean here without the proper attire was likely to be his little sister, Lucy.

My God! Lucy must be nearly eight now. How could I have been away from home so long? She won't even know me when I get back! he thought, horrified.

He sat there, slightly stunned, and realized that five years was too long to be away from home. Just one more day savoring the sights of this gem of a country and its amazing history and he would be on his way back into the bosom of his family.

Presently, his thoughts returning to his existing surroundings and curiosity getting the better of him, Thomas asked airily as he swatted a sand-fly away from his face:

"I wonder who it was that burned down the Great Library here in Alexandria, El Mahib…infidels."

"Er, no, Effendi. Legend has it that it was Arab invaders. The foreign sciences that the Greeks brought here with them were considered a threat to Islamic religious beliefs. (The foreign sciences included not only mathematics, astronomy and medicine but also magic, alchemy and astrology.) But the burning of the library is a…how do you say…paradox…to historians because the early Muslims actually welcomed the Greek intellectual tradition. But then there were some who said that those who agreed with Greek logic held heretical views towards all religions. Often astronomers and physicians would claim that their work revealed evidence for the wisdom of Allah. At the same time however, they would look down on theologians for using their authority as a cover for genuine knowledge."

"It's very interesting that you should *say* that El Mahib. Ever since Darwin's theories came to light, that very same debate has been discussed in the drawing rooms of England. In fact, it was my father's pet subject…"

* * *

On Thomas's last day in Cairo, he said a fond farewell to El Mahib and took a dahabiya from Cairo to Ismailia along one of the interconnecting canals where it linked up with the Suez Canal. From here, he would travel by steamer down the Suez aboard the British cargo ship again to Port Said.

His dream of sailing down the Nile would soon be coming to an end so he made a point of savoring every last minute of it. Stretched out on a deck chair under the striped awning of the dahabiya he watched Delta life pass by as he sipped languorously at a long Tom Collins. A Thomas Cook's Excursion Tour Boat passed by and he waved to the passengers and raised his glass. Several like-minded American tourists waved back.

At Port Said, he made a fleeting one-hour side trip to the banks of Lake Manzala to view the natural bird sanctuaries there teeming with white pelicans and pink flamingoes. A lot of these birds he realized would be migrating northwards in the summer with the tourists and the swallows. He felt glad that he would be following suit and soon be home in balmy old England.

Once back aboard his trusty British cargo ship which had been unloading the last of its cargo at Port Said, and having seen all that he had to see in the time available, he felt more secure in the knowledge that he was going home. Home to his family once more…to his mother, to his brother Jeremy, and to his sisters Emma, Geraldine, Charlotte and Lucy. Not forgetting a visit to his father's grave there. And not forgetting Rusty, the dog, for that matter. He wondered if Rusty would remember him after being so long away. He was just a very small puppy when he left. One thing was for sure. He would not be averse to a little 'puppy pampering' himself and was looking forward to all the comforts of home.

Twenty-One

Louisa lay motionless in her hospital bed, forgetting momentarily where she was. Confused, she anxiously clutched at the bedclothes, not feeling them in her bandaged hands. The skin down one side of her face tingled and she felt dizzy and nauseous. There were burns on her hands which felt quite numb, her right arm was very weak and she had a terrible headache. She was extremely tired and to top everything off, there was a roaring ringing in her ears.

A door slammed and there was a faint smell of disinfectant in the air. Suddenly, she remembered where she was…in the City Hospital in York, the very same hospital that Theodore Bycroft was sent to after his accident in the belfry last year. She realized that he must be here again…perhaps even next door. Her short-term memory was poor but she did remember that the doctors had said something about police and Theodore rescuing her from lightning in the church. What was she doing in the church to have been hit by lightning? She couldn't remember. What was Theodore doing in the church? She couldn't remember that either. It was a miracle that they were both still alive.

She did remember however seeing a blue flash, feeling as if the inside of her head was on fire, having great difficulty breathing and a terrible pain over her right arm. Then there was the horrible taste of metal in her mouth and complete numbness. But she was feeling a little better now and would soon be allowed visitors.

She took a sip of water beside her bed and tried to sit up, but couldn't get comfortable. She felt almost as uncomfortable as the time when she wore that confounded musical bustle for the Queen's Golden Jubilee which played the National Anthem whenever she sat down! She smiled at the recollection. Strange how she could remember things like that and yet not even remember what she had for breakfast yesterday morning.

She finally managed to get herself comfortable and was then able to let her mind drift. She tried to remember the train of events leading up to the lightning strike. She thought of home, the children, her husband…of course…her husband was dead. She was alone. A dark cloud descended upon her. Darkness and despair. She remembered lying awake alone in her bed at night…a banging…the belfry door…going outside during a storm to shut the door…a specter…the banshee! Of course, the banshee! It was the banshee that must have caused her to panic and somehow end up in the church. But why was she not dead if she had set eyes upon the banshee? Perhaps she was yet to die? Who would take care of the children? Or perhaps one of the children was meant to die? If she herself was the target, why was the banshee showing mercy and letting her live? Just for the satisfaction of seeing her maimed and becoming a martyr? Was the banshee just being spiteful…making her suffer a fate worse than death? Public humiliation, scandal and persecution! Social ruin?

"Oh, woe is me," Louisa said aloud. She tearfully thought of her dead husband and of the confrontation he had with Theodore in the tower. If only she hadn't been quite so enamored of Theodore. Then none of this would have happened and she would not have been scarred, physically or emotionally. She had no hand in her husband's death. She was no less a scarlet woman than she was an accomplice to murder. Why wouldn't folk believe her?

She looked at her hands, heavily bandaged with poultices and wondered what her face must look like. The nurse that came in last had reassured her that the red marks on her face were fading slightly so that was at least some consolation. She dreaded looking in the mirror just yet. Maybe tomorrow.

She knew she had compromised herself by becoming friendly with Theodore. Certain people in the village had ostracized her ever since her husband's death even though she was innocent. So why should she suffer? Was it because she had been a vicar's wife and should be above reproach? At least she hadn't had to suffer the social stigma of divorce. Heaven forbid! The last thing she needed was to suffer the loss of her children. That would be more than she could bear. Please God that her children should not be taken away from her! She would do anything to save them from harm. She must visit her husband's grave as soon as she got out of hospital, she vowed and must pray for succor at the altar.

* * *

There was a knock at the door. It was Jeremy with the nurse.

"A visitor for you, Mrs. Picard. Do you need your pillows plumping up? You're looking better than you were first thing this morning."

"Thank you, nurse. Hello Jeremy, nice to see you."

"Hello, Mother dear." He bent to kiss her marble patterned cheek, asking, "May I?"

"Of course, dear."

"Sorry about your brush with death."

"Yes, it was close, wasn't it? But we have Mr. Bycroft to thank for saving me."

"Yes, so I heard. They tell me he's just down the hallway."

"Really?"

"So what were you doing at midnight in church playing the organ?"

"Was I?"

"Yes."

"I don't remember that."

"It was in the middle of a thunderstorm, Mother. Very dangerous. Especially when the organ happens to be electric."

"Oh…electric…oh…yes. I forget things you know…even what I'm saying mid-sentence sometimes…"

"You won't do it again, will you, Mother?"

"What?"

"Play the organ during a thunderstorm."

"No Jeremy, of course not. Now, tell me about what you have been up to."

"Well, I've brought you some marmalade, some of the famous variety made from those juicy Seville oranges from Oxford."

"That's nice. The real McCoy."

"Yes. And I have some news for you as well, Mother."

"Oh?"

"I've decided to take up Holy Orders."

"You're going to take up Holy Orders?" she reiterated after him, not quite registering what he had just said. "You mean you're going to become a vicar and follow in your father's footsteps?"

"Yes. After Father's death and now with your close shave, I've decided that it's the proper course of action…as a younger son…and as a gentleman of honor and integrity as well, you might say. So I'm putting my entomology studies on hold and entering Wycliffe, the C of E college at Oxford. Wycliffe tends towards the evangelical approach, but that could be useful if I decide later to become a missionary in darkest Africa. I would have that option you see, to go and convert the natives there. But at this stage, my sights would be set purely on the vicarage in Bingham."

He paused and thought ruefully that he would now have to mend his ways and put Nell and his drinking buddies behind him if he was to be changing his vocation to one of such piety. Privately he wondered if he had enough grit to sustain such abstinence. He looked apprehensively at his mother for her reaction.

"Oh, that's marvelous dear. That's wonderful news! Your father would be so proud of you. Give me a hug."

They embraced and then Jeremy stepped back and said with a frivolous smirk:

"And don't worry, Mother, I shan't get myself expelled like P.B. Shelley did by writing anything stupid like *The Necessity of Atheism*. I shall be a most diligent student."

Louisa laughed and then Jeremy cleared his throat and said on a more serious note:

"There is one thing though, Mother. I was wondering if…to make up for the sacrifice, that is…whether you would mind if I were to build an apiary at home?"

"An apiary? I don't see why not. I'm sure it would mean we would get more plums than we do at present. Of course, dear. Build one if it makes you happy."

Jeremy smiled his appreciation.

"Thank you, Mother. I will never lose my interest in bugs and insects; I can tell you that. So, tell me what has been happening at home since I last visited?"

"Well now…everything has been ticking along as usual…except that Geraldine announced recently that she wants to attend Ladies' College."

"You mean she wants to go to one of those posh establishments where they have to wear hats and gloves and aren't allowed even to *look* at young toffs?" He carried on in a mock female voice and recited the well-known protest:

'Miss Buss and Miss Beale
Cupid's darts do not feel.
How different from us
Miss Beale and Miss Buss.'

"Yes…I fear that she is going to become something of a bluestocking," Louisa said, with some misgivings.

"Oh well, I suppose if that's what she really wants to do…" Jeremy said, trailing off.

"But I can't *not* give her the opportunity, Jeremy. I wouldn't hear the end of it if I didn't. The only thing is, we shall have to get a lodger in to help pay expenses. I can see that I will have to speak to the squire about that."

"Yes, the squire will know where to find you a lodger, I'm sure."

"And then of course, Thomas is coming home at Easter," she said suddenly smiling.

"My gosh, there's nothing wrong with *your* memory, Mother!" he exclaimed, laughing jovially.

He turned around and out of the blue, Geraldine, Charlotte and Lucy appeared at his shoulder, bearing chocolates and accompanied by Betty, the curate's wife, who was chaperoning them (under sufferance).

"Why, hello you lot," Jeremy said. "I didn't hear you come in."

"No, we crept up on you," blurted out Lucy, unable to contain her exuberance.

"Hello girls, hello Betty," said Louisa.

Betty smiled and the three girls rushed to their mother's bedside.

"How are you, Mother? Are you alright? Do your face and hands hurt?" they all asked at once.

"I'm getting better thank you girls. Settle down. It's thanks to Mr. Bycroft that I'm still alive. He saved my life you know."

Betty winced noticeably as she envisioned Theodore Bycroft giving Louisa some kind of mouth-to-mouth resuscitation but smiled disarmingly to cover up her gaffe.

"In fact," Louisa went on, "Geraldine, would you mind writing a thank you note to Mr. Bycroft while I dictate? It's just that I'm a little restricted with my hands like this. Then we can ask the nurse to deliver it later."

"Certainly, Mother. I'll just find a pen and paper in my purse."

"Are you ready?"

"Yes."

"Dear Mr. Bycroft," Louisa began. "Thank you for helping to save my life. If it had not been for you, I would most certainly have died. I hope that you yourself are not too badly damaged and wish you a speedy recovery. Thank you once again most sincerely, yours, Louisa Picard."

"There, that's it," said Geraldine. "I'll give it to the nurse when she comes in."

They chatted on and then Emma and John arrived from London with a bunch of grapes and some petunias for Louisa. Emma thought petunias might be appropriate as their meaning, according to her flower dictionary, was *'never despair'*.

* * *

Just down the corridor, Theodore Bycroft lay propped up in bed with huge bandages covering his hands. His face appeared as if bruised and he was feeling very sorry for himself. Not only had he an already gammy leg but it was now numb as well, his head ached, he was feeling dizzy and his ears rung. He stared miserably at the ceiling wondering how long he was going to be laid up like this when an unexpected visitor suddenly arrived for him unannounced.

"Theodore!"

"Why, hello Hugo. How are you? Come on in."

Hugo ventured into the room clutching an envelope in one hand.

"My gosh, Theodore, I thought you were a goner at first. It's good to see you're still alive and kicking."

"Still alive, yes, but not kicking. My bad leg's worse, I fear."

"Oh, that's no good. Look, I've brought you something to cheer you up," he said, handing him the envelope. Then suddenly realizing Theodore's inability to open it, he opened it himself and planted the card within upon Theodore's chest so that he could see it.

"What's this then?" asked Theodore.

"It's a Valentine's card, a belated one," he said ingratiatingly.

"But there's no signature."

"It's anonymous. It was supposed to be a surprise. But I must confess, I made it myself. Do you like it?"

"You what?"

"I made it myself," he repeated proudly.

"For me?" asked Theodore, surprised.

"Yes."

"But…you should be giving this to a lady friend…not to me."

"But I thought…"

"Oh no, not me. You've got the wrong end of the stick, me lad. When people call me a 'man's man' they don't mean a 'man's man' in *that* way. In fact, I'm really a 'ladies' man' to be more exact…always have been…it's just been this wretched leg. Besides, you wouldn't want a clapped-out old man like me. Why don't you find yourself a younger fellow who's more in one piece?"

"But I've never felt like this about a man before…What about the blue hyacinths you said you were bringing me?"

"Oh, they were to be a florist's mere 'thank you' gift from man to man for putting me up for the weekend," Theodore replied with a toss of his head. "Sorry Hugo, you've got it all wrong. Now just you tear up that card and I won't say a word to anyone."

Tears were welling up in Hugo's eyes. "But Theodore, I can't," he pleaded.

"Then I will," said Theodore. So, saying, he lifted the card up between the wrists of his two bandaged hands, placed it between his teeth and ripped.

"There. It's done," he said significantly.

"I have never in my life been so humiliated," remonstrated Hugo, upset. "I feel as if my heart's been ripped out of my chest."

"Oh Hugo, don't be so melodramatic. It's just been some silly schoolboy crush. It's not cricket you know, to fall for another man. Look what it did to Oscar Wilde. You wouldn't want to end up in prison, would you?"

"Don't *do* this to me!" cried Hugo in despair. "You are torturing my soul!"

There was a pause and then Theodore said matter-of-factly:

"Sorry Hugo. You're a smashing fellow as a friend, but you just overstepped the mark."

"Oh my God, I can't stand it! You're rejecting me…and after all that I've done for you. I don't understand it. What has happened to make you change? Louisa?"

"No, not Louisa. Nothing really. I never *did* care for you in that way. Purely as a confidante…nothing else. Now I really must get some rest if you don't mind."

"Yes, of course. I'll go then. Sorry to have disturbed you. I hope you get better soon. I'll find my own way out…"

Tearfully, Hugo retrieved his hat and coat, seized the torn-up pieces of valentine and stuffed them into his coat pocket. He fled out the door almost toppling a nurse as he made a mad dash for the nearest carriage outside the hospital.

"Bingham please," he blurted out to the driver, trying unsuccessfully to hide his distress.

All the way home Hugo sniveled with self-pity. He realized that Oscar Wilde was right of course when he had said that 'In this world there are only two tragedies. One is not getting what one wants and the other is getting it.' He mulled over how this applied to both Louisa and himself regarding Theodore. On the one hand, Louisa had been a married woman, a vicar's wife (and now a widow, he noted) and he, Hugo, was of the same gender as Theodore. Louisa's so-called 'liaison' with Theodore had created a scandal in the village and now here he was himself, only just prevented in the nick of time from making the same mistake. What an ass he had made of himself! But just what *was* it about Theodore that made him so damned attractive? He had that magnetic quality, that certain charisma that was impossible to resist. Just the way his moustache bristled when he spoke was so endearingly captivating. But now here he was, Hugo, just a lowly and oversensitive church organist, rejected by the man of his dreams whom he had supported and cajoled through all the lengthy trauma of being a cripple (and who was spurned by the ladies because of it). Now Hugo had been thrown on the scrap heap. So, what was he to do? He hoped that he would never set eyes upon Theodore Bycroft again and that that cruel beast of a man would banish himself to London forever.

* * *

156

Down the hospital corridor, Lucy Picard was making faces at another little girl visitor from the doorway of Louisa's room.

Why doesn't she go away and stop staring at me? she thought.

Suddenly, her attention was diverted by the sight of a man rushing from a room just down the corridor almost tripping up a passing nurse. She recognized him instantly. It was Hugo, the church organist, looking quite agitated and in a great hurry. Curious, she forgot all about the other little girl and slipped out of Louisa's room unnoticed, to investigate. She tip-toed down the corridor to peep around the doorway of the room from which Hugo had come. She was right. It was Mr. Bycroft in there, all bandaged up. She took a deep breath and said from the safety of the doorway, "Oh, you look poorly, Mr. Bycroft. You were so brave trying to save Mama."

Theodore looked up in surprise, wondering where the small voice had come from until he noticed the small blonde head peeking around the doorway.

"Oh hello. It's Lucy, isn't it? Mrs. Pickard's daughter. Come in. I didn't see you there."

Lucy shuffled in, somewhat reluctantly.

"Well, really it was just a natural reaction on my part," Theodore went on. "Lightning is very dangerous when you're touching anything metal…even inside buildings."

"Oh."

There was a pause in the conversation as Lucy looked guiltily all around the room before having the courage to say, "I'm sorry Mr. Bycroft…about the jam, I mean…I only meant to make you a *little* bit sick…like when Rusty, our dog, eats something he shouldn't and sicks it up again all over the carpet. I didn't mean to hurt your leg…honest, I didn't."

Theodore was stunned. He couldn't believe what he was hearing at first. Then realization slowly dawned on his face.

"Oh…it was you, was it? Did you put something in the jam, little girl?"

"Yes…some of Grandpapa's old medicine."

Theodore heaved a great sigh of relief. So it was not Louisa after all who had tried to poison him! This was all very much out of the blue, he thought. He looked gravely at Lucy standing shamefaced at the foot of the bed, and was on the point of scolding her when he thought better of it. She was only a child after all.

"It doesn't matter Lucy. What's done is done. You know you've done wrong and I can see that you are sorry for it. I survived the storm and at least I can still hop about a bit."

"You can? You can hop?" Her face lit up. "Oh goody! You can play hopscotch with me then when you get better!"

She smiled brightly and skipped merrily out of the room and along the corridor towards her mother's room. She was blissfully unaware that just a few yards away, someone was waiting for her, hands on hips. She skipped straight into the enfolding skirts of a very stern looking curate's wife.

"Lucy! Where have you been you naughty girl, running off like that? I don't know what's the matter with you. Now just you come away from there. You don't want anything to do with the likes of Mr. Bycroft there. Now come along!"

Lucy was hauled away in the direction of her mother's room leaving Theodore alone to digest the latest news.

Shortly afterwards, a nurse entered Theodore's room with a note. It was the note dictated by Louisa. The nurse opened the note up for him and held it for him while he began to read. A huge smile began to spread slowly over his handsome features.

* * *

After a couple more days, Theodore was able to hobble around more easily, so he decided to pay Louisa a visit. He wrapped himself carefully in his dressing gown and with the aid of his stick, hobbled to Louisa's door.

She was sitting up in bed, attempting to read, her face now with only the merest hint of marbling upon her otherwise flawless complexion.

"Louisa…" he said hesitatingly. "I trust you are feeling better? Thank you for your note. Lucy has explained everything."

"Oh…Theodore…it's you."

"Yes."

"I'm so glad you received my note. I am extremely grateful to you for saving my life. I trust you are feeling better too? And you say you have been talking to Lucy?"

"Much better, thank you. And yes, Lucy and I had a little chat the other day. All is forgiven. She's just a child after all."

"Oh Theodore, I'm so glad that all's well that ends well. So, we're friends again?"

"Yes. We're friends." He smiled reassuringly.

* * *

Easter had almost arrived and it was now two weeks since both Louisa and Theodore had been back at their respective homes in Bingham after having spent two weeks in hospital. Spring was in the air and Louisa had received flowers quite openly from Theodore via a delivery boy as she was now no longer a married woman, but officially a widow of one year's standing. She had received a bunch of heartsease (another name for wild pansies, meaning 'you are in my thoughts') and a bunch of peonies (meaning 'my apologies' for their previous misunderstanding). This put a spring in Louisa's step and even helped to keep her mind more alert. The amnesia caused by the lightning strike was diminishing and she was becoming less susceptible to such strange little foibles as putting the crockery in the coal-range or the milk in the linen cupboard.

For Easter the church was to be decorated with traditional daffodils ('you are the only one'), primroses ('I can't live without you'), trailing ivy ('eternal faithfulness') and candles, all from Theodore's florist shop at Louisa's special instruction. And Thomas's homecoming was scheduled for the day before Good Friday.

The Picard family was abuzz with excitement for Thomas's homecoming and had all descended upon the vicarage in time to set up a banner over the front porch on which was written in big red letters, "WELCOME HOME THOMAS." Louisa had even put floral arrangements around the house of oak leaves ('welcome') and periwinkle ('happy memories') in honor of his return to the fold.

When Thomas finally put in his appearance at eleven o'clock on the day, there were hugs, kisses, tears, laughter, squeals and much barking in reciprocation from the dog. Thomas was surprised that Rusty still remembered him after such a long time. Emma introduced John, her fiancé to Thomas and they shook hands warmly.

"Welcome to the Picard family," said Thomas. "Thank you," said John, grinning.

Thomas was surprised at the change in his mother and noticed as they embraced that her hands were scarred. He looked at her questioningly so she said, "Ah yes…a slight accident. I was struck by lightning in the church. I suppose I'm lucky to be here really."

"What? Oh Mother! How on earth could that have happened?"

"I'll tell you shortly…at lunchtime. But I'm alright now, thank you dear."

The squire who happened to be passing by, on hearing the commotion coming from inside the vicarage, popped his head inside the open front door and called out:

"I say…I say…Can I come in?"

"Is that you, Squire?" called out Louisa. "Do come in."

The squire wandered into the drawing room and upon espying Thomas standing there in his magnificent uniform, exclaimed.

"Good heavens, lad! I can remember the time when you were just knee high to a grasshopper! And now look at you. You must be over six foot. You just tower over your mother! I say, that uniform certainly is fetching, isn't it Mrs. Picard?" Then turning to Thomas, he warned, "You'd better watch out for the ladies, young man! In that uniform, they'll be all over you like a rash!"

Thomas smiled forbearingly, exuding grace and confidence in all his sartorial elegance. He was very much like his mother in that respect (except that he was male of course) and could behave like the perfect gentleman when it behoved him to do so.

They shook hands warmly, the squire feeling distinctly frumpish and unprepossessing in the presence of such a suave young man who cut such a dash. The curate was the next to pop in and he said as he pumped Thomas's hand:

"So you've decided to join us landlubbers for a while have you? Nice to see you back."

Thomas grinned and said:

"Would you two gentlemen like to stay for a drink?"

They accepted and stayed for a short time while Louisa and the girls prepared the midday meal…roast pheasant, kindly donated by the squire after a successful shooting spree out on the moors the day before. They exchanged pleasantries with Thomas, Jeremy and John over a few whiskies and then discussed the ins and outs of the Boer War, the British Navy, wireless, Cecil Rhodes, the Suez Canal, Egypt and brass bands in that order. Then not wanting to outstay their welcome, they wished the family a Happy Easter and departed, the squire calling out to Louisa as he left:

"I'll be introducing your prospective lodger to you straight after Easter if that's alright, Mrs. Picard."

"Oh, thank you Squire," she called back.

At lunch, Thomas was plied with all sorts of questions from his family, eager to know of his recent exploits. Lucy was first up and managed to ask after swallowing a huge piece of pheasant that was too big for the size of her mouth and that made her eyes bulge with the effort:

"Did you see any p…pirates anywhere?"

"No…or yes really, I suppose. But it was only the remains of an old pirate ship off the east coast of Africa…no pirates. It had just been left to rot in the sun on the rocks."

Then Louisa chipped in with, "It's a wonder you didn't get a chance to wave to the Duke of York and his wife. They would have been going around the rock of Gibraltar at the same time as you, wouldn't they, only in the opposite direction?"

"Yes, that's right, on their way to the colonies on board the S.S. Ophir. I did notice their ship off the coast of Portugal actually, but I couldn't recognize anyone on board with my binoculars."

"What do the natives look like in Africa, Thomas?" asked Charlotte with shy naivety.

"Black."

"Oh come on, Thomas. That goes without saying," said Jeremy exasperatedly. "So tell the poor girl Thomas, what do the natives really look like?"

"Well, the Hottentots wear bones through their noses and sticks in their hair and hardly any clothes," he said staring hard at Charlotte. Charlotte blushed. And then turning to Jeremy he said, "And they cook up missionaries in big black pots…"

Jeremy did a double take.

"So, Mother's obviously told you I'm taking up Holy Orders. But the missionary business is on hold for the moment. Maybe later on."

"You mean, once the natives have become more civilized?"

Jeremy remained silent. Changing the subject, Geraldine asked tactfully:

"When you were in Egypt, Thomas, did you see any of that real oriental dancing?"

"No. I was told that was just for inside the harems."

"Oh, I'm disappointed," said Geraldine, "especially after all the publicity about that dancer, 'Little Egypt' performing in America a few years back. A real Salome she's supposed to be, isn't she, Mother?"

"Yes, a real *femme fatale*," Louisa agreed.

"Who is 'Little Egypt'?" Lucy prodded her mother.

"Oh, she is an oriental dancer who created a scandal amongst polite society in America with her exotic dancing," explained Louisa.

"So how does she dance? Like this?" she asked, trailing her hands seductively under her chin and making a silly face.

"Yes, something like that dear."

"So will you be coming to our wedding, Thomas?" asked Emma.

"When is it?"

"In about one year during summer, that is, after I've finished my course. John and I wondered if you would like to play a French horn solo. Geraldine's going to sing for us as well."

"I'd love to. But it depends where I am at the time. I will definitely try and get some more leave. Heaven knows, I'm due some."

John finally cleared his throat and asked:

"So, tell us about those new submarines they're building in the navy, Thomas. Do you think you will ever man one of those?"

"It depends. They're building some Holland submarines at Barrow now, but you know what some of the Admirals have been saying…that they're so 'damned un-English'. Gentlemen are supposed to fight each other face to face wearing easily recognizable uniforms, not underhandedly or under water. Still, the navy's treading warily and the first sub is due to be launched around October this year, I understand."

"Do you know how deep they'll go?"

"Around one hundred feet, travelling at seven to eight knots. And they will stay down for about four hours."

"Interesting."

"Will you sing us a sea-shanty after lunch, Thomas?" asked Lucy.

"Yes, if you like. How about *The Walloping Window Blind?*" he asked.

"Ohhhh…yes!" said Lucy excitedly.

Once lunch was over, Thomas leaned back in his chair, patted his stomach, stretched and then announced magnanimously, "That was delicious, thank you, Mother. What I've been missing at sea! Now I'm only home for three months everyone, but during that time, Mother will be my first concern. And don't worry about me, Mother. I've given up smoking for good. But I'm now growing a moustache!"

He grinned roguishly and tweaked his bare upper lip. Everyone cheered and drank to that and then the Easter eggs were passed around early. And over the top of rustling wrapping paper, he sang:

'A capital ship for an ocean trip
Was the Walloping Window Blind.
No wind that blew disturbed the crew
Or troubled the captain's mind.'

When he had finished the final verse, there was much applause and everyone else followed suit with their own musical items. The celebrations continued far into the night and there was much contentment at the vicarage that night.

* * *

Easter itself was naturally a more subdued event. A light sprinkling of spring rain fell gently over the moors as if mirroring the melancholy mood of Good Friday throughout the four full days. The Picard family was happily reunited and outside, a cocky fat pheasant strutted along the top of the low stone wall beside the church while a squirrel skittered up a nearby tree with a mouthful of nuts. But the tranquility of this pastoral scene was broken somewhat when the curate's wife met Louisa after the Sunday morning service.

The congregation had just adjourned onto the lawn outside the church and the people had begun chatting amongst themselves and thanking the Reverend McAlister for stepping into the breach when they needed him most. A small group from the Ladies' Guild was chatting animatedly when suddenly Betty, the curate's wife, abruptly detached herself from the group and headed resolvedly in the direction of Louisa who had been exchanging pleasantries with Millicent, the squire's wife. Betty had just heard the news from Mrs. Duval of Jeremy Picard's intention to build an apiary in the vicarage grounds, and made it her business to quiz Louisa upon the matter.

Her ample bosom heaved as she approached Louisa busily and expostulated incredulously:

"Lordy Louisa! First spiders and now apes! Wherever will Jeremy get his apes from? For my part, I could never abide monkeys!"

Louisa looked at her in disbelief. Didn't this woman know the difference between insects and hairy arboreal quadrupeds?

"Bees Betty, bees…He's going to keep bees in the garden so we can have fresh honey."

"Oh…" she said, looking askance and somewhat po-faced, "Did I make a paux-fas?"

She was immediately aware that she had made some sort of blunder by the mere look on Louisa's expressionless face.

"Don't you mean a *faux-pas?*?" Louisa asked in measured tones.

Betty clutched her bosom in mock horror.

"Oh, so I do! Silly me! How could I have made such a mistake?"

She squawked with raucous laughter, clutching her sides with mirth.

Really! Sometimes Louisa wondered how on earth this woman had had the nerve to become a teacher's aide at the church school with all her various malapropisms and quirky little transgressions of English grammar.

When Betty had finally calmed down and regained her composure, she said:

"Well…that explains that then." She paused to catch her breath again. "The young people of today can be so unpredictable. Fresh honey? That sounds wonderful!" She smiled and smoothed her hair in a conciliatory manner. "And I hear he's going to take over from his father as the new vicar?"

"Yes. Once he's qualified. The Reverend McAlister will be with us till then. Jeremy decided to follow in his father's footsteps after all…all things considered."

Betty looked suitably impressed, her hand flying immediately to her breast again.

"Well, I never…" she declared, sounding slightly flustered.

Twenty-Two

Shortly after Easter the squire introduced to the Picards, their new lodger, Mathew Middleton. He was a Methodist of good farming stock from north of the Dales. He was to be employed at the local blacksmith's shoeing horses until he had earned enough money to study for a teaching career in London. So he said, anyway. He was a sturdy lad of about sixteen, shy but handsome and possessing an accent typical of his place of origin. On his first day at the vicarage, Lucy bumped into him at the door to the reading room. She stood in the doorway barring his entry and said with a certain measure of importance:

"My Papa's dead. He fell under a bell and it killed him dead."

"Oh aye. Oi heard that someone pushed 'im under t'bell…some florist or other."

"Oh no. You mean Mr. Bycroft? That's what some people say. But they're wrong. He saved Mama's life and he gives her flowers."

The curate's wife who just happened to be passing by on her way to the vestry, on overhearing this, said in an undertone, "And that's not the only thing he gives her, I'll be bound!" She gathered up her skirts and stalked past with as much haughtiness as her small plump stature could express.

"Mr. Bycroft and I play hopscotch. He hops at the same time as doing tricks in the air with his walking stick. He is ever so clever. And brave too for saving Mama from being killed by lightning. And he buries ha'pennies in the garden that turn into pennies. And he always lets me win at hopscotch…Do you want to play?"

"Aw, no thanks miss. Got t'git mi readin' done a'fore dinner."

He pulled his forelock and dutifully walked into the reading room.

***

A week later everyone was seated at the breakfast table together with Mathew, the new lodger, except for Emma and John who had returned to London.

Charlotte had become quite enamored of the taciturn young man with the developing muscles, swarthy complexion and curly dark locks and had suddenly decided that she too would like to become a teacher when she grew up. She thought Mathew was just perfect, overlooking his accent of course, to which she turned a deaf ear. At every opportunity, she would shyly glance up at him from under her shock of red hair across the table and blush modestly. He in turn would respond to her attentions by grinning with much aplomb. On this particular occasion, Charlotte was seated opposite Mathew at the table and Lucy was to the left of Charlotte. Lucy, who although she was only eight, was not unaware of such goings on and suddenly decided to become spokesperson for the little gathering.

"You know what they say about Charlie, don't you?" she said overzealously.

"Charlie is me darlin', me darlin', me darlin'," she sang teasingly in a cocky voice.

Charlotte suddenly blushed to the roots of her hair and gave Lucy a mighty backwards kick under the table which caused the table to lurch slightly to one side.

There was an embarrassed hush and Louisa and Thomas looked at each other blankly. Then Lucy continued in her obstreperous mode, directly addressing Mathew with:

'Adam and Eve and Pinch Me
Went down to the river to bathe.
Adam and Eve were drowned
Who was saved?'

She looked challengingly at Mathew, who having already been suitably humiliated in front of everyone present and now being provoked by the blatant stare of this young slip of a girl, said naively through his mouthful of porridge:

"Pinch Me."

Lucy needed no further encouragement. She lurched across the table in an effort to pinch Mathew on the upper arm, but in the process knocked over the condiments and spilt the contents of the milk jug all over the clean tablecloth. Mathew in surprise, reacted by spewing nearly all his porridge in her face.

"Lucy!" scolded her mother. "Behave will you! Now go to your room!'

"Don't worry, Mother, I'll see that she goes," said Thomas. "And I'll make sure she gets cleaned up first."

Thomas excused himself from the table, stood up and folding his napkin neatly, laid it very deliberately back on the table. Then in one quick movement he swung around and scooped Lucy up and over his shoulders. She struggled there kicking like some crazed animal and yelled, "A pinch and a punch for the first of the month and no returns!"

"You little boor, Lucy, or should I say Boer? Joke everyone, joke!" he called out as he carried the squirming child out of the room.

"Silence is golden, isn't it?" resumed Louisa, quite taken aback by Lucy's outburst. "That's not like Lucy. I don't know what's got into her lately." She sighed.

"It's Mathew, Mother. She doesn't like the fact that Mathew and I are going to study teaching together," said Charlotte… "aren't we Mathew?" she said, looking wishfully at Mathew.

Mathew nodded, his copious curls bouncing around his face.

"Oh, really dear? That's news to me," said Louisa wearily as she sponged the table cloth where Mathew's porridge had landed.

"Well, if Geraldine wants to become a doctor, then I can become a teacher," she retorted.

"Yes dear, of course you can," said her mother solicitously. "Although why Geraldine's throwing away her talent with that beautiful singing voice on some highfalutin idea of becoming a doctor, I'll never know."

"You *said* I could, Mother," remonstrated Geraldine, "as long as we got a lodger in to help with the cost."

"Yes of course I did dear. Don't worry. I know you can do anything if you put your mind to it."

"*I'm* all for you wanting to become a doctor, sis," said Jeremy. Then with a wicked glint in his eye he went on to say, "As long as you don't ask me to do your dirty work for you and go out body snatching from the church cemetery at night so you can cut up fresh corpses and practice blood-letting them with leeches on your dissecting table!"

"Jeremy!" said his appalled mother.

"Ugh! Do you think I'd do that?" retorted Geraldine. "Lay my hands on local stiffs? You must be mad. Just you stick to your stick insects and I'll go through the proper channels for cutting up cadavers at the medical school…when I get there." She reflected a moment and then said, "They *did* get paid well apparently though…the old resurrectionists…for supplying bodies to surgeons to practice on in the olden days…" Then turning to Jeremy, she said, "But it wouldn't have been as easy as going down the bottom of the garden at night like you do Jeremy to catch crickets."

"You're not wrong there sis," he agreed, balancing his spoon on his forefinger and tapping it gently so it see-sawed from side to side. "It used to be a real racket in the olden days because with the shortage of bodies they used to bribe the sextons and the undertakers. And to avoid blackmail the surgeons were forced to pay exorbitant prices for the bodies. There were even more murders to increase supplies."

"Oh Jeremy, *do* be quiet," said his mother.

"Sorry Mother."

"At least, Queen Vic's gone now," continued Geraldine, "so she can't keep going on that women ought to be kept out of the professions. She disliked the idea of 'young girls and young men entering the dissecting room together.' At least, there will be a little bit more freedom by the time I get to that stage."

"I'm not so sure my dear," said Louisa. "Remember that these are pioneering days for women and you will most likely have to make certain sacrifices."

"Sacrifices? But you are a pioneer, Mother. You are one of the first lady bell ringers. You haven't had to make any sacrifices have you?"

"Well, there was your dear father, Alfred…"

Her voice trailed off and her eyes began to fill with tears.

"But…"

Jeremy gave his sister a warning look.

Just then, Thomas re-entered the room, minus his little sister.

"Oh dear, I'm feeling a bit poorly," said Louisa. "I think I shall have to take the waters again soon. It always does me a power of good. These headaches and this blessed insomnia make me very tired, children. What is so annoying is that I can't even seem to handle my embroidery any more. It is *so* frustrating. Even the simplest little thing takes me twice as long now. Would anyone like to accompany me to Ilkley Moor next weekend? The waters there are so beautifully soothing."

"I will, Mother," said Geraldine. "Will next Sunday suit? Sally and Avril and I were going to go cycling in the country then anyway. We could all go together on our bikes if you're feeling up to it or you could go by carriage and we could meet you there. What do you say?"

"That would be lovely dear. But I think it would be better for me to travel by carriage if you don't mind."

* * *

The following Sunday, Louisa and Geraldine were preparing at the vicarage for their outing to Ilkley Moor. Geraldine had decked herself out in stout roomy serge knickerbockers and trilby hat and coat with turned up collar ready to go cycling while Louisa was her usual fashion-plate self in gored skirt and pouter pigeon blouse. When they were almost ready to leave, Louisa remonstrated with surprise:

"Why, hello Geraldine! You've got Jeremy's hat on and his overcoat!"

"Yes. Why…don't you like it?"

"Well…it makes you look like a young man, you know…and that's so…you know, effeminate."

"Oh."

Geraldine looked down with some dismay at her specially put together outfit and wondered if it really did give the opposite impression of what she was trying to say.

"But I'm one of the 'New Women'. All New Women wear rational dress. We're making a statement. Sally and Avril are wearing their brother's clothes too."

"So what is the statement that you are all making then?"

"Reform. Reform for women's freedom."

"Oh well then, don't let me stop you. As long as Jeremy doesn't mind. Don't lose any of his things on the way, will you dear?"

"Don't worry, Mother. I'll be careful."

They kissed goodbye and Louisa waved to her daughter as she departed in her carriage.

169

Just what is the world coming to? she asked herself. *Young women wearing men's clothes! My daughter wearing men's clothes! I don't know…I just don't know.*

She felt a sudden surge of relief however when she recalled having seen Geraldine only the day before yesterday busy at her embroidery. At least, she is not an 'unwomanly woman' and in that case in no danger of becoming a suffragist either, she thought. She would hate to think of any of her daughters becoming involved in politics. So unladylike. Louisa followed the late Queen's ideas in a lot of such matters. Speaking of royalty, look at Princess Alexandra, she thought. Now *there* was a lady who knew how to dress. Such elegance!

Soon after Louisa's departure, Sally and Avril appeared at the vicarage on their bicycles. They too, were wearing their brother's clothes…although Sally's coat was too tight and Avril's too big, as Sally had a much younger brother and Avril a much older brother.

"You both look great!" enthused Geraldine. "You too!" beamed the other two girls.

"Give us a twirl," said Avril. "That's better. Sally said you would be wearing Thomas's sailor's hat, but it looks like she was wrong and I was right."

"I could if you like…I'm sure Thomas wouldn't mind."

"No, that looks fine. Very chic."

They all stood back and admired each other once more before Geraldine announced:

"Right-o girls, let's be off then and test the waters."

The three girls mounted their bikes and headed out the front gate. Just as they turned into the lane, they heard wolf whistles coming from the direction of the vicarage. Then there was an ear-splitting howl. They looked back and saw Thomas and Jeremy standing on the front porch with huge grins all over their faces.

Between them stood Rusty, prancing on his hind legs singing, with the two boys egging him on. Then Mathew appeared with a sheepish grin and joined in the malarkey with a ribald attempt at mimicking Rusty in a doggy duet. Such a masterly demonstration of his vocal register almost belied his lingual background. The three girls ignored them, secretly satisfied with themselves as the wolf whistles persisted, and cycled off with their noses in the air towards the main road to Ilkley, three abreast.

"Men! They just don't know how lucky they are, not having to wear skirts!" said Geraldine. "It's so nice not having to be laced up into a corset for once. I can ride more easily and I can actually breath properly now. So much better for us singers."

"Yes, let's throw away our stays!" agreed Avril enthusiastically. "No more fainting ladies in the choir stands if you please!"

"So, are you really giving up your singing and going to Ladies' College then, Geraldine?" asked Sally.

"Yes. To Cheltenham Ladies' College first, as a steppingstone to St. Hilda's College where I'll become one of the 'Hildabeasts'. I'll have to get used to the stiff collars and ties they wear there first." She laughed. She paused for thought and then said, "Do you know, I was watching my sister Charlotte mending Mathew and Thomas's socks the other day…why can't boys darn their own beastly socks? That's what I'd like to know."

"They're helpless, that's why," said Avril. "They need a woman to look after them. I say, Gerry, your brother Thomas is a bit of alright. I haven't seen him for ages. He's completely changed from how he used to look. Is he going to be in church this evening? If so, I think we should all make a special effort to be back on time for the service."

They all laughed.

"The trouble is," said Geraldine, "*he* thinks he's the salt of the earth too!"

"And Jeremy's a good-looking sort as well," said Sally, "as long as you don't mind his spiders and all."

"Yes well, now that you two have sorted my brothers out between you, we'll just keep on pedaling shall we and enjoy the fresh country air," said Geraldine, changing the subject.

"Don't try and change the subject Gerry," said Sally. "We're worried for you. Quite a few chaps are afraid of clever girls you know."

"Yes, well I'm not brilliant, I just like a challenge. And besides, you and Avril are going to be nurses, aren't you? So, what's the difference?"

"I suppose you're right…"

They kept peddling on and then Avril suddenly piped up with, "Did you hear about Amelia Jacobs at that London Ball a couple of weeks back? She insulted a young man by refusing to dance with him. Apparently, she said to him point blank, 'No thanks. I don't dance with younger sons!'

There was a united gasp from the other two girls. "That's terrible!" they said.

"That's what her friend Cynthia told me," said Avril, as the other two girls pedaled on in silence pondering the utter recklessness of such a breach of etiquette.

****

They met up with Louisa after a couple of hours at White Wells, Ilkley, attracting some attention as they sauntered into the ladies changing rooms wearing their androgynous outfits. Louisa was pleased to see them and was already 'taking the cure' in her top-to-toe bathing costume. The three girls joined her and they were all soon delicately perspiring together in the same hot spa.

"Oh, this feels just so wonderfully relaxing, doesn't it girls?" said Louisa, luxuriating in the soothing waters. "You must all be appreciating this after your long ride?"

"Oh, it wasn't that strenuous really, Mother. You could have done it if you had put your mind to it."

"Perhaps next time dear, when I'm feeling a bit better," said Louisa, tucking a stray piece of hair back under her mob-cap, oblivious of the stark contrast that her scarred hands made with her face. "Let's have lunch after this at Polly's Tea Shoppe just down the road and then go exploring."

"Great idea," the girls agreed as they lay there soaking and losing themselves in the sensuousness of the spa's waters.

****

After a delicious lunch at the tea shoppe (which included such delicacies as Yorkshire Fat Rascals), Louisa and the girls strolled over through one of the local parks. The wind was getting up a bit and suddenly a freak gust caught the brim of Geraldine's hat and hurled it into the air. It fell and scudded along the ground with Geraldine racing after it not far behind.

Then the same thing happened to both Avril and Sally. The only one whose hat stayed firmly upon their head was Louisa. It was all of her decorative hat pins that did it.

Geraldine scooped up her hat, laid it across her chest and with feigned seriousness and great gusto began to sing the Yorkshire National Anthem:

'Wheear 'as tha binn since ah saw thee?
On Ilkla Moor baht 'at
Wheear 'as tha binn since ah saw thee?
Wheear 'as tha binn since ah saw thee?'

The two other girls, spurred on by these off the cuff theatrics, gleefully joined in, improvising in close harmony and clasping their hats solemnly across their chests in similar vein:

"On Ilkla Moor baht 'at
On Ilkla Moor baht 'at
On Ilkla Moor baht 'at."

When they finally finished the last verse, they all fell about laughing.
"We should be in a barbershop quartet, not a choir!"
"Either that or in Music Hall," quipped Louisa.

* * *

Later that afternoon Louisa took the carriage back home and the three girls cycled slowly back towards Bingham. After about an hour's cycling, they stopped for a break and had a sip of lemonade that Sally had brought with her. Then Avril suddenly remembered the cigarettes that were in the top inside pocket of her brother's coat.
"Here, have one of these, you two," she said, offering them around.
"Cigarettes?" asked Sally.
"Yes. I've even got matches in here I think, she said, feeling further inside the pocket."
"Really?" said Geraldine.
"Yes, well we've got to look the part, don't we?"
"Oh look!" said Sally. "Clara Butt, the famous contralto is on this cigarette card. I bet she never smoked."
"It won't do you any harm," said Avril. "Just try it at least."

Avril lit up a cigarette with much decorum while the other two girls watched and then slowly inhaled. There was a dramatic pause and then she wretched and coughed, completely ruining the effect. The other two girls then lit up as well and joined in the charade. Soon they too, were coughing. Not wishing to waste such expensive tobacco however, they persevered until they had perfected the technique and were puffing away daintily with just short sharp puffs. They re-mounted their bikes and cycled home, each with a cigarette in one hand delicately poised over the front handlebars.

Once they reached Bingham, it was time for church and they could hear the church bells ringing in the distance.

"Oh, let's not miss church," said Avril. "Thomas will be there in his uniform."

"That's right," said Sally. "Let's not miss that! He's such a dish!"

They immediately all stubbed out their cigarettes on the handlebars and rode up to the church. There they parked their bikes outside in a neat row, side by side. As they sauntered nonchalantly up to the front door, they were accosted by the curate. He cleared his throat and then announced rather stiffly:

"Excuse me please, but it is customary for *men*…I will not say 'gentlemen'…to remove their hats upon entering church!"

The three girls looked at each other quite stunned.

They each then obediently (if somewhat piously), removed their trilbies and suppressing their giggles, went to sit in the back pews, peering around for Thomas.

Twenty-Three

After his three months was up, Thomas rejoined the navy. Louisa was much saddened to see him go. It was as if he had only been home three weeks, let alone three months as the time had flown so quickly. But she was not the only one sorry to see him go. There were his brother and sisters and all his female admirers including Sally and Avril who were going to miss his worldly presence too. Bingham would certainly be a much quieter place without him. The sonorous tones of his French horn practice for instance, would no longer be heard wafting across the neighborhood every night before dinner. Hearing a brass instrument in the house again had so much reminded Louisa of her father and the antics he used to get up to with the children and his 'oom-pahs' on the euphonium. She missed those good times too.

Jeremy was back at Oxford taking Holy Orders…but not before he had set up his apiary. Jeremy's bee-hives had kept him busy every couple of weekends since Easter. He had single-handedly built two wooden box hives and set them up by the woodshed behind the greenhouse. He had got stung a few times after introducing a couple of queen bees to entice swarming, but as he said to his mother, it was now less likely that he would ever suffer from arthritis. Elderly beekeepers were hardly ever afflicted with that, he said. He also estimated they would get at least another twenty five percent more plums and a good thirty pounds of honey per hive. Louisa was impressed with her son's enthusiasm but was shocked the first time she saw him emerging from behind the woodshed when collecting honey. He had smoked the bees out of their hives and was walking stiff-legged like a tin soldier blindly through the smoke towards her. He seemed to her like an apparition appearing out of the apiary because his face was literally crawling with a kaleidoscopic carpet of swarming bees. Louisa had shrieked at the sight of him and dashed into the greenhouse for safety.

Apart from that little unexpected encounter, Louisa was in full support of Jeremy's rewarding new hobby. Moreover, it was certainly helping to keep his mind off Nell and his drinking binges. Emma and John had now returned to London and interestingly enough, Hugo, the organist, had also gone to London in order to try his hand at learning to become a butler…but mainly it was to avoid the presence of the 'wicked' Theodore who had remained in Bingham.

Mathew was settling in nicely at the vicarage and Louisa quite appreciated having an extra male about the house for doing odd jobs like chopping firewood etc. Besides, Charlotte was impressed with his physical prowess and took great delight in watching him with his shirt off as he demonstrated his skill at such work. Drawing such an admiring audience made Mathew execute his tasks more willingly so that any extra chores got done effortlessly and without any fuss. It was the ideal set-up.

As for Geraldine, she was still itching to get to Cheltenham Ladies College but was obliged to complete her education at the church school first before becoming a Cheltenham boarding pupil. And Lucy of course, was still attending the church school and constantly on the lookout for stirring up trouble between Mathew and Charlotte.

Meanwhile, in spite of Louisa and Theodore's monumental efforts to carry on their lives in as inconspicuous a manner as possible, they were still both subject to whispered jibes behind the hands of passing villagers…even from people completely unknown to them. Of course, they never walked out together as that would be *asking* for trouble. But whenever either one or the other was out in public, there would be the inevitable knowing looks, the whisperings and seething undercurrents of slander hovering upon the lips of those close at hand. Sometimes, Louisa even got the impression that certain people, thinking of her as a sinful woman, wanted her cursed by bell, book and candle and excommunicated from the church!

Louisa was finding this all very difficult to cope with because by now her feelings for Theodore were running deeper. She was starting to fall in love with him. She was a widow now so she should, by rights, be free to fall in love again, but she felt like her life was being put in full view as if under a microscope. It was affecting her nerves in more ways than one.

However, both Louisa's and Theodore's physical aches and pains were slowly healing and they had both just re-started bell ringing again; Theodore as a one-legged ringer and Louisa as a one-armed ringer, as her right arm was still a bit weak. But as Theodore always said to her at each ensuing practice, "Once a ringer, always a ringer," to which Louisa would reply, "We make a great team, don't we, with me and my one arm and you and your one leg? What we should really do is make the trip to Ireland and sip from the bell of St. Odoceous to see if its healing powers really work!"

"I would be delighted to escort you there, my lady," he would reply.

And then she would smile coyly at him.

The rapport that was rebuilding between the two, soon became obvious to the other ringers, but they discreetly refrained from comment, for the time being at least.

* * *

At practice a month later, the ringers performed exceptionally well and Louisa, as captain, congratulated everyone (including herself) for making absolutely no mistakes. Consequently, at the end of the evening she allowed the other ringers to leave early so that just she and Theodore were left behind to tidy up and remove the baffles from the bell clappers upstairs. Then once the last of the ringers had closed the belfry door behind them and were out of earshot, Algie nudged Gareth and quoting Gilbert and Sullivan, sang somewhat facetiously:

*'If you walk down Picadilly with a poppy or a lily in
your medieval hand.
And everyone will say, as you walk your flowery way
If he's content with a vegetable love which would
certainly not suit me
Why what a most particularly pure young man,
this pure young man must be!'*

Then he winked and said, "I couldn't resist singing that little ditty. What do you reckon about that florist? He's sweet on Louisa isn't he?"

"I think you might not be wrong somehow," Gareth agreed. "The two cripples seem to be enjoying each other's company a lot, don't they?" He chuckled.

* * *

Not everyone found this blossoming liaison quite so amusing however. From not too far away, a single pair of eyes peered from the shadows, watching and waiting.

They were fixed intently on the belfry door, trying to fathom the identities of the persons leaving the tower in the half light. It was dusk and the night was just starting to draw in. A chimney sweep was just finishing up his last job for the day and stood on a roof top silhouetted against the bright twilight wielding his long-handled brush over one shoulder. Meanwhile, the mystery observer remained a little longer in the obscurity of the shadows until certain that the coast was clear. Then they made a move. They approached the belfry in a suspicious manner with something concealed under their coat.

Then stealthily opening the belfry door, they peered in. Their eyes were met at once by a set of rules mounted on the opposite wall:

'There is no music played or sung
Is like good Bells if well Rung
Put off your hat, coat and spurs
And see you make no 'brawls or iares,
Or if you chance to curse or sware
Be sure you shall pay sixpence here.
Or if you chance to break a stay
Eighteen pence you shall pay.
Or if your ring with gurse or belt
We will have sixpence or your pelt.'

The intruder stood still, absorbing the atmosphere of a bygone era, but their little reverie was disturbed by muffled sounds coming from upstairs in the bell tower. Louisa and Theodore were in a clinch near the top of the spiral staircase. They were oblivious to the fact that there was an intruder downstairs.

Without any further hesitation, a hand with malicious intent, fumbled furtively amongst the coat-tails hanging by the belfry door. It swiftly whipped out a paraffin lamp from under its owner's coat, upended the tank and drizzled paraffin all over the dangling coat-tails. There was a surreptitious scratch as a Lucifer match was struck and the coat-tails ignited. A faint crackling sound began as the coat-tails caught fire. This was followed by a slightly more audible scraping sound and a click as the latch was lowered and the key turned on the outside. The key was extracted and then there was the sound of brisk footsteps as the intruder disappeared into the dusk.

The only sign of carelessness evident upon this inauspicious visit was an innocuous looking cigarette card that had inadvertently fallen upon the floor from the intruder's coat pocket. It lay face up depicting a famous cricketer and the edges were starting to curl slightly in the heat.

On the rooftops nearby, the lone chimney sweep wiped the sweat from his brow as he whistled a few bars of *Jimmy Crack Corn*. He suddenly stopped mid-whistle as someone in rather a hurry passed by in the churchyard below. He tipped his sooty cap further back on his head and scratched the spot where it had been. From where he was standing, he couldn't tell if it was a man or a woman, but they definitely had something hidden under their coat.

* * *

Suddenly, Louisa smelt smoke. She pushed herself away from Theodore's embrace and peered down the stairwell. Smoke was wafting up the stairs and it was getting warmer.

"Theodore, there's a fire downstairs! Quick, let's get out of here!"

On full alert, Theodore tore himself away from his ladylove and yelled, "Follow me!"

He grabbed Louisa by the hand and clattered down the stairwell with his walking stick at full pelt dragging Louisa behind him. They could hear the crackling of flames getting louder as they ventured further down the stairs and could feel the increase in heat. At the bottom of the stairs, they were met by a curtain of flames.

"Stay here Louisa and I'll check the door!"

He navigated his way through the flames while Louisa waited, but the belfry door was locked.

"Someone's locked us in!" he yelled. "It's locked!"

"Oh no!" Louisa wailed. "I left the key on the outside of the door tonight!"

"Don't worry. I have an idea. Just go back upstairs and stand by the windows. But whatever you do, don't touch those clappers and keep right away from the bells!"

"But what about you?"

"I'll be up in a minute. Don't worry. Just hurry."

Louisa stood staring after Theodore through the flames for a moment and then ran back up the stairs, coughing through the smoke. Theodore hobbled as fast as he could towards the winch mounted on the wall which controlled the copper window louvres upstairs.

The handle was hot. He wound the handle anticlockwise so as to unbaffle the window slats and set them at a forty-five-degree angle to the ground. Next, he rushed towards the bell ropes and untied first the tenor, then number 4, number 3, number 2 and then the treble bell. As each rope was untied, the bells rang out in sequence in a 'backwards toll', (an ascending scale)…the universal signal for an alarm. It was the same signal that was used to trigger the Massacre of St. Bartholomew. Then, using the pocket knife that he always carried with him to cut wild flowers, he hacked off the brightly colored sally of the tenor bell and braving the flames, scuttled back upstairs with his jacket smoldering. He was lucky that the wooden staircase didn't give way as he went.

Louisa was waiting for him with bated breath. "Oh, you're on fire!" she screamed. "Quick! Roll on the floor!"

This he did, while Louisa stood watching, horrified. He got up coughing, ripped his jacket off and stamped the embers out.

"Quick. Help me pull this tenor rope through the hole in the floor and over the pulley. Then put it out the window."

"Right."

That was soon done and then Theodore started battering the copper louvres with his walking stick.

"What are you doing that for?" Louisa asked.

"To make the gap bigger. You and me are going down the rope outside and you're first."

"But I can't…"

"Just do it," Theodore commanded, "or we will both be burnt to death."

Forcibly restraining herself from bursting into tears, Louisa reluctantly picked up the rope with one hand and looked out the window. It was a long way down, even in the dark.

Obediently, she hoisted her skirt and climbed onto the window sill, rope in hand. Then just as she was easing herself under the lower louvre, she froze.

Silhouetted against the flames, which by now had reached the top of the stairwell behind Theodore, a wizened face had sprung into view. It let out a horrific howl. It was the banshee. Louisa was transfixed and almost let go of the rope. She was vaguely aware of Theodore's voice calling out. "What are you waiting for?" as she teetered on the window ledge between certain death and a possible exit, but she was unable to move. It was as if her life was hanging on a thread between the real and the supernatural. Suddenly, she became aware that the banshee appeared displaced and disorientated. Of course, its normal habitat was around water, so what was it doing here? So just whose existence was more in danger? Her's or the banshee's?

Suddenly, she got her answer. With a sickening suicidal scream, the banshee suddenly started sizzling like a mirage in the desert. Its image began to fade as it started to quickly melt before her eyes. Soon there was nothing left but a single searing plume of steam rising up like a shriveled up will-o'-the-wisp. This condensed into a small cloud and suddenly fell with a loud splash just in front of where Theodore was standing. All that was left of the banshee now was a small and insignificant puddle, wet on the floor.

Louisa couldn't believe her eyes. Was the banshee finally abandoning its calling and making the ultimate sacrifice by throwing itself at the mercy of its own antidote…fire? If so, why? Whatever the reason, Louisa was now triggered into action. She nervously licked her lips and found herself automatically going hand over hand down the bell rope. Vaguely she could hear men's voices down below, but her mind was elsewhere.

Did this final (she hoped) sighting of the banshee mean that her mother's ghost had finally done its duty and was now leaving for other realms? Perhaps, disappointed at losing its powers for not having caused someone to die after its last appearance, it had decided to end it all in shame. So why hadn't she, Louisa, died after having been struck by lightning? Perhaps it was a bogus banshee unable to do a proper job. Or perhaps it was a banshee that just couldn't face going into the twentieth century? Louisa was confused. But before she knew it, a strong pair of hands was helping her onto a ladder. The volunteer fire brigade had arrived.

When Louisa finally set foot on the ground, she was in a daze. Theodore was soon by her side, slightly singed, blackened and reeking of smoke. Firemen had by now broken down the belfry door, installed their ladders and were hosing down inside the bell chamber.

"Anybody else inside, mister?" one of the firemen asked.

"No, just us two, sir," Theodore replied, coughing hoarsely.

A small crowd of onlookers had gathered in the church grounds, carrying lanterns and there were two horse-drawn hook and wagon carts parked nearby which the fire brigade had brought. A couple of policemen were also on the scene, Constable Kenny and his assistant, Addison. An anonymous young couple had donated their coats to keep Louisa and Theodore from shock and then once they had spotted them, Louisa's girls, Geraldine, Charlotte and Lucy swarmed around their mother, obviously upset, with Mathew hovering behind them.

Sergeant Addison approached Louisa and Theodore and announced:

"Constable Kenny and I have some questions to ask you two this evening if you don't mind Mr. er…and Mrs. er…?"

"Mr. Bycroft and Mrs. Picard," said Theodore helpfully.

The policeman did a double take, but refrained from comment. He obviously hadn't recognized them in the half light.

"Yes, well then, if you would be so kind as to answer a few questions in say, half an hour?"

"Of course, officer."

The squire and the curate and their respective spouses then appeared on the scene, horrified at what had happened.

"A fire? A fire?" the squire expostulated. "How on earth could a fire have started in the belfry? Was it an accident or was it arson? Our poor village church that we've only just had restored! It's abominable!"

His little wife, Millicent piped up with, "Who is responsible for such sacrilege? Dissenters? Heathens?"

The curate put his penny's worth in saying, "It's going to cost us hundreds to get it back into original condition again. I don't know how we're going to do it!"

His wife, Betty, said to Louisa, "You're welcome, Louisa to come and stay the night with us, if that is of any help."

"Thank you, Betty, but I will manage just as nicely at home in my own bed, thank you. But I could murder for a cup of tea. Anybody else?"

The three girls were duly sent off to bring cups of tea to the little group while the rest of the flames were extinguished. The crowd dispersed slightly after that and then Louisa and Theodore were taken aside to be interviewed. Constable Kenny conducted the proceedings.

"Er, tell me, Mr. Bycroft," he began, "what time does bell ringing practice normally finish?"

"Nine o'clock, sir."

"And both you and Mrs. Picard decided to stay late?"

"That's right, officer. We were going to unbaffle the clappers first before we shut up shop for the evening."

"And at what time did you notice the fire?"

"Probably at about ten past nine, I would say, sir."

"And the other bell ringers?"

"They left about ten minutes early, sir."

"Would you agree with that, Mrs. Picard?"

"Yes. The others were let off early because we had such a good practice."

"Were you both on good terms with the other ringers?"

"As far as we can tell officer," said Louisa. "Everyone was in extremely good spirits after tonight's practice."

"Interesting," said the constable. "And who was the last to leave the belfry after the practice, Mrs. Picard?"

"Algie and Gareth. They left together."

"I see."

There was a considerable pause as the constable heeded all their answers.

"We would like to ask you both to come down to the station at eleven o'clock tomorrow morning in case any further evidence is uncovered. Thank you for your co-operation."

Louisa and Theodore thanked him and returned to their little group of supporters ready to partake of a nice hot cup of tea while the police cordoned off the belfry.

* * *

Next morning, Louisa and Theodore each arrived separately at the station at the appointed hour.

"Good morning Mrs. Picard. Good morning Mr. Bycroft," the constable said. "Do sit down. I trust you are feeling a little better after the trauma of yesterday evening?"

Louisa and Theodore smiled their acknowledgement.

"Now, you may be interested to know," he continued, "That since the fire has been extinguished, we have uncovered certain clues. In particular, it seems that an accelerant of some sort, possibly paraffin, must have been used to allow the fire to have developed to the extent that it did in the time frame involved. All the wooden paneling downstairs was damaged, the bell ropes burnt, and the outside door almost completely burnt except for the latch. Not so much damage upstairs, just the internal door now a pile of ashes and smoke damage all up the stairwell. The staircase has gone. Strangely enough, one of our men recovered half a cigarette card on the premises. Do you know anyone who collects portraits of famous cricketers?"

Louisa and Theodore looked at each other blankly. "I'm a cricket fan myself but I don't smoke," volunteered Theodore. "A friend of mine was the same. But we both own smoking jackets," he added incongruously.

"Oh? And his name, Mr. Bycroft?"

"Hugo. Hugo Blanchard."

"He used to play the organ at the Anglican church here," explained Louisa, "but now gone to London I hear to learn how to become a butler."

"Really? Is that so…?" He paused for thought and then said, "Now you may not be aware, but Scotland Yard only just set up its Fingerprint Department a few weeks ago under Edward Henry. He's a brilliant man. We're sending for one of his officers to come down in a few days to take prints. So, we hope to have this little mystery solved sooner than you think."

"So, you definitely suspect arson, Constable?" Theodore asked, looking concerned.

"That's what we're thinking at the moment. We will be taking prints of all persons you have had contact with in the past few weeks as well. So, we will need a list of these people in two days' time, if that's alright."

"Oh, my goodness," said Louisa. "It's horrible when you think about it isn't it?"

"You were both extremely lucky to get out alive Mrs. Picard. Don't forget that. If it weren't for Mr. Bycroft's quick thinking, who knows what might have happened. But it does seem as if someone has it in for you, so I urge you both to be very cautious over this next little while."

"Thank you, Constable," they said. "We are much indebted to you."

They shook hands and showed themselves out. They were both a little shaken now that their suspicions had been confirmed.

"Whoever could stoop so low…?" Louisa asked Theodore as they bid each other goodbye outside the entrance to the police station.

* * *

Two days later, someone's dog, in chasing a cat under a hedge not far from the church, uncovered an empty paraffin lamp with a key tucked in its tank. The dog's owner contacted the police who salvaged the items for Edward Henry's man to examine. And a local chimney sweep had also come forward offering information. He reported having seen a person acting suspiciously in the church grounds on the night in question and that the person seemed to be in quite a hurry and was hiding something under their coat.

After all the requisite information had been collated and fingerprints taken of a good many people down at the station, it was just a matter of time before the police came up with a result. Several weeks later, they had their prime suspect.

"We have a match!" cried Edward Henry's man.

And so it was that the curate's wife was summoned to the police station.

She arrived at the station in a little bit of a dither and sat herself down ready for her interview with the constable and two other police officers.

"Now tell me, Mrs. Hogarth," Constable Kenny began, "what were you doing on the evening of 16th July, Wednesday, at a quarter to nine in the evening?"

"I was out in the garden, sir, tending to my dahlias before it got too dark."

"Have you got someone who can testify for you upon that?"

"Yes, sir. My husband, the curate."

"That's right, you're the curate's wife, aren't you? And how long has your husband acted as curate in Bingham, Mrs. Hogarth?"

"Nearly twenty years now. Seventeen to be exact. Quite a long time really, sir."

"Yes, quite a long time for a pillar of the church and the community to be in office. And how long have you known Mrs. Picard, the ex-vicar's wife? About the same time? Nearly twenty years?"

"Yes, that's correct, sir."

"And are you on good terms with her?"

"Yes, sir."

"Then how is it that we have your fingerprints on this latch here which belonged to the belfry door and on this key to the same door and on this paraffin lamp?"

The curate's wife looked stunned and was silent for a few moments, unable to fathom what was going on.

"Mrs. Hogarth? You were saying…?"

"Oh…nothing."

The constable cleared his throat.

"Mrs. Hogarth, we have undisputed evidence which points to the fact that you not only recently touched this latch but also this key and this paraffin lamp. Can you give us an explanation?"

"But I…you can't…I didn't…"

"You did it, didn't you, Mrs. Hogarth?" the constable said forcefully. "You opened the belfry door, poured paraffin from the lamp around the cloak room area and then lit a fire, didn't you Mrs. Hogarth. And then you put the latch down behind you and locked the door behind you before throwing away the evidence under a hedge." He paused for breath. "You don't smoke, do you, Mrs. Hogarth?"

"No, sir."

"No, so we are led to believe. There is the question of the cigarette card you see."

Suddenly, realizing that she had been backed into a corner, Betty looked exasperatedly from one to the other of the two policemen on either side of her and confessed. "Ah, yes. My husband, the curate, well, you see he enjoys the occasional cigarette. But I collect the cards. So, whenever I go out and buy him cigarettes and matches, I always check to see whether there's a famous actress on the card inside. All I need is Sarah Bernhardt to complete the set."

"But it wasn't Sarah Bernhardt?"

"No, it was W.C. Grace, the famous cricketer."

"Correct. One hundred percent correct, Mrs. Hogarth. It was indeed the 'Demon Doctor' himself, with his beard singed off, wasn't it?"

Betty gulped.

"So, what happens now?" she asked awkwardly.

"You are under arrest, madam," announced the constable, "for the crime of committing arson and endangering the lives of two people. It will not be necessary for your husband to give evidence, however, as the evidence we have speaks for itself. There is just one question that needs answering however." He paused. "We have reason to believe that although you say you are on good terms with Mrs. Picard, you do in fact hold feelings of hostility towards her. Is that correct?"

"Yes, well, that Picard family is a rule unto itself. They have been conspiring against my husband for years and now all hope for my husband's career advancement to the position of vicar has been dashed with Jeremy Picard now taking Holy Orders. On top of that, Louisa Picard is a two-faced little madam who is seducing her ex-husband's killer right under everyone's noses. She should be excommunicated for aiding and abetting his crime. I was hoping that by getting rid of those two pieces of riff-raff, Jeremy Picard would finally get the message that Bingham is jinxed for him and his family and that he should leave voluntarily, as he could be next. Why the devil he wants to stay, I don't know…"

"I'm sure you are of a minority who thinks like that," said the constable. He sat up straight. "Well, Mrs. Hogarth, thank you for our little chat. That will be all for now. We will be putting you in a holding cell here until further notice…"

"It's true, it's true…they killed the ex-vicar together."

"I'm sorry, Mrs. Hogarth, but we have evidence to the contrary. Now off you go."

The other two policemen took hold of each of her arms to lead her away.

"And why my husband had to act so neighborly with that bigot Bycroft and help dig stumps out of his garden is beyond me…" she persisted as she was taken away.

* * *

Betty Hogarth, the curate's wife, was soon afterwards transferred to Holloway Prison in London where she was forced to wear coarse serge clothing and eat thin oatmeal gruel for ten years. Her only reading material was a bible, a prayer book and a hymnbook. The poor curate was so embarrassed by his wife's behavior that he left the district, never to be seen again.

It was nearly six months before the belfry was restored to its original condition. All ringing was stopped for three months until the bells were cleaned of smoke damage, the bell frame cleaned and the ropes and pulleys restored. Several volunteers from the congregation and the bell-ringers themselves had done all the work and it was not complete until just before Christmas. It had meant many long hours of volunteer labor, scrubbing walls, floors, brickwork and mending loose tiles on the roof where they had warped under the heat. Where there had been superficial scorching, charred wood and smoke damage in the bell ringing chamber, it needed to be completely repaneled with new woodwork. And then there were the rope shutes that needed unclogging and a new spiral staircase that needed to be built. In the meantime, Jeremy Picard had been helping out the Reverend McAlister as temporary part-time curate whenever his timetable allowed.

The people of the village had been utterly staggered by Betty Hogarth's confession of guilt and equally staggered by the accuracy of the new fingerprint techniques. There was a new deterrent to crime everywhere now. The villagers just could not get over the fact that their curate's wife had committed such a crime. In fact, they thought much worse of *her* now than they had of Louisa. So that was at least some consolation for Louisa.

But now that everything was finally ship-shape in the belfry, Louisa had developed an irrational fear of ringing there, in case some strange mishap should befall her again. She knew there was no chance of encountering the banshee again so that was at least some comfort, but it was as if she felt responsible for anything else that might go wrong. For instance, she now had an inordinate fear of thunderstorms and hoped against hope that the tower would not be struck by lightning and ruin all their new handiwork. She did recall with some trepidation however, her ex-husband's words about some bell-ringers in Alphington, Plymouth. About seventy years previously, the belfry was struck by lightning and one of the ringers was killed.

"I wonder which bell he was ringing?" she asked herself. "Please God, don't say it was the treble bell! The treble bell is *my* bell!"

Consecrated bells were supposed to have the power, merely by ringing, of putting out fires, abating thunderstorms and protecting the community from pestilence and evil. She was thankful therefore, that her Alfred had blessed these bells before they were hung, bless him!

But what she was relieved about most of all, was that *"that woman"* had been taken to heel and shown the error of her ways. Holloway Prison was the place for the likes of her, although Australia would have been even better, she thought. It was just unbelievable that someone as close to her as the curate's wife, who had had the run of her very own household on many an occasion and who had had her absolute trust, could be so spiteful…

Twenty-Four

Winter turned to spring and spring turned to summer and by the time that the second Boer War was over with the signing of the Treaty of Vereeniging on 31st May 1902, the Picard family was really looking forward to Emma and John's wedding in late June. Emma had passed her exams and her wedding would be a welcome relief from the goings on at the church and its belfry over the past two years. Thomas would be home just in time for the wedding and he had assured Emma by letter that he had been diligently practicing his French horn. Hugo had been asked as a special favor to Emma to accompany both Thomas and Geraldine on the church organ for their solos and to her delight, he accepted. He had now long since forgotten Theodore and had found himself an altogether much more amenable young man in London. Besides, Theodore would be escorting Louisa to the wedding. Thomas had also arranged for a friend of his, one Angus McPherson from the Navy Pipe Band, to pipe Emma into the church.

Finally, the big day arrived. It was 29th June, Emma's wedding day and the church was beautifully decorated with orange blossom ('chastity'), trailing ivy ('fidelity in marriage') and forget-me-nots ('true love'). The bells rang out and all Emma's Irish relatives arrived, John's London relatives, the squire and his wife, the ladies of the Guild, Louisa's lodger and several friends of the young couple getting married. The Reverend McAlister was officiating at the service and Thomas had been picked to give Emma away.

Emma looked radiant in white satin, tulle and orange blossom and was attended by her three sisters as bridesmaids. John's brother was his best man. Louisa was extremely proud of her girls…and her sewing expertise, as in spite of her handicap, she had spent the past six months making all the bridesmaid's dresses.

When Emma made her entrance, the skirl of the pipes playing a strathspey and reel sent shivers up everyone's spines as the haunting notes echoed around the chancel. Geraldine, having had some experience of cross-dressing herself, glanced appreciatively across at Angus in his kilt and gave a secret nod of approval to Sally and Avril sitting over near the front pews. They in turn, reciprocated with significantly raised eyebrows and by mouthing the words, "Nice legs!"

Emma and John exchanged their vows and then Thomas played Bach's *Jesu, Joy of Man's Desiring* transposed especially for French horn and organ accompaniment. The acoustics of the church were superb and did justice to both Thomas's solo and Geraldine's rendition of Bach-Gounod's *Ave Maria* for soprano and organ. Both were stirringly beautiful and Louisa was almost moved to tears.

When the happy couple emerged from the church, the white pigeons were released and the bells rang merrily. They were showered with rice, old slippers and blessings before they made their way to the vicarage for the reception in the vicarage grounds under a huge marquee.

Everything went without a hitch, the sumptuous wedding breakfast, the toasts, the speeches and then afterwards Emma and John left on their honeymoon. Emma looked lovely in a travelling dress of eau de nil cashmere with salmon pink trimmings and hat to match. It was almost too much for Louisa and she could not stop herself from shedding the odd tear or two.

* * *

Three weeks after the wedding, Louisa held a small family get-together at the vicarage. Emma and John had by now returned from their Isle of Wight honeymoon and settled into their new London home. So there was just Thomas, Charlotte, Mathew the lodger and Lucy there as Jeremy had returned to Oxford and Geraldine to Cheltenham.

Louisa gathered Mathew and her remaining children about her in the drawing room and made an announcement over poised glasses bubbling with champagne.

"Children, I have an announcement to make. Mr. Bycroft and I are to be married."

There was a collective gasp all around, dead silence and then a burst of congratulations. Theodore, who had been hidden behind the drawing room door, entered the room with a huge smile on his face. Thomas shook his hand and offered him a glass of champagne.

"Thank you, Thomas," said Theodore graciously.

"When will you be tying the knot?" Thomas asked.

"Next week," Louisa replied as quick as lightning.

"It's all been arranged. We're going to get married at Gretna Green in Scotland and then honeymoon in Edinburgh. We'll be returning to London to live in Theodore's quarters there. Jeremy will be back in Bingham permanently next week and will have finished his Holy Orders so he will be able to help care for Charlotte and Lucy. It's all been worked out. Plus, he will be able to take my place on the treble bell."

"My goodness, Mother, you *are* a dark horse!" quipped Thomas. "But you're so clever, I wouldn't have put it past you," he said, reaching for another drink.

Louisa smiled. "So, I'll be telephoning the others straight away to tell them the good news."

"Wonderful!" Thomas took a sip from his glass, considered it from every angle and then said tentatively, "So you're not asking Jeremy to marry you in the church here?"

"No…we want something much more low key, don't we Theodore? All things considered…We don't want to draw attention to ourselves, do we? Much as we would have loved Jeremy to do us the honor."

Theodore nodded.

"And naturally we will be popping up here from time to time to visit."

* * *

Louisa and Theodore were thus married at Gretna Green and exchanged posies and rings, although they did not on this occasion ring their own wedding bells. Thomas went back to sea in another month and by the time Louisa and Theodore reached London they were just in time for Edward VII's coronation in August. The city streets were thronged with well-wishers.

Both Louisa and Theodore joined the London Ringing Society which enabled them to travel all over the country to bell-ring in different belfries. In fact, Theodore even bought an antique set of dumb-bells, (a wooden machine resembling a windlass), which he set up in the attic with ropes threaded through the floorboards so that Louisa could practice strengthening her weak arm and so that they could both practice bell ringing at home without disturbing their neighbors. Theodore's pet name for Louisa became Esmeralda and Louisa's pet name for Theodore became Quasimodo. They were devoted to one another.

As the years went by, Thomas was eventually promoted to the position of Captain in the navy, Jeremy became much respected as the new bell ringing vicar of Bingham and Emma gave up nursing to become a full-time mother to six children. Geraldine became a doctor who became involved in the Fabian Women's Group promoting equal opportunities for both men and women, Charlotte and Mathew both became teachers and Lucy, after becoming enthralled by the Cake Walk, later became a vaudeville entertainer in London.

As for the banshee, Louisa was never bothered by it again although she often wondered about it since its demise. Why had it come to haunt her causing her all that angst and then taken it upon itself to self-destruct? It was just another unsolved riddle like the riddle of the sphinx in Egypt. She tried to put it out of her mind and concentrate on other more pleasant things. Besides, she really didn't care if she was connected to the nobility or not. The fact was, that she was happier now than she had been for a long time…

In fact, Louisa and Theodore were spotted in the summer of 1906 out on a Sunday drive to Brighton. Theodore was at the wheel of a very early model open-topped Ford car and they were motoring from London to join the Ringing Society in a peal at a Brighton belfry at noon. Louisa looked very svelte wearing a large straw hat fastened on with hat pins and a voluminous chiffon scarf wrapped over the top and under the chin and slung insouciantly back over each shoulder. Her jacket had wide lapels with a long peplum that folded neatly over at the back like the wings of a ladybird. Theodore was likewise decked out in his Sunday best in a suit and bowler hat.

They were enjoying the country air blowing in their faces when suddenly Theodore began frenetically ringing the car's bell and swearing under his breath. There was an elderly lady driver ahead who was hogging the road and only travelling at about five miles per hour in a much later model than theirs. As they passed, Theodore turned around and raised his bowler hat at the lady driver and smiled graciously. He was always such a gentleman, even when in haste.

Louisa gave him a disapproving look once they were well clear.

"Once a ringer, always a ringer," Theodore said simply, without a tinge of guilt.

Louisa smiled at him and laughed.

"Just so long as we're not late for the Duchess!" she said.

Theodore did a double take.

"Alice my dear, we are not in Wonderland yet…and besides," he said, fumbling in his coat pocket with a wry grin, "this fob-watch has stopped."